ORANGEVILLE

W9-AJL-131

Library

ORANGEVILLE PUBLIC LIBRARY

The Living End

**Center Point
Large Print**

**This Large Print Book carries the
Seal of Approval of N.A.V.H.**

The Living End

LISA SAMSON

Orangeville Public Library
1 Mill Street
Orangeville. ON L9W 2M2

(519) 941-0610

CENTER POINT PUBLISHING

THORNDIKE, MAINE

For Marty, one of the warrior women.

This Center Point Large Print edition
is published in the year 2004 by arrangement with
WaterBrook Press, a division of Random House, Inc.

Copyright © 2003 by Lisa E. Samson.

All rights reserved.

The text of this Large Print edition is unabridged. In other
aspects, this book may vary from the original edition. Printed in
Thailand. Set in 16-point Times New Roman type.

ISBN 1-58547-496-7

Library of Congress Cataloging-in-Publication Data

Samson, Lisa, 1964-
   The living end / Lisa Samson.--Center Point large print ed.
   p. cm.
   ISBN 1-58547-496-7 (lib. bdg. : alk. paper)
   1. Self-actualization (Psychology)--Fiction. 2. Widows--Fiction. 3. Grief--Fiction.
4. Large type books. I. Title.

PS3569.A46673L57 2004
813'.54--dc22

                                                    2004006941

Acknowledgments

This book was written during a very difficult time for me, so I'd like to thank those who bore with me, lifted me up, and gave me grace: Will, Tyler, Jake, and Gwynneth—my precious family; my sister, Lori—the babealicious one; Tim—pastor, brother-in-law, and caring friend; Jennifer—best buddy of the Tattooz; my Monday "prayer, share, and care" ladies; my agent, Claudia Cross—it's always a hoot with you; at Water-Brook: Dudley—thanks for the extra weeks; you are a gem and have very fine taste in literature! Erin—editor extraordinaire. And of course, the delightful Don—the world's most friendly, truly caring publisher; Jack Cavanaugh—for the phone calls; and the gangs at the Greek Village Restaurant and The Winters Run Inn where I write when deadlines are looming. Writing about a suicidal woman during my own time of depression was the most mentally exhausting thing I've done. I'm glad it's over, and I'm sure most of you all are too!

Thanks be to God who gives us the Victory. Jesus, well, You know, don't You? You always do. Your love is my breath.

December

My definition of beauty? Jimmy Stewart and Donna Reed in any one of a number of embraces during the holiday film *It's a Wonderful Life.* Keep your pyramids, your mountain ranges, and your gems and jewels. The planes of those two faces, not flawless by any means when compared to the likes of Errol Flynn and Grace Kelly, mesh to form perfection. In a sense, perhaps their lives—well, their characters' lives at any rate—mesh to form perfection as well. And isn't that the point of the movie?

I sit and cry as I do every year, weeping as George Bailey, having seen life without his existence, runs through town screaming with joy and yelling, "Merry Christmas!" Joey runs his fingers through my hair, sniffing, and wiping his eyes with his other hand. I know what he's thinking. He's thinking what a wonderful life *we* have, naturally. For who can watch this movie and not celebrate the fact that they merely exist in this big old wonderful world?

September

How is it I've come to be sitting here in this aspirin room, hovering inside my own nervous energy?

"We've done all we can."

I shake my head, a gelatin shake, more vibration than information. In direct opposition to my movement, the doctor slowly nods.

"I'm sorry to have to tell you, Mrs. Laurel, that there isn't any more we can do for your husband. The most we can do now is make him comfortable."

"How much longer will it be?" Vibrating words cricket-hop across my tongue, springing out into oxygen in which the odor of bodily secretions, feces, puke, urine, and spilled solutions have been masked by cleaning products. I've been reading the labels on these things the past twenty-four hours, and it amazes me they don't eat right through their containers. "How much longer, then?"

"Three days, maybe four or five. Could be today. I regret not being able to tell you anything more specific."

Not Joey. Not my Joey. My lively Joey, for thirty-five years now. The doctor's hands display no wrinkles.

The sterility in here disconcerts me. Yet an earthiness pervades because diseases are living things. They do not infect linoleum that cannot die, or sliding glass doors, or ball-bearing–lined curtain rings. So cold and stand-offish, these things. Unworthy even of death. Only the living deserve to die. In a way, maybe death is the ultimate compliment.

Maybe Joey's right where he belongs. The friendliest guy in the world, yes sir, that's what everybody said about Joey. So full of life, curiosity, and contentment. And after all these years, I can only agree. This room crushes his persona.

I feel old now and sweaty and stinky in this clean hospital room. We always loved a clean house, Joey and me, which is probably why we never adopted after I came down with cervical cancer and underwent an early hysterectomy. Joey held me after the surgery, and I cried.

I want to hold him now and have him feel my love and commitment and maybe even what little strength remains, the way I did when he held me in his bamboo arms. Just one more time, I want to see the moist sparkle that never left his eyes. Oh, he's been a saucy thing all these years. If I had a dollar for every time he swatted my behind, the tomcat, I'd be richer than a headmaster's wife ought to be!

I wonder how the folks at the school are taking this?

I haven't called them!

Nobody knows but me.

But this is good.

The doctor fidgets with his lab coat lapel. "You have the option to remove him from life support, Mrs. Laurel."

"Is he suffering now?"

"No."

"Then keep him on."

I dream all the time about suffocating. Some people dream about drowning. Some dream about fire. Others have falling dreams and crashing dreams, suicide dreams and bomb dreams. Shooting dreams and stabbing dreams and dying dreams.

Oh, dear God.

Would he suffocate without the ventilator? Would he somehow feel it, somehow know I made the decision? I mean, people say all the time after they wake up out of comas that they heard everything going on in the room. One time one of Joey's students, a boy named Spike, told us when he was seven he—

"You might want to do whatever you need to do to prepare yourself, Mrs. Laurel. We have a wonderful social worker and a chaplain here who can help you. Again, I'm so sorry."

He leaves the room with his callow head hanging a bit. It was one thing when the policemen started looking young, but now the doctors blush with youth and an uncertainty only the older folk detect. Joey and I always laugh about it, though. We love growing old together. He calls us "The Coots." Of course, he's been calling us The Coots since I turned thirty-five and he was about to turn the ripe old age of forty-one.

Twenty years ago.

It's not often that I wish to go back in time, but right now?

There we'd been, lunching at the Golden Corral yesterday, and Joey fell face forward into the strawberry-gelatin-with-bananas salad. Right there at the salad bar. A stroke. Massive they said.

But Joey never does anything halfway. If cyclones actually left places better than they found them, they would resemble Joey. I keep reliving the conversation that preceded the incident. Joey's eyes glowed like they do when excitement surges inside him. Which happens often. With a rise of his brows, he pulled from his pocket a piece of paper, the object of much thought, judging by the chamois texture of its folds. "I have news, Pearly."

I remember feeling the emotion I'd felt so many times with my husband: that childlike expectation, that hippity-hop dance of the brain that would jangle down into my limbs each time my parents and I waited in line on the amusement pier at the ocean. The lights blinked in time with my heart, and the smell of caramel corn and hot dogs and cotton candy rose on the salty air of the warm sea breeze above the smell of tar and creosote and Coppertone. Oh, Joey's made life a carnival, that's for sure, with his verve, his zest, his tap dance of an existence. All this and a brain to boot.

I catch my reflection in the sliding glass doorway of the hospital room. I haven't slept since the stroke occurred and they flew him here to shock trauma. My hair foams from atop my head down to the bottom of my chin in a silver halo of disarray. My jeans gap around my middle, my waistband far away from my empty stomach. I am haggard and starved of so much right now, wispy and insignificant in this large complex. One of the many suffering molecules in the mass of humanity. I look as old as Joey. And almost as gray.

At least his face shines smooth and clean. I wiped off the salad before the paramedics arrived. That would have humiliated Joey, to be found with that substance glistening on his face.

I reach for a wet wipe and freshen my face and neck, but the paper cloth heats up too quickly. I throw it in a garbage can filled with tubing and empty foil-lined packets. Such crisp edges define their boundaries, nothing like the paper Joey pulled from his pocket yesterday afternoon.

He held out the paper. "Take it, read it, and tell me what you think. Personally, I think it's rather brilliant."

I laughed. "Joey, you think everything is brilliant."

Which explains why he married me. The man is hardly choosy.

"Open it. I'll pretend to ignore you while you read."

There before my eyes marched a list, typed out on Joey's old Selectric with the script type ball. Remember those days? I thought my job at the insurance agency couldn't get any easier than that! But then computers came, and my goodness, that old Selectric, all one hundred and fifty pounds of it, became a horse and buggy almost overnight. Joey always has admired my ability to keep up with technology in office machinery.

Oh, the list. He was right. Brilliant. Up at the top, in all caps, which does look a bit odd in script, are the words WHILE I LIVE I WANT TO . . .

A nurse enters on white rubber clogs, but I hear her. "Hi, Mrs. Laurel."

"Hi . . . Cindy, is it?"

"Yes. How's our man?"

"The same." I shrug.

"Well, let me hang another bag, and I'll leave you alone."

"No hurry."

She props reading glasses on her nose, then pushes buttons on the IV machine. She turns, her cherubic yet lined face beautiful even in the sickly, fluorescent light shining from above the bed. "Are you hungry? I can order up a tray for you."

"No, thank you."

Her beeper sounds, and she checks the code. "Well, honey, let me know if you change your mind, okay?"

I just nod. I'm not up to much more, really. After she

pads out, I pull Joey's list from my pocketbook. Darn it, I wish he had written it out in his own hand. I could really use the sight of that right now. But they are his words, at least, and I run my fingers over the black letters and read them again.

1. *Go whale watching in Alaska.*
2. *See the mysterious figures on the plains of Peru.*
3. *Climb a pyramid in South or Central America.*
4. *Walk the Appalachian Trail.*
5. *Spend a winter on a mountain.*
6. *Try every entrée at Haussner's.*

I had laughed at this. "Joey, we'll be going to Haussner's for years if we do this!"

"Exactly! Brilliant, isn't it? I've always wanted to be a regular at that restaurant."

I looked around at the cheesy steakhouse décor. "Well, we may have to curtail our trips here."

"That's true. But I think we'll manage." He sat back and leisurely sipped on his tea. I read the last item and smiled.

7. *Get a tattoo.*

"So, what do you think, my dear? Are you game?"

"For the list? Well, of course!"

"Won't we have a wonderful time?"

"Yes, Joey. When do we start?"

He sat forward. "This is my news: I'm thinking about retiring from Lafayette."

I couldn't believe my ears. "But . . . well, my goodness. Isn't this sudden?"

He nodded. "Yes. But I've been thinking lately. You've given up your entire life for me, Pearly. And now, well, let's simply enjoy each other, travel, complete something *together*."

"This list?"

"Precisely. Can you imagine the pictures you'll take, my dear?"

I blushed. "Oh, Joey, I haven't taken out my camera in years."

"Then it's time to now, don't you think?"

I cocked my eyebrow. "Is this your annual 'You need to start taking pictures again, Pearly' conversation? Because if it is . . . you're going a little extreme here with all these things to do. There must be a less expensive way to convince me."

"Are they at least activities you think you can stomach?"

I ran my fingers down the list. "Yes. The whole South American angle is a bit mysterious, though, Joey. I never knew that interested you."

He smiled and took my hand. "Well, to be honest, Pearly, I actually put some of these down for you, too."

"But why would South—"

"Hold that thought. You know, I think I'd like a little more of that broccoli salad. Would you like something else?"

And he walked away. Really walked away. But I watched him go, as I always do, fascinated by him even after all these years. Oh, my, I love this man so much, love the way his smile never quite leaves his face, the way the cowlicks at the back of his head make a C— well, made a C before he went bald—the way he's stayed so trim and fit, and how many women my age actually are married to a man with a flat stomach and a nice firm tush? But Joey's blue eyes, faded now, never cease to find the good, the beautiful, and the righteous, even in the most unlovely of places. And now here I sit in a hospital room.

Before I place the list back in my pocketbook, I run my index finger along its folded edges, rubbing, rubbing, fraying the edges further. Turning off the light over the bed, I wait now. I gaze at the rose-colored vinyl lounge chair, my pillow still indented where my head once lay. No heartbeat thumped through the pillow last night the way it always thumps through Joey's T-shirt when I drift off against his chest. I wonder if sleep will ever own me again, or if it will see itself as merely a surprise visitor, a wayward cousin coming only when I least expect it.

What abrades my well-being the most right now is that Joey has lost his scent. I haven't been home to stuff my nose into his pillow or his winter coat. I'd stick my nose into his old running shoes if I could. Everything smells like hospital here. Even Joey.

So I perch on my chair and tuck his slender hand inside mine. It's cool. Sickly city daylight filters through the drawn blinds in vertical strands.

"Where are you, Joey?" The sound of my own voice, soft yet intrusive in this room, embarrasses me. What will the nurses think if they catch me talking to an unconscious person? I never liked the sound of my voice anyway, too thin and trepid, and it skips sometimes. It seems more wrong than ever here.

Can you hear me, lovey? Do you know I'm here?

How long will you stay?

I don't know what happens after death. But if anyone can come back and tell me, it'll be Joey. He loves to teach.

Oh, God.

I can't quite tell if I'm praying or cursing right now. I think it's a prayer. I really do. And I'm sure Joey needs some. So I say, "Oh, dear God, I pray to You," just to make sure. And nothing else comes to mind.

The big hand sits atop the twelve, the little hand on the five. How can a woman survive over half a century and still have to think when she sees a clock with a face? Give me digital.

I went down to the cafeteria a little while ago. Nausea and lightheadedness had set in, so I fixed a cup of tea and bought a poppy-seed muffin. Only half of it went down before I threw it away and decided to take a walk. I know the machines are keeping Joey alive, so I figure I'll get as much fresh air as one can here in the city before I venture back up to the ward.

Humans hope naturally. It's one of those things that separate us from the animals, I guess. A five-minute conversation in the waiting room proves that. And yet there seems to be a competition, some unspoken "my relative is worse off than yours" contest. Well, I can tell you, I'm not the winner today. There's a set of parents whose two-year-old is dying with cancer. That puts my situation into an aching perspective. Yes, things could be much worse, but the fizz atop my world dissipates nonetheless. I don't even deserve to feel the way I do, then, not if I compare myself to them. Plus, seeing that little family unit together there on the couches—Mom and Dad, a fourteen-year-old daughter, a twelve-year-old son and grandparents galore—the futility of my own existence rears up with ready claws. Woo boy, I married a man and worked at an insurance company all my adult life. There are no accompanying worriers here by my side. And this made me content? Why? Didn't I once see this day coming? Didn't I once think that maybe I needed people to fall back on for such a time?

This is too much thinking. Joey's still here. Perhaps a miracle will occur. Yes. Surely miracles have happened for people less worthy than my husband.

But I saw the CAT scans earlier, and even to someone who knows so little, it looked bad. There is no hope. My whole world is fading away inside that head of Joey's. They're trying to be nice about it, to fashion their explanations in terms I can grasp if not fully understand, but I know better. I know my Joey, and I know he isn't there. Not really.

It looks so normal on the outside, that head of his. Same gray hair, nonexistent on top, scanty lashes, mouth soft in repose, white beard neatly combed. So typical in outward appearance. But what's new there? We see only the surface when it's the underbelly that seethes and swarms and empties out.

But Joey and I have a good *inside* life together too. In thirty-five years of marriage only a few arguments erupted, and one so ridiculous—over what bag of potato chips we should take to his first end-of-school picnic as headmaster, green onion versus barbecue. That shook us both up so much it changed us. Sometimes it only takes something small.

The commuters scurry home now, and I long to throw myself into their hustle-bustle, into their Habitrail-without-the-tubes existence. Where are they going? What kind of house awaits them? What kind of home? Will they stay in their work clothes before attending to dinner and baths, or will they change into their sweats or pajamas? Do they need to stop at Safeway for the ingredients to their meals, or are their larders full? Perhaps happy hour calls?

I should call school. They love him so much. He gives them all he possesses, not only in his teaching and administrating, but in the informal sessions around our kitchen table with the older students. I love those nights. Having grown up on a farm on the Eastern Shore, I know how to feed people.

There they sit, gabbing about literature, authors, poets, the novels and short stories they're all writing. Words fly like water droplets off twenty simultaneously shaking wet hound dogs. Joey always includes me, saying things like "What do you think of that idea, Pearly?" or "Weren't you reading a book with that sort of premise recently?" He's only being sweet, because that is Joey. But their passion far exceeds mine.

I love Joey's mind. All the fascination that swirls around inside it has always intrigued me. Joey is the sponge; I am the soap dish on which he sits.

We travel a lot, just Joey and me. But there are things left to do. A list to be ticked off. See the pyramids for one. Joey always did talk about that. Although I always thought he meant the Egyptian pyramids. Joey laughed at himself for that one. "It's so typical, Pearly. But how can one understand the mind of men without seeing the pyramids firsthand?"

He'll never get there now.

Joey dropped his mind there in the Jell-O salad and can't go back to pick it up.

My breath catches like a fly in a spider web. It stops. And so does the world. Joey is gone. My Joey is gone. It struggles, caught, unable to free itself. My head spins, almost lifting me off the pavement as colors flood my vision in swirls of gold and violet. I rub my eyes and shake my head.

I want to succumb there on Green Street. I want all the flowers to fade. I want all of life to recognize that something is happening that shouldn't be. I want the drivers to stop and salute Joey's window. I want them to drive home and say, "Well, all is not right in the world tonight, honey."

But they continue driving, lost in their own tragedies. How many people have I driven right by, judging their everyday, fleshy shells, failing to see the drama beneath the stony, placid faces? I'm walking by them right now, committing the same crime of dispassion.

I turn around, right there on Green Street, and head back to the hospital, the early summer sun line-driving its light across the eastern faces of the buildings, cars tumbling past on their way to seemingly better things, the hollow heels of pumps and loafers drumming on the concrete sidewalk.

I decide.

He'd hate living like this. He'd hate that the world he loves so much moves on while he twilights in never-never land.

The Golden Corral is Joey's "nasty little secret." The fact that he met his final fate there almost makes me want to laugh. "Actually, Pearly," he once said, "I fit in here about as much as a Dostoevsky in the romance section."

"Are you Dostoevsky or the romance section?" I asked.

"At this point, I have no idea. And I don't think I actually care."

Joey's poetry, essays, short stories, and novellas have achieved that smaller measure of success the cream of writing does. I call him "Mr. New Yorker" to keep his head from swelling. But his books have given us a nice little nest egg, primarily from the speaking invitations they garner. Still, he's said more than once, "I should just write a couple of genre novels under a pen name and make some real easy money."

"Providing they become bestsellers."

His brows sailed high. "Why wouldn't they?"

Oh, Joey. His naiveté endears him to me. I've chosen to limit my view; Joey comes by it naturally.

No bestsellers now. I always felt that writing one wouldn't be as easy as Joey suggested, but I never said that. I never said anything like that to Joey. The world beats us down enough without our spouses pummeling our abdomens.

I hold my lighter, which sports a picture of a sunflower, up to a cigarette and inhale. Checking the tip to make sure it's lit, I stick it back in my mouth. I've been quitting for years. One day on, one day off. It's agony, that's for sure. And yet I go back, like the same polluted wave onto the same seashore, back and back and back, grating along the sand, depositing tenacious slime and muck. But if I can't smoke a blasted cigarette before I tell them to take my lifelong love off life support, I don't know when I can.

I sit in the park across the street from University Hospital. Teaching hospitals give me cause for nerves. My mother died in this hospital. It seems like everybody in Baltimore dies in this city of a hospital. They actually have a food court now. It will rain soon.

Ozone blows in with the air, cutting through the smog of Baltimore and running across my warm face. I breathe in the fresh scent of a soon-coming shower. The cigarette burns down quickly. Too quickly. I light up another.

And another.

And the sun is below the horizon, and the world plums to night.

I wanted to go back up to that hospital room, but something stopped me right at the massive revolving door that sucks people in and out of the complex. I realized I didn't want to enter our home with Joey already dead. I needed an interim going-home. I couldn't just lock up and head to our Sunday outing at the Golden Corral and then unlock the door with Joey dead. That didn't seem right.

I'm sitting on the back deck of our house right now.

We reside in the town of Havre de Grace, about forty or so miles northeast of Baltimore City. It sits at the confluence of the Chesapeake Bay and the Susquehanna River. Our backyard affords us a limited view of the Bay, and it overflows with my flowers and Joey's herbs. A concrete pool sits in the middle, a place for Joey's summer boarding students at Lafayette Classical School to convene after hours. We've built our life around these stunning boys and girls, handpicked from a world of foster care and violence and neglect and stupidity. I've enjoyed our life. I've enjoyed watching them arrive, unpack, and learn how to grow. They're smart, these kids, or they wouldn't be here in the first place. We're not for everybody. We're for those who *want* to be here. We're not a reform school. Joey says that kind of education is a job for better people than him!

I closed up the pool last week. September isn't for swimming or leisure. It's for cutting back plants, mulching, tending to their needs. It's for driving through tunnels of turning leaves, for the blue of the water reflecting a deeper sky, for cheering Joey on at the soccer games he referees, for making autumn wreaths and arranging pumpkins and gourds. It's for spicing up cider and picking out which Halloween candy to distribute even though the trick-or-treaters won't be by until the end of October.

I used to love the month of September.

I can't bring myself to open up the door yet, so here I sit. I see Joey there in the water, wearing plaid trunks, goggles, and a bathing cap. I see him trying to do the

22

butterfly stroke, wanting desperately to do the butterfly stroke, year after year, and never being able to raise his body up out of the water as high as it needs to go. He's never given up, though.

He stands in the water, his older-man chest drooping a bit, and he waves, his lion grin spreading over his sharp canines, his beard dripping water.

I wave back, then remember the cover protects the pool and the leaves are just beginning to turn. I remember it is already dark and all that I see really lives inside my head.

What will I do once I get inside? Shower, I guess. Rid myself of hospital stench. That settles it. I arise from the lounge chair and let myself into the back door of the Tudor-style house we bought twenty years ago, when Joey's speaking engagements began to pile one upon another. The mullioned window over the kitchen sink holds black diamonds, and the brick floor glimmers when I turn on the kitchen light.

Pumpkin, our tabby cat, races in and rubs against my legs. I pick him up, feel comforted by his purring, and tend to his needs. Poor thing. Only a few drops of water bead in the bowl, and no food, not even a stray bit of kibble by the baseboard, promises a bite. The kitchen table, long and scarred yet glowing with orange oil, sits empty, and I know it will never be completely peopled again.

One instant, one Jell-O salad flash.

I flip the light switch by the back stairway, illumining one part of our art collection that zigzags up the stairwell walls. Nothing valuable, really, just student art Joey offered to buy when someone needed cash. And a few of my photos from college days, when my dreams were my own and my life was only about me.

I cannot go up to our bedroom. So I walk down the hallway and into our living room.

He's everywhere in here. His old typewriter on an antique secretary we found in Tennessee. His collection of steins from all over Germany. His attempts at string art, macramé, watercolors, woodcarving, and bottle cutting litter the walls and mantel.

This place, which everyone always said was warm and cozy with its knotty pine support beams and floors and golden stucco walls, just appears gloomy and faded as I see it through my own eyes. My own lonely eyes.

Old sofas. Odd end tables and knickknacks. Antiques of various periods and nationalities that once mingled like old friends at a cocktail party now look like strangers gathered together at a newly opened bar. They're almost begging me to stick a Purple Heart sign on them and banish them curbside.

I realize how much Joey filters my view. My eyes catch a prayer book resting on his favorite chair near the front bay window. An Episcopal prayer book. A mysterious Episcopal prayer book. Joey loves the mystical mumbo religion affords. I've never understood it. Never really wanted to, honestly.

My lack of interest seems silly now. But I needed to keep some part of myself separate from him, and even though I could have chosen his book collection, his big band recordings, or his love of imported beer, I chose to divorce myself from his religion. I believe I picked the right thing, because Joey never brought up what went on at mass, and he only insisted I accompany him to the Christmas Eve candlelight mass.

But there were times when he'd sit out on the deck overlooking the gardens, and he'd stare at the sliver of water visible through the next block of houses, and the sun would penetrate the leaves like strips of bridal veil, and he'd look as though he weren't really there at all.

That's the only way I know how to explain it.

He has a journal he's kept for years.

My skin recoils under the hot droplets of the shower, and I wonder if the water will wash away my liver spots as it sluices away the hospital. My true wish, however, is that it would sluice me away, disintegrating Pearly Laurel to nothing more than liquid spiraling around the lip of the drain, swirling down into the pipes to work her way into nature via a smelly treatment plant, to come back as something like a mushroom or a forsythia bush.

I comb my white hair back into a tight ponytail and throw on the last outfit I'll wear while my Joey is alive. I choose carefully. Joey's always loved the way I dress in artful, flowing, handmade pieces. I love wearing things others have loved in the creating. It makes me feel as though I'm part of something far bigger than my own risings and settings.

I pull on a pair of black pedal pushers, a black tank top, and an embroidered batik throw. Joey loves this throw that sparkles with silk thread and little mirrors.

I stand in front of the mirror of our small London hotel

room. No big swanky places for Joey. "I want to hear their stories, Pearly." Joey's never cared much for the affluent, who, unfortunately, are the ones who read his writing and support the school. But they sure love him! Who couldn't love a guy like Joey?

Joey approaches me with a smile and swats my behind. "Hi, lover." He kisses my earlobe.

He doesn't say "Hi, lover" in a sexy manner but in a comfortable "Hi, sweetie" way.

I brush my bobbed brown hair, each harsh stroke electrifying it to more mammoth proportions. Oh goodness. Sighing with drama, I reach for a barrette.

Joey's smile broadens. "You need to learn to love your hair, Pearly. I do." And he hands me a package. I gently tear open the tissue paper, and an exquisite yet simple delight fills me as a beautiful embroidered shawl spills onto my hands, its tiny mirrors capturing the evening sunlight streaming through the window.

So I loan my hair to nature's whims that night as we walk along St. James's Park, feeding the ducks and swans. Joey finds an old couple to mine for stories, and I settle in beside him, content to listen.

The phone rings, jerking me out of my sleep. Sleep? Oh, dear. I had sat down on the sofa to recompose my decomposing self. Just for a minute, mind you.

But the morning sun now shines through the picture window in front of me, casting white diamonds on the wood floor. The leaves outside, just starting to yellow, jangle on their stems like golden charms on a bracelet.

I scrape the receiver up from the end table and

punch the ON button. "Yes?"

"Pearly?"

"Hello, Maida."

Maida lives across the street. She calls the Bay her backyard. Lucky Maida. A spinster, she's spun like an electron in that huge house all her life. She maintains the place all by herself. "Me and Time-Life Books," she says. Despite its frightful resemblance to some odd three-dimensional patchwork quilt with its various widths of siding and trim—usually whatever's on sale at Hechinger's or Home Depot—the house stands in solid defiance to men everywhere. Maybe too solid, like a pair of orthopedic shoes, or one of those sea captain beds with the hideous cannonballs on top.

"Something's wrong over there. I can tell."

Maida thinks she's clairvoyant as well as handy.

I'm glad she called. I need something usual. "Maybe the fact that the car was gone all the night before last had something to do with it?"

"Oh, no, it's more than that."

Maida's my age or thereabouts, but no gray hair sprouts from *her* head, just cool, ashy brown. And she lets it air-dry in a curly halo around her head. No bar-rettes for Maida. No bright colors either. Maida wears khaki bottoms and white tops. Period. Every morning during the school year she straps on her Clarks and foots it down to Lafayette School, where she is the cook. If Maida carts food over to the house, you can be sure the pot's cubic inches are pretty much that of a Custom Cruiser.

"Well, you're right about something being wrong."

I tell her everything, and she cries, sniffing whenever I pause. I stop several times to swallow the tears. But I manage the story somehow, leaving out the Jell-O salad aspect for my sake and Joey's dignity.

"I'll be right over, hon."

"Don't bother, Maida. I'm heading back down to the hospital after I eat some breakfast. I guess they'll take him off the ventilator soon after."

"You want company?"

"No, thanks. It's always been just Joey and me. It needs to be that way at the end."

Maida understands. "Let me know when you need me, babe."

"Will do."

"And I know you will need me eventually. So if I don't hear from you by tomorrow, I'm coming over."

"Yes ma'am."

Later today, when I invite her to the funeral, she'll offer to make food for the gathering afterward. And I will accept.

"Can you call the school for me?" I ask.

"Will do."

"And State Farm?"

"Sure."

"Hey, what's happening with Brock?"

Brock fills the role of king of the heartthrobs on the soap opera Maida would mainline if possible. *Loves, Lies, and Lifetimes.* Last time I heard, he and the show's main vixen, a platinum blonde named Shelby, had traveled back into their past lives, back to ancient Egypt where she is Nefertiti and he a young slave named Jahi.

Heartsick with love for his queen, he puts himself in danger every other day merely to touch the hem of her garment. Finally, the Egyptian palace guards throw him into prison.

Maida taps the receiver. "Are you sure it's the time for mundane conversation?"

"More that you can believe."

"Well"—she lowers her voice as though she gossips about living souls—"Shelby-slash-Nefertiti has visited the prison in the middle of the night to see if the reports of Brock-slash-Jahi are true. She sees him wasting away and takes pity on him, and she kisses him on the lips. Well . . . his eyes open, and she's smitten because she sees the love in them—isn't that romantic—and she kisses him once more and leaves quietly. But . . . that night she can't sleep, and she's smiling like crazy there in her bed on her Nile boat."

"I see an affair coming!"

"Of course! But it's going to be difficult considering he's a prisoner now."

"But she's the queen, right? What's her husband's name again, the pharaoh?"

"Who cares?"

"That's for sure, Maida."

"Be nice, Pearly. But get this . . . back in present day, Shelby's being investigated by this private detective!"

"Why?!"

"Her dead husband, Rafe—remember that slime bucket? Well, he isn't really dead!"

"But he was ground up by an industrial meat grinder last year! I actually saw that episode."

Maida sucks in air and whispers, "I guess it wasn't him after all."

"It sure does make you wonder about your ground beef, though, doesn't it?"

Maida laughs. "I'm glad you haven't lost your sense of humor, Pearly."

"Sometimes it's all a person has."

"That's the truth."

"I've got to go on down to the city soon. It's time."

That's all. Just . . . it's time.

I'm fifty years old and standing before her casket, looking down at a farmer's wife's hands now cold. Still dry, though. Mom's hands were always so dry and cracked. They smelled of Lubriderm and dish soap. They spent countless hours smoothing my head as it lay in her lap during evening TV viewings.

Pop died three years ago. My Mongoloid brother, Harry, who went to live at a boarding house in Princess Anne when Mom got cancer, stands here holding my hand. Only six of us attend the viewing, the funeral, the interment. My cousins Peta and Cheeta as well as our old neighbor from childhood, Shrubby Cinquefoil, stand in silence. We don't know the priest, and he didn't know Mom, so we tell him to skip the eulogy. He sighs in relief.

The priest intones some Bible verses and then we stroll away, hand in hand in hand, Joey, me, then Harry, to our car. My feet feel much too light, as if some foot fairy changed them from flesh and blood to Styrofoam. "I'm glad her suffering is over."

Joey squeezes my hand. "I enjoyed having her around. You'll have more free time on your hands now. That might be difficult."

He opens the car door, and I slide in, looking into softened eyes. "Will you get the rental company to come for the bed and all?" I ask.

Joey nods and shuts my door. We deposit Harry at the home, drive an hour to the ocean, and sit near the breakers until the horizon tops the sun. I sleep the entire way back to Havre de Grace and I dream about my mother, only she isn't sick, and she laughs as her dark hair blows in the wind, a tendril sticking into her bright pink lipstick. She laughs more and doesn't pull it free.

Joey's always enjoyed reading poetry to me, and I pretend to understand. Sometimes I actually do. But always, no matter how cerebral or lofty the words and thoughts, the sound of his voice is enough.

"I think I'll have a little more of that broccoli salad. Would you like something else?"

Yes, I'd like something else. No kidding I'd like something else!

I'd like you just like you were. I'd like to feel your feet under the sheets near my calves, and I wouldn't tell you your toenails need clipping. I'd like to see the mug you could have easily placed in the dishwasher yourself sitting in the sink. I'd like to observe you when you don't realize it as you read or play your guitar. I'd like to watch you eat a failed meal on my part and pretend it's a Julia Childs masterpiece. I'd just like to watch Julia Childs with you. Even that would be enough.

I circle around the yard in my black pants and shirt, a cup of coffee in my hands. I stroll into the small, wooded portion in the back east corner. The moss I planted years ago cushions my bare feet, and the newly decaying autumn leaves insulate me from the sound of town traffic two streets over. Decay seems plain nervy right now. People really should die in spring, when at least you'd have the comfort of new life erupting all around you like the first laugh of a baby.

Rocking on the bench swing we placed here this past summer, I light up a cigarette. Joey guaranteed a smooth installation, but we ended up enlisting the help of Maida, who laughed like Phyllis Diller almost the entire afternoon. I can't sit here. I can't sit still. I walk back through the yard, look at the pool. This time I don't see Joey. I only see the cigarette smoke curling in front of me, the rest of the world blurred and remote. I throw the butt into the planter I filled with sand and bury the burning end, feeling sorry for it somehow, to be extinguished so soon. I decide maybe another nap would be prudent. I have yet to sniff Joey's sneakers.

Back in the kitchen I call the doctor. "I'll be in early this afternoon. How is he?"

"His kidneys are beginning to shut down now."

"Then I'll be there in an hour or so."

"Just have the nurse page me, Mrs. Laurel."

"Thank you."

Only a little time remains to drink him in. I begin my search for Joey in the kitchen.

Green tea in bags. Early morning, rumpled Joey.

Salted cashews. Reading the newspaper Joey.

Five corkscrews. The better mousetrap Joey.

A bottle of Australian merlot. For our anniversary Joey.

Bamboo skewers he's never used. I'll do dinner for you Joey.

Skippy peanut butter. Hey, it's for the students Joey.

Fresh ground coffee. Bought it for you, lover Joey.

A mug fashioned during his pottery phase. Can't get rid of anything Joey.

A clay ashtray he sculpted with his first-grade fingertips. Can't imagine kids making ashtrays at school nowadays Joey!

His grandmother's stoneware tureen. We always use it for Irish stew, sweet and sour meatballs, cabbage and noodles, and the soups I love to make when the weather turns.

Soup is the freshly washed down comforter of food. That's what Joey always said.

I examine the box of tea, then set it on the counter near the door.

A few minutes later the bathroom throw rug, a huge sunflower, cushions my feet. I only bought it last week. It made me feel so delighted, so sunny and at home with my world.

Straight razor in a shaving mug. Fluffy bristle brush. Cake of shaving soap. Relics of a bygone era. My father's razor, his father's brush.

Contact case and solutions. Extra pair of glasses.

Polo cologne.

Dark blue Oral B toothbrush, bristles fountaining out to the sides.

Colgate. Almost empty. No other tube in sight.

Listerine. The green kind. Almost empty. No other bottle in sight.

My goodness, I've been lax in the toiletries shopping! Did I instinctively know he wouldn't be needing them?

Prescriptions. Toprol. Rocaltrol. Baby aspirin. The high blood pressure cornucopia of ailment blockers.

Spots from shaving soap on the mirror.

Before I realize what I am doing, I find I am licking them off the reflective surface. I do not open my eyes for fear of what I will see.

The tang constricts my tongue.

I grab the closed straight razor and run from the room into the hallway. I cannot raid the bedroom yet.

So I crouch on the floor against the wall of the upstairs hallway, right beneath a photo of my brother and me taken thirty years ago. Hugging myself, I rock a bit, willing my arms to belong to someone else. Mother? Father? Grandma Peta? Joey?

Who?

The clock over the fireplace downstairs *thunks* the quarter-hour. We purchased that clock in a dim, dusty London antique shop ten years ago. Had the greatest laugh with the owner, a froglike, woody-scented man named Gavin, over the Royal Family and whether or not their teeth are to the manor born or if they surgically give themselves those overbites to make up for their lack of a chin.

Even now I smile at the memory and allow my feet to slide out from beneath my rear until I sit with my legs straight out. Oh, dear, but my knees have become knobby over the years. So much living we've done, Joey and I.

I tap my toes along the walnut shoe molding anchoring the other side of the hallway. I slide my hands through the dust as though I'm making an angel. I chuckle now, a slide show of winter days with Joey projecting behind my eyes. The man always slipped and slid—and with absolutely no grace. He reminded me of a cartoon character at times like that, a thousand arms waving up and down at his sides, a protracted "Oh, nooooooo!" blowing from between his lips.

I climb to my feet, feeling positively arachnoid as all twenty digits make contact with the floor.

I groan.

I heft.

Through the doorway, my sight catches on the skirt of our four-poster bed. Its white Hardanger embroidery dusts the floor, reminding me of my embroidery phase that lasted for the decade between 1975 and 1985. Joey even tried his hand at a little needlework during that period. Did well too, but he soon tired of it and moved along to something else. I can't quite remember whether it was model boats or wood-burning.

I rise completely and finally enter the pale blue room. Plate shelving encircles the entire room, Delft pieces resting along it. I pull the stepstool leading up to my side of the bed over to the wall and pull down a tiny porcelain frog that belonged to Joey's mother. I kiss its cool surface and place it back on the shelf. Dust clings to my lips. I rub it off with the back of my hand, but my tongue still seeks the remainder. I grimace at the grit and climb back down.

My eyes circle the room like a radar scanner, blipping on Joey's things:

Tortoise shell reading glasses. Very William F. Buckley.

A man's jewelry box lined with dark green felt.

A compartmented teak tray littered with odds and ends—one each of the new state quarters, paper clips, cuff links, and an old two-dollar bill. "Someday, I'm going to spend this on something really special, Pearly," he'd say. "I don't know what it is, but I'll know it when I see it."

"Two bucks isn't much, Joey."

"Maybe not. But I'm sure it will be all I need."

I slip the bill off the tray.

Truth is, we never spend much time in the bedroom. Just sleep and make love here. Oh, Joey is such a tender man. He treats me like the diamond tiepin that glints in the tray. I saved up for five years to buy that piece of jewelry. Five years of stuffing extra bits of change and dollar bills into a ginger jar proudly displaying the words *Harford County, Maryland* in calligraphic-style letters on its belly. He wears that pin every time he wears a tie. I grab this too.

Downstairs once again, I place the razor and the two-dollar bill next to the box of green tea on the kitchen table.

I close the door on Joey's study. I cannot enter the room that for the most part he alone inhabited.

Finally, the sunroom floor at the back of the house

splays beneath my feet. The late morning sunshine streams from windows on three sides and warms the room. We sit out here together more than any other place. For three seasons of the year.

Faded red lounge chair.

Pipe holder/ashtray combo nearby. Never been used. Joey just likes the idea.

Small oak bookshelf he bought at a yard sale on Harford Road a few years back. I remember it well. "Handmade, Pearly! Five bucks!" And he smiled his purity upon me. So untouched yet so instinctive. I've never lost my amour for Joey. Oh, the amour.

1966

I walk down Charles Street. Finishing up my freshman year, I'm set on being a photojournalist someday, traveling to places like Vietnam and exposing the evils of the war machine. Right now though, I am tired. It's Saturday, and I worked all day downtown waiting tables at Burke's Restaurant. The bus dropped me off a few blocks back from my apartment near campus.

Something's happening over on the lawn near the Carroll Mansion, the centerpiece of our campus.

Music. Singing.

Well, that's not too strange nowadays here at Johns Hopkins. All this war stuff brings out all sorts of creative urges in people. Self-expression, you know.

I reach into my bag for the little Instamatic I keep with me all the time, because you never know what will pop up in front of you. And I'm learning to do all sorts of groovy things in the darkroom. Someday, Pearly, someday people will actually *pay* you for your pictures. I am determined to give them their money's worth. I'm going to be the best. And not only the best but the boldest. I will go into the line of fire. I will turn around and grab that shot while the rest of the world runs away.

As I cut across the lawn toward the gathering, the music clarifies, and so does their garb.

Bogus.

Jesus Freaks.

Kumbaya. Kumbaya.

Put your hand in the hand of the man.

As I said, bogus. It's all bogus.

Who knows, though? Some good pictures might surface. Maybe somebody'll get mad and act like one of us heathens! That would be rich. A fight at the Jesus Freak meeting. Oh, yes, I can see it now—and can't help but chuckle.

Standing before them, I'm thinking I'll at least capture some interesting faces here. Lots of closed eyes and enraptured expressions. Don't often see that out in the open for public consumption! Too bad I don't carry my 35mm with me all the time. I'd like to zoom in on some of them.

My mind photographs the group before my camera does. A dozen or so sit in various positions, cross-legged, legs stretched out in front, one girl on her knees, together composing an oval. Several young women, much like my own circle of friends in appearance, sing a high descant of alleluias. Pretty, even I admit. One woman, much older than the others, at least forty-five, wears a lavender suit with a cameo pin on the lapel. Her long hair dips from her crown into a thick bun.

Weird in this crowd.

She lightly taps a tambourine, face clear of concern, smoothed by some cosmic, inner peace, I guess. Hey, whatever works, you know?

But what's an old lady doing in a group like this?

Young men fill in the rest of the circle. I have a feeling some of these people are graduate students because they look a little less self-conscious.

Next to the woman in lavender sits the guitar player. He's beautiful. Definitely a grad student. Hair, prematurely white, waves back from his smooth forehead into a ponytail at the nape of his neck. Eyes closed, he finger-picks delicately, prayerfully, I guess, at the strings. His voice rises only slightly above the others as he sings, "alleluia to the king." He intrigues me. I am a voyeur suddenly, peering like a Peeping Tom into someone else's Holy of Holies.

I snap one picture only. Of this man. I feel shame. I've become one of the exploiters. But I cannot leave without this.

I rest for a moment in Joey's chair and lean down to examine his bookshelf. The sun illumines the dust particles in the air, my breath moving them in mad circles like tiny rockets. I lean back into his chair, lay my hands on the small stack atop the case. A prayer book, a New Testament, and a diary. Breathing through my nose, I try to smell him. Oh please, Joey. Be here. Please, just be here now.

Grabbing all three books, I run from the room, shutting the glass door behind me, allowing the dust to settle back into its own comfortable existence. I hope it takes a long time to do so.

Placing the books on the counter with the rest of my collection, I walk into the pantry behind the kitchen. I've been threatening for years to turn it into a darkroom. But something has always stopped me. Fear? Anxiety? Reluctance to find out that I really didn't possess what it takes to succeed, to make a stand for the glory of the picture, to be brave enough to be in the right place at the right time?

Maybe some cereal now. Maybe that would go down. I grab a box of Joey's cereal—I'm a fried-egg-on-toast type myself—and step back into the kitchen. I loved this place yesterday, its warm, barn-red walls and wrought iron light fixtures. And the armoire desk Joey bought me for my last birthday. I'd been wanting one ever since they came out. My photo albums rest on top. I grab my special album. Only my very best pictures of Joey reside there. I sit down at my polished table and look through, all the while chomping on Grape-Nuts and wondering if the demonic nuggets are doing a number on my tooth enamel.

Not many pictures, really, fill the album pages. But they fill my heart to bursting with the love I've borne for this man for over three decades. He was so handsome and striking as a younger man, so carefree looking and intelligent. And in his later years now, he still has that Swiss, too-steeped-in-life's-wonders-to-notice-what-others-think air about him. Well, he used to anyway.

After my date with Euell Gibbons and his evil nuggets, I am as ready as I can be. I stack all the items in a tote bag, gather my purse and throw, and head out to the car. My heels resound, as though I am walking on empty caves. They used to bury people in caves, didn't they?

Time to kill Joey. I wonder where that thought came from. But I know exactly where. This feels so awful, worse than putting our cat to sleep five years ago, a calico named Mr. Stuffin'. I hear all the things we said to each other on the way to the vet's.

It's better this way.

He needs to be put out of his misery.

He doesn't understand the pain he's in.

Why should he suffer for our sake?

Are we keeping him alive for ourselves or for him?

It's better this way.

Joey reaches for my hand. "It's better this way, Pearly."

But my hand still rests on the door handle of the car. I could have sworn I felt his touch just then.

I bite my lip almost the entire way into the city. By the time I walk into the ward, it is swollen and numb like the rest of life around me.

The doctor won't be in for another hour or two. Emergency surgery. I ruffle through the Joey items in my tote bag, and since he cannot speak to me aloud right now and never will again, I open the journal. I don't know when he began this particular volume, or this first passage, because Joey journaled in whatever book lay at hand.

Oh good, this passage rings somewhat familiar. They always include it during funeral scenes in movies and, well, funerals in real life. I've attended plenty of those over the years. We all do, I guess.

Meditations on the 23rd Psalm

No. 1: The Lord is my shepherd.

The Lord: Jahweh, Jehovah. Almighty God. Eternal, unchanging, beautiful, terrible, just, merciful, compassionate, slow to anger. His mercies are new every morning. Faithful and true. All-powerful, all-knowing, everywhere at once. The Lord.

This is my shepherd, this stunning Being who created me in His image, so that my hand would fit flawlessly in His own. The Lord is my shepherd. And with pillar of fire and cloud He leads me through the wilderness, through the deep waters of my Red Seas, through the bitterness of my Maras. He leads me through disease and the pestilence of my own sin, my own wanderings away from His care. I am unworthy, and my wounds of humanness ache as I look upon the Hand that holds my own, the Hand of the second person of the Trinity, my Lord Jesus Christ. And the Hand, through which my own gaze, my sinful sight passes, pulls me across the mountains, valleys, and rocks, pulls me like a Father would a child, with a certain, steady yank across streams—sometimes raging, sometimes deathly calm—into His arms. For sometimes simply the Hand is not enough, sometimes the embrace of Deity is called for, and He knows when to extend such affection and when to continue onward. I do not know this. I possess not this Divine sense of timing, for I would be drunk upon the Holy embrace all the day, willing to stand unmoving. But the Lord is my shepherd and forward I must go.

I cannot read on. Joey's told me everything I need to know, and now I wait, wishing for silence so that I can hear his heart beat. But only my own pulse thunders in my ears, sounding like my mother's old dryer. I feel dry but cannot leave this chair for a drink. The moments wane, more precious now, so few of them left to us. Well, to me, I guess. Joey's gone. Remember, Pearly?

So I pull the tote bag onto my lap and rummage through its remaining contents. I lay Joey's belongings out on the tray table. The Bible, the prayer book, the journal, the razor, the tea, the diamond tiepin, and the two-dollar bill.

"Something special. I'm saving it to buy something special."

Joey's beard has always been so special to me. So soft and comforting.

I grab the bill and head down to the pharmacy, where I buy a travel-sized can of shaving cream. I want his beard. I can't imagine it being buried with him. He threatened to shave it off every summer, but I talked him into keeping it, year after year. It's my beard, really. He kept it for me.

"I just need to shave my husband," I explain to the Middle Eastern young man behind the register.

"Yes ma'am." Yezmaahm.

"Do many women come down to buy this?"

"Yes ma'am. That's two fifty-three."

I hand over the two-dollar bill and some change.

I stop at the nurses' station. "Have you got a Ziploc bag or the like, Cindy?"

The nurse sitting at the computer nods. "Just a minute, Mrs. Laurel. I always keep an extra one in my purse for emergencies."

"You got kids?"

She nods, her auburn hair reflecting the lights. "Yep. Five of 'em." She hits one key and turns to face me. "There. That's done. I swear, they got computers to make things easier, but it only serves to keep us at the keyboard a lot longer than we should be. I did not get into nursing so I could do a bunch of data entry. Now let me get that bag."

She reaches into a drawer and pulls out a large canvas bag. I lean forward and am amazed at the variety of items inside, the most unusual being a garlic press. Why in the world would anyone be walking around with a garlic press inside her purse?

"Here you go! Found it!" She hands me a bag.

I try to chuckle as I take it. "You've probably put some amazing things in Ziplocs."

"Oh, yeah. They find all sorts of things they simply have to keep, things deserving of a Ziploc."

I lean onto the counter. "You sound like you enjoy being a mother."

"Oh, I do! How many kids do you and Mr. Laurel have?"

I shake my head. "We weren't able to."

Her face falls. "I'm so sorry! I'm such a boob. I really should be more tactful."

"You're not a boob, Cindy. Most people do have kids."

"He doing any better today?"

"You haven't heard?"

"Heard what? I just got on."

"We're taking him off the machines."

Her heavy chest heaves in a sigh. "I'm sorry, Mrs. Laurel."

I simply nod.

"Is there anything you need me to do?"

"I'll let you know. I just want to shave his beard now."

"Want me to help?"

"No thanks."

"Buzz me if you need *anything*."

I smile as best I can and turn away.

Joey's skin in these parts hasn't seen the light of day in twenty years. I lather up the beard with probably too much cream, but having never really done anything like this before, I figure it's better to overdo it than underdo it. He looks like a whipped-cream dessert.

Grabbing a kidney-shaped bowl, I examine the terrain, hoping against hope I won't shave open an artery or something very damaging. Oh, right. Like that matters. Actually, perhaps bleeding to death falls into a more humane category than suffocating.

I drag the straight razor down from his sideburn, and I kiss the pink skin, leaving my lips to linger after each stroke. I taste the invisible remains of the shaving cream.

"When did a cement truck pull up and fill my insides?" I whisper to my husband. "I want to say something to you, Joey, but nothing sounds right coming out into this room here. It's cold and it's lonely and so unworthy of you."

The music stops, and I hear the sound of a single pair of feet loping in my direction on the grass behind me. I turn, and he stops abruptly, right in my face. Yes, it's the guy with the guitar. I knew it would be him. Out of that entire weird group, he would run after someone.

What a tan!

"Whoa!" he says. "Sorry! Didn't expect you to pull up short like that!"

His voice sounds scuffed, naturally hoarse. Sexy. Very. His hair, striated with sun-soaked silver, shines even more brightly close up. I want to rub my hand over it, or tug the ponytail.

I smile. "That's okay. I heard somebody running up behind me."

"I'm not exactly the Indian Guide type."

I cross my arms. "So can I help you with something?"

"Well, no. I noticed you standing there for a bit and wondered if you had any questions or anything?"

"Questions?"

"About God. People hanging around on the fringes usually have questions about God."

How's this for direct? I shake my head. "Nah."

His robin-egg eyes go round. "Really? None?"

"No."

So I'm lying.

He shrugs. "Well, then. But just in case you find you do have some, we meet over at the lawn in front of the art museum, weather permitting, every Thursday at five for Bible study, singing, etcetera."

"You a graduate student?" I change the subject.

"Yes."

So I'm right.

"What about you?"

"Freshman. Journalism."

"Brilliant."

"Yeah. I like it."

He shuffles from one foot to the next. "Would you like to grab a cup of coffee?"

I decide I need to know more. Journalistic curiosity, of course.

"If you tell me your name."

"Joe Laurel."

"I'm Pearly Kaiser."

"Brilliant name! Worthy of an explanation, surely."

"Pearls were my mother's favorite gem. They've always brought good luck to our family."

That satisfies him. "Brilliant. Interesting name matching an interesting woman."

Woman? I look down at my speckled arms. Me? A farm girl from the Eastern Shore? We walk toward the coffee shop in the basement of an apartment building across the street.

"When you say 'brilliant' do you mean, like, 'groovy' or something?"

"Precisely."

He's a *smart guy*.

"What are you getting an advanced degree in, Joe?"

"Education and literature."

"Brilliant," I say.

"Groovy," he says.

"No. I really meant brilliant."

And Joe blushes. "You know you have a beautiful smile, Pearly."

"Brilliant?"

"Precisely." His grin injects me with a warmth like that of stepping onto a warm school bus after waiting at the stop for fifteen minutes in the bitter cold. Without mittens.

Though I've only just met him, I slip my hand into his, and he holds tight. I know I'm embarking on a journey. Several times I've heard wives say they knew they'd met the love of their life upon first introduction.

Am I experiencing that now?

It sure feels like it.

You're such a dummy, Pearly. This guy's only trying to sell you Jesus.

I feel like a tree that's had the heart of its branches cut out to make room for the power lines. Trees in that condition sadden me. They become inorganic, more object than life form.

There's something I need to know about Joey. Something definite I need to take away with me today besides the beard, which, now washed free of the shaving cream, inhabits the Ziploc in my tote bag.

I admit, I do fixate on moles and liver spots. But what other marking, besides a wrinkle, behaves more like a yardstick than age spots? Why human beings enjoy measuring their surroundings and the items contained therein mystifies me. But I can't claim to be otherwise. I suppose I could choose to count wrinkles, but it could take so long, I would definitely lose count, and my close vision isn't what it used to be either. At this moment, exactly twenty moles and ten liver spots adorn my hands like mud puddles in a snowscape. They are not evenly distributed, for my left hand has more liver spots than moles, and my right hand more moles than liver spots. Two raised moles decorate each hand, moles which I would love to bite right off, but then the scars would be far worse!

I take Joey's right hand in my own, thankful no IVs spear it. They installed a central line yesterday. Counting, I pair one wonderful thing about this man with each blemish. His hands are not as littered as my own.

Loving.
Hard-working.
Witty.
Kind.
Batty.
Understanding.
Patient.
Hopeful.
Gullible.
Absent-minded.
Sweet.
Innocent.
Curious.

Holy.

Giving.

Trusting.

Strong.

I am done with both hands. Seven liver spots: two on the right, five on the left. Ten moles: five tiny ones on the left hand, three tiny ones on the right, and two raised ones on the right as well.

I write that down on the back of my social security card.

I count the marks on his face. Fifteen. I write that down too. Reaching into the drawer of the nightstand, I remove his silver pen, a gift from me for our twenty-fifth anniversary, and place everything back into my tote bag. I search for one more memento.

Joey's feet stick out from the bottom of the pink cotton blanket. Yellow terry socks with skid pads stretch over them. He always had pretty feet, none of those finger-toes so many males sprout.

Joey's last socks.

I smile. Joey would smile too if he could read my mind. "For heaven's sake, Pearly. They're socks!"

But Joey's almost dead.

I pull them from his feet, settle my hands inside them, and wait.

I look better than I ever have before, and that's not being vain. I should look better today, for I am a bride.

The blue Chesapeake waltzes in the golden June sun, and the corn has just begun to sprout a tender green in my father's fields behind me. Mom's purple irises wave in the zephyr, blessing the air with their perfume, and everybody's waiting for me to appear at the door and sashay up the grassy aisle between the bright white rental chairs. An insane desire to "mash potato" my way to Joey makes me giggle.

Dad squeezes my hand. "Nervous, Pearly?"

"No, Dad." For through the screen I see my love, handsome in a charcoal gray suit and a light blue tie that matches his eyes. I never thought of myself as corny, but this man brings out all the corniness I must own. Like writing his name on scratch paper, ringing it with hearts. Or lying next to him on the couch and just staring into his eyes for, how long? Hours usually. All those falling-in-love things that will fade with time but will always be looked upon with fondness. For time will not split us apart as it does some couples. It will only serve to meld us together until we are truly one heart, one mind, one soul.

See? How corny can you get?

I don't care.

It's all brilliant to me.

Yet something about watching him through the screen saddens me, for the old screen sags, and I see we are young and taut for but a season.

He sports a haircut for the occasion. "It's the least thing I can do for Dad," he said yesterday when we walked across the lawn toward the rehearsal. Joey's mom died years ago. His father's sister Evelyn, a "gay divorcée" in from Las Vegas last night, is his only other relative attending. A tight floral sheath girdles her curves, and a smart hat, resting on beige blonde hair and matching her purse and shoes, tops the classy yet impertinent ensemble. When she first saw Joey yesterday, she left a big lipstick mark to the left of his mouth and didn't wipe it off.

Joey didn't either.

I wear my mother's wedding gown from the forties, only we pinned some flowers here and there to freshen its look. A lovely *something old.* I made the veil for *something new* by sewing yards of chiffon to a crown of roses and daisies from my cousin Peta's garden. Some Indian beads of Grandma's circle my left ankle. One of the beads is blue. Sad, right?

I borrowed some deodorant from Dad which has to count for *something borrowed* because nothing else on me qualifies. Sadder still!

Oh, who cares? I'm marrying the love of my life. I've known Joey for three months, and that's plenty, because when you know, you know.

His priest, a man named Father Damien from their Episcopal parish on Charles Street in Baltimore City, waits there with Joey at the head of the aisle. My father pushes open the screen door, both of us wincing as it groans and wails. The aroma of pit beef cooking and crabs steaming in the side yard summons that overall aura of childhood, and I begin to shake. I step onto the porch, and Father Damien whispers something to Joey. Joey looks at me, and we smile.

How can I live without you?

The doctor said he would be done by now. The twilight thickens into a deeper dusk, a gauzy world tottering on the edge of velvet. Machines hum and click, and alarms sound every so often. I see that nothing collects in the round, malleable cavity of the urine bag.

How can I live without you?

Nine o'clock, and Joey's chest still rises and falls in that jerky *pip* and *thunk* of the confident ventilator. I feel as if I am the one expiring with each tick of that horrible second hand on the clock over the doorway, dying to the beat. I will the doctor to arrive soon, and each time I picture his shadow falling across the tile, another shot of adrenaline releases. I am skittish and nervous and sick.

The time has come. I keep thinking that. The time has come.

But the time isn't coming because, according to the nurse, this emergency surgery turned into a doozie. I just tried to smile at her.

She brought me a sandwich a few hours ago. Turkey and American cheese on rye bread. I actually ate it. I couldn't believe it. How can I eat at a time like this? What's wrong with me? Don't I love him the way I think I do?

Every minute delivers a wash of tears that I refuse to free, because I don't want to spend the last moments of Joey's life crying. There'll be time enough for that.

Or will there? And then what?

Then perhaps the time to pull the plug on myself will have arrived.

I feel antsy.

Joey's clothes lie folded in a white plastic hospital bag

in the closet. I decide to go through them in a last effort to connect with a living man.

His watch. I put that right in my tote bag. I gave that to him for his fortieth birthday. Real gold too.

Khaki green Dockers. Nothing in the right pocket but the receipt from that blasted Golden Corral. I rip it into little shreds, then sit down in my chair. His wallet in the left pocket. I'll need that, I'm sure. I briefly examine the cards inside: health insurance, driver's license, social security, Klein's check-cashing card. My picture. Oh, my, there it is, my senior portrait from high school. Now where did he find that?

I move on.

Boxers I bought him at The Gap. Bumblebees fly all over the mustard-colored cotton.

Soft, well-worn white undershirt.

Stewart plaid shirt. I lift it out, burying my nose in its pliancy. Ah yes, his smell. Oh dear God, his smell is right here. I fold it neatly and put it in my tote bag with the other Joey things. I decide to throw in the T-shirt and the boxers, too. I hug the bag to myself, and I stare at Joey until my eyes burn and I forget to breathe.

The doctor joins me at the bedside thirty minutes later. "How are you doing, Mrs. Laurel?"

"As well as can be expected." Isn't that what you're supposed to say?

"I'm sorry to keep you so long."

I shrug. I can't say, "That's okay," because it's not. And yet it is, too, right? I didn't want Joey to die sooner, did I?

He clears his throat. "We'll get started in a few minutes. Again, I'm so sorry."

Again, I shrug. This time I shake my head as well.

Ten moles. Seven liver spots.

"I think it's time to set him free, Doctor."

Joey believes in heaven, and I doubt skin blemishes flourish there, at least I hope not. So these things remain my own.

A few minutes later a male nurse enters and explains the procedure. I wish he were Cindy, but then I wouldn't want to put her through the ordeal. And maybe he's a specialist at this. If so, I feel for him. I try to listen to the words, but only "blah, blah, blah" makes it through. Until he says, "When it's over, we'll come and get you in the waiting room."

Oh, so I don't sit here? But surely that can't be? Don't you sit there, holding the dying hand, waiting between the click of the shutdown and the final self-issued breath? No?

I am relieved. I don't want to watch Joey die, I just realized. Some people do, I suppose. And I don't blame them. I say, "May I have one more minute with him?"

"Of course. Take as much time as you need."

He leaves, and I lean over Joey. "If you suffocate now, I'm sorry. I'm so sorry. I just don't know what else to do."

I take a chance and say, "If you hear me, squeeze my hand."

. . .

I kiss his lips one last time, flesh lingering on flesh, tears cementing them together for only seconds. I taste my lips as I straighten. Salt. Water. Him. I thank him for a lifetime of love, take a mental photograph, and leave the room before my abscessed heart erupts. The male nurse hurries up to me. "Shall I show you to the waiting room?"

"No, thank you. I know where it is."

I look back one last time, and I am staring down a well at Joey and the well is deep and the candle at the bottom is flickering wildly, its light growing smaller and bluer and truer, and soon it will follow the way of all that is temporal.

I walk past the waiting room, my feet unable to make the turn. Down the elevator, through the revolving door, I find myself in the thriving lights of a nighttime city.

Joey's blushing like crazy.

Oh, no! He's a virgin!

Inwardly, I roll my eyes and think this is one of those negatives about getting married so soon. He never made sexual advances during our courtship, something I found refreshing. Most of the guys on campus had paws on the ends of their arms, the clumsy buffoons.

Not that Joey and I didn't make out. We did, but he always stopped short of touching me "down there."

"You're too good for that," he'd say, then he'd get up from the couch in his apartment and suggest we do something else, "anything else."

I am not a virgin.

Crud.

Never in a million years did I expect to marry a virgin.

I mean, only lecherous *men* sowed their wild oats and settled down with an innocent.

I feel really dirty right now. And unexpectedly dirty, as though my Harley went out of control, skidded through a manure pile with me on it and crashed through a set of sparkling French doors right into a circumcision gathering or a first communion or a first-time mother as she rocks her newborn to sleep.

"Oh man, Joey."

I don't have to say anything else.

"You're experienced, aren't you?"

"Yeah. Sort of."

"I figured as much, Pearly."

I don't know whether to yell at him or cry. I just say, "This is awkward."

"Have you made love with anybody since we met?" he asks.

"No."

I stare out of the motel window and onto the highway. The neon sign flashes *Vacancy* every other second. Tawdry-like, as if it should really be saying, *Girls, Girls, Girls!* "This isn't a good setting to lose your virginity in, Joey." I turn back to face him. He's so vulnerable looking right now. I am in pain! I am immoral. I kind of suspected I was immoral, but right now I know it for sure and it is humiliating. None of those guys were worth this! Why didn't I see that then? And it wasn't like I even enjoyed it all that much. I just wanted to fit in and play the role of free spirit at one and the same time.

Now only car seats and crummy apartments and closets in classroom buildings come to mind, and I can hardly remember an accompanying face. It's all just genitalia and sin. This stinks more than the elephant emporium down at the zoo.

Then he smiles. "I'm twenty-eight years old, Pearly. If it makes you feel better, I've done everything but *the act,* and being a red-blooded male, I wouldn't care right now if we were in an abandoned factory!"

I chuckle despite my mortification.

"I have one favor to ask," I say. "Just don't expect me to teach you anything."

"Why's that?"

"From what I've heard, I'm not all that hot in bed." At least that's what Bob Lansing told me last year after I said I wasn't into commitment. "Maybe we'd do better to start from scratch. Maybe you'd better just lead the way."

Reaching out and touching my cheek with his fingertips, he tells me he loves me, that we're beginning a brand-new life together. "Brand-new, Pearly. Do you understand what that means?"

I do.

He smiles into my eyes and seals that informal vow with a soft kiss on my lips, lifting me out of the bargain basket at costume jewelry and placing me in a guarded case in the fine jewelry department, setting me aside now for him and only him, under the lock and key I willingly place in his hands.

The silence usually fills me.

Joey loved silence. He fed off it, nourished by its possibilities. "Pearly, silence has no boundaries."

I didn't understand that. I only understood that the sound of his breathing was all I needed to hear.

I flick a glance at the car clock. 9:42 P.M.

He's dead by now, Pearly.

At exactly 53 MPH I negotiate the skyway ramp leading from downtown to I-95. Now at its apex, I soar above Baltimore. Joey soars as well, I'll warrant. If there's anybody destined for heaven, it's Joey.

I examine my hands, keeping one eye on the road. But I see Joey's. Seven liver spots. Ten moles. I cannot go back to the hospital. I seek a greater silence, one with indelible boundaries encased by an impermeable membrane, only memories of a good life allowed to tumble and squeal within like lively kittens on an acre of early summer grass.

Joey would have understood.

I begin tumbling into a world of past-tense.

Joey would.

Joey did.

Joey had.

Joey was.

Only a very few modifiers can now be put with Joey *is*.

Dead.

Cold.

Decaying.

Gone.

"Nevermore," quoth the raven. I can say without hesitation that Edgar Allen Poe never envisioned his sinister bird as the mascot of an NFL team. And that seems to be the only thing I can say for certain right now. Joey thought the entire matter amusing, after all, "Nobody can replace the Colts, Pearly, nor should they try."

Forty minutes later, I pull over at the first gas station on Route 50 as I continue the journey to our vacation house on the Chesapeake Bay. I place both hands atop the steering wheel, and once more I count the liver spots and moles. I count until I can no longer see, a tear for each blemish magnifying the marks of a life lived for no other purpose than to love a man now gone, then spilling over.

Why I gave up on myself I don't know. It was never a conscious decision. I just delighted in my husband, that's all. So easy to do if you know Joey.

A phone booth sits vacant near the car, so I ring Maida after the tears dry. Thank goodness for her palindromic number or I'd have never committed it to memory in the first place. The first click of her answering machine sticks my eardrum, and I blurt before she can greet the unknown caller. "Joey wanted to be buried. We have a plot at Harford Memorial out on Route 155. Bye!"

Opening the jointy door, I sit upon the small cement slab in the booth and light up my first cigarette since leaving the hospital.

I stare at the pack.

Merit Ultra Lights.

Merit Ultra Lights? Ridiculous!

See, Joey is dead.

I crush the cigarette right away and walk into the Snak Mart. For some reason, I picture the hinged door of the phone booth waving in the balmy breeze and flying away into the darkness with a chipmunk laugh. Laughing at me. What a nutcase I am! Where is this craziness coming from?

"Marlboro Lights," I say to a cartoon character of a youth sporting bright red hair, an apple green shirt, and yellow shorts that expose the beginning of a butt crack and a pair of graying boxer shorts. I'll bet a father is raising this boy, someone who's never heard of Clorox.

He acknowledges my nonexistence, and I stare at the dazzling confectionary of tobacco delights. Oh, the packs line up so pretty with all their colorful boxes and sleeves. The glittering cellophane, too. Of course, the red on the pack of full-strength Marlboros catches my eye. It's usually the first to do so anyway.

Should I?

I haven't smoked these things since I met Joey. He just didn't seem to be deserving of a paramour who smoked full-strengths. Surely, it's one thing to smoke—that's bad enough, however fun and relaxing and sociable—but Reds? That points its finger right to a precipice of death. In point of truth, I can hardly imagine classy, willowy women like Grace Kelly or Audrey Hepburn or Cyd Charisse lighting up a Marlboro Red as they're sitting at The Carousel Club or The Florida Room. Or maybe I'm wrong. After all, I love them from my childhood. And those childhood loves can't be trusted. That's what makes them so wonderful.

Now Mae West holding a fired-up Red? Absolutely. Marlene Dietrich, too, or these days, Madonna or Pink or another one of those attention addicts. Well, Madonna I'm not, but I'm going to buy them anyway.

"Marlboro Reds," I say. So there. I look around me. No one present but cartoon boy to witness my crime. "I haven't smoked one of these since I was nineteen. But you see, my husband just died, and I thought—"

The phone rings. He lifts the receiver and tucks it under his jaw and ear in one swift motion. "Oh hey, Brian." He slips a pack out of the overhead rack. "That'll be $3.65," he mouths, designating me the unimportant one in this trio of communicating humanity.

I pay with a five.

He hands me a one spot and slides the change down long, sensitive looking fingers into my outstretched palm. I curl my own fingers around the coins, feeling his warmth. I hold my fist to my face. He doesn't notice, for he's saying, "I'm back. So how'd it play out with Tiffany?" He turns his back, and I drag myself past the cheese nips, the pink hairy snack cakes, the fifteen thousand flavors of bubble gum, the beef snacks, and the jerky bags.

He must not have heard me, that boy. Or perhaps I only imagined I spoke.

Outside now, I light up the full-strength smoke, inhale a deep, lung-sanding drag, sucking it into each individual sac of alveoli. Shoot, if I'm going to die eventually anyway, I might as well go whole hog. I decide to start collecting little tar beads deep inside myself, willing each drag and its black tailstream to absorb another saline tear, another day of my life. Maybe the insides of my lungs will glimmer as though lined with hematite, hardened and unable to sustain the body of my dead soul much longer.

I sit on the hood of my car as the final strands of autumn beach traffic slide by, weighed-down cars of late-going, thrifty vacationers bound for Ocean City.

Eleven o'clock already. I can't believe it, but my stomach rumbles. I find the next all-night drive-through, a Burger King not far from the Bay Bridge. But looking at the backlit menu, nothing sounds appealing. I figured I'd have a sporting chance with the flame-broiled aspect in play.

"Can I take your order?" the voice questions me.

I freeze. Not good. Too much pressure. Too much, too much. How can I possibly decide in less than thirty seconds? Not only does the sandwich need selecting, but beverage options, dessert options, condiments, and side dishes remain as well. Onion rings or fries? I blurt out the first words I read, "A milkshake? Chocolate?"

"What size?"

"I don't care."

"Excuse me, ma'am?"

"You pick."

"But—"

"Pick one!" I scream at her. This is not good. I gun the accelerator and whiz by the window, hiding my face behind the flap of my left hand. My wheels screech as I pull out onto the blacktop of the highway, barely missing a tractor-trailer.

He flips me off.

Don't you know? I think. Don't you know I'm dying inside? Can't you see the last thing I need tonight is somebody giving me the finger?

Of course not, Pearly. You're just another stupid woman driver to that guy.

The tollbooths of the Bay Bridge span the highway, and I pull out four dollars as I brake in front of the window. "Here you go."

"Have a good night," a pillowy man says. He smiles sadly, and I wonder if he has lost something precious too. I wonder if I'll develop a skill enabling me to identify other lonely halves. And yet I do not feel lonely, exactly. I was alone quite frequently in my life with Joey. I feel lost. I suppose that's it. Lost and insignificant, like a hairpin behind the sink cabinet, easily replaced, too unimportant to fish out with a coat hanger.

Despite this thought, I smile at the tollbooth operator and raise my eyes to the Bay Bridge, that five-mile span connecting Maryland to its better half across the Chesapeake Bay. Its lights stutter, red blinkers flashing up top where the birds soar, swaying in the arms of the winds. Closer to my comfortable range of vision, the other lights speak directly to me, green Xs over the open lanes, red Xs over the others.

Cables, horribly big, alarmingly small, disappear into each of four stretching towers, four mountainous harps holding up a roadway upon which the tires of the cars hum a tune, my tires providing the bass line.

Once across I pull off to the side, exhausted. Joey always drove across the bridge.

I rest on my hood once more, chain-smoking half the pack of Reds, hoping to join Joey all the sooner. I have the feeling he was holy enough for the both of us. Or at least I hope so. With him gone, I see myself for the wretch I am, for I cannot hide behind his glory any longer.

By my thirty-eighth birthday, I realized we'd already have adopted if we really intended to. We talked about it from time to time to time, and I even secreted away two pairs of booties, one set blue, the other pink, at the back of my underwear drawer. I still wonder why we never did. Maybe Joey didn't possess my ache. Or maybe I feared that Joey, ever throwing himself into his interest du jour, not to mention his position at the school, would transfer his affections from me to the child.

As if I knew *then* that he'd land face down in the Jell-O salad! And even if I did, that would hardly be a noble motive for adopting. No child deserves that much responsibility.

It's past eleven now, dark and cool. But I cannot drive any farther. Guilt creeps in through my opened tear ducts. I left Joey alone to die, to be buried. I hate myself more than usual.

I wonder what they're doing with his body right now? They've scoured the hospital looking for me, I'm sure, have called my home and left several messages. No doubt they're wondering right now which funeral home to call.

In Cambridge I pull over into the parking lot of the HG Restaurant. Joey and I always stopped here on our way back from our vacation home, a cabin we built on the shores of the family farm. Home cooking. And decoys for sale in every nook, on every shelf, beside every window. Although darkness shrouds the distance, I know the landscape has ironed itself out by now, that trees and fences outline level fields, and chicken farms spread their arms every few miles. Produce stands stagger in drunken construction down either side of the road leading east, and here I stand now, outside my car, unable to turn around and, upon thought, less able to simply disappear.

Wouldn't that be lovely? Poof! Pearly is gone, like some character in a *Twilight Zone* episode who fades from view at the same rate her dead husband's body cools. Maybe I should have been the popular fiction writer! I'm probably more delusional than most novelists.

I run across the highway to a phone booth at a closed gas station. I call the doctor's beeper number and then punch in Maida's number.

"Hello?"

"Maida, it's me again."

"Are you all right, Pearly?"

"I'm fine. I'll be fine. I need you to take care of some things for me. I'll call you in a couple of weeks."

"Pearly?"

"Listen, the doctor should be calling you any minute, okay?"

"Well, okay, but you know—"

I hang up, picture her phone ringing again and the doctor filling in the details.

Crossing the road, I decide to sleep in my car for a bit, gather a few groceries come morning, and then decide where the road will take me. Maybe I'll find some hidden avenue, some twilight-zone route that leads me back to my real life.

Have many people convinced themselves that someone who's died actually isn't dead at all? For instance, do they tell themselves that he's really away for an extended sabbatical or something where he can't write letters or call? And can you write letters to him destined for some imaginary address?

I slam the dishtowel onto the counter.

"Look, Joey! You knew I wasn't a Jesus Freak when you married me! If it was that important to you, why did you marry me in the first place?" And why didn't I use something louder than a dishtowel to get my point across? What a waste.

"I thought maybe you'd get an interest."

"We've been married three years, Joey. Don't you think it would've happened by now?"

"Yes."

"So get a clue, smarty-pants."

He turns around and walks into the bedroom of our little apartment.

I yell, "I mean, when I got cancer I was going to swing one way or the other!"

"But you're still alive," he hollers back. "God kept you living."

"Yeah! Without a uterus!"

The bedroom door clicks shut. The snow falls outside the kitchen window, the Bay is quiet, and the timer at Concord Point Lighthouse has signaled the nightly illumination to begin.

I feel like dirt. Joey deserves better. I can be so mean sometimes, and I don't know where I get it from. Mom certainly wasn't like that. But in my defense, I'm twenty-two years old and will never achieve the pinnacle of womanhood. Oh sure, I know women like Bella Abzug and Gloria Steinem would say otherwise. But honestly, what do they know? Who bestowed on them such clout anyway? I was given ovaries, a uterus, and a birth canal for a reason. Not putting them to use is like wearing clown makeup and never being funny.

I wash up our lunch dishes and continue staring at the falling snow.

Joey emerges. "I'm sorry Pearly."

"Me too. This is one area we have to be different, Joey."

He nods. "Can I ask for one compromise?"

"What's that?"

"Just Christmas Eve. Will you just go to church with me on Christmas Eve?"

"Okay. But it's just for you."

"I know."

He hugs me and kisses me tenderly. He wants to tell me something, but he holds back, and I am grateful.

I stop in Salisbury, only thirty minutes from the cabin now, and head into the Giant grocery store. We stayed at the cabin only a week and a half ago, so I won't have to clean. I buy a big bottle of root beer, a box of granola, some skim milk, which I loathe but use anyway since Joey started on the low-fat kick, a pound of ham, some rye bread, and tomatoes. I buy a carton of Marlboro Lights while I'm at it. Black lung has already erupted from those Reds, and the thought of bringing one to my lips makes me want to throw up. Next I head to the liquor store for a case of Shiraz and a bottle of Bailey's for my nightcap.

I sit outside the store on a bench formed from recycled store bags. I recall the little white wrought iron bench and cocktail table my grandmother arranged near the weeping willow by the Bay, at the western edge of the farm. Lighting up a cigarette, I remember family life. Not a large family really; we were, however, dovetailed together by hard work and an appreciation for common genetics. Only four of us remain: me, my brother, Harry, and my cousins, Cheeta and Peta.

Peta inherited Grandma's name. Cheeta's real name is Concheta. Her mother, my Aunt Sally, just liked the name. "So much more exotic and substantial than Sally," she said many a time. They're older than I am by ten years and consistently top the list of the strangest people I've ever met in my entire life, a high honor considering that during my freshman year at Hopkins I met Tiny Tim *and* Andy Warhol through bizarre circumstances that included an ice storm, a car crash, and four boxes of silver tinsel. My cousins live on the property in the old farmhouse where I grew up. They don't know I'm coming. Cheeta will have an all-out fit, and Peta will boss me around and shower me with all sorts of unasked-for advice.

I light up a cigarette and slip out the bottle of Coke I pulled from the cooler near the register. I've disappeared for all practical purposes, so there's no hurry to get to the cabin. Actually, I know that once I arrive, only crying and smoking, drinking wine and eating ham sandwiches, and staring out at the water will consume me for days and days.

Goodness, but that sounds so good.

After taking one more pull on my smoke, one more slug of my Coke, I head back to the car. This is Joey's first full day dead. It is my first full day alone. It is only ten in the morning.

But maybe the miracle happened. Maybe he continued to breathe on his own! Right? Couldn't that have happened?

I rush to the pay phone and call Maida. The answering machine clicks on. Must be at work. I call the school.

"Maida, please?" I disguise my voice.

"I'm sorry," some volunteer manning the phone says, "but she's not here."

"Can you tell me where she is?"

"She's busy planning the funeral of Dr. Laurel."

"So he's really dead, then."

My voice loses all shine. I hang up the phone, sagging against the booth, breathing deeply, realizing that something deep inside me had hoped in and had been utterly disappointed by both God and man.

I luck out. Cheeta and Peta have apparently deserted the farm until tomorrow afternoon. I learned this from Shrubby Cinquefoil, a waterman with property north of the farm on the Bay. Shrubby's skin reminds me of

70

those dried pigs' ears people give their dogs to gnaw on. His colorless eyes, bleached by years of "drudgin'" for oysters or tending his crab pots, convey his general distrust of humankind with a spaghetti western squint.

"Do you know where they went, Shrubby?"

"No, and I don't wanna know."

"Why's that?"

"Cheeta's been making googly eyes at me lately."

"Cheeta? Really?"

"Durn right."

I don't have the heart to tell him she switched to contacts recently.

"Not only that. I ain't no gossip. What them ladies do is their own durn business. I got enough troubles of my own."

I sit in my car, window rolled down, breeze across my face, sun in my eyes. Such a beautiful day, and it's a miracle I even noticed. "Well, I'll be at the cabin if you need me."

"You stayin' long?"

I can't tell him about Joey. "I'm not sure."

"You know, you're the only Kaiser I could ever stomach."

Poor everybody else. Still, "Thanks, Shrubby."

Plus, Shrubby, my age almost exactly, remembers the time I caught him skinny-dipping with Margie Carruthers on the same day I caught him making out with Debbie Phillips. He's been married four times and divorced three. They managed an annulment on number two, which has become fodder for many a speculative conversation in these parts ever since.

Shrubby remains mum.

"Hang on a minute," he says and hurries off to his shed by the water. I scan the September Bay, feeling Joey's approval with me here at his favorite spot on earth during his favorite month of the year. Perhaps coming here is a more fitting tribute than sticking around Havre de Grace.

Har har.

Shrubby returns with a pail hanging from the bony fingers of his right hand. "Here's some oysters for ya. Need me to shuck 'em?"

"No way, Shrubby Cinquefoil! Don't be insulting."

He salutes.

"Thanks for the oysters."

"Get outta here, Pearly. A man's got work to do."

I drive across his property and onto ours, forsaking the driveways.

I am rich. I've found an old notebook of Joey's here at the cabin, right on the built-in bookshelf next to the fireplace. He looked and looked all over our Havre de Grace house for this thing several years ago and, sighing, finally assigned it to the category of disappearing socks, lost safety pins, and missing ballpoint pens. Then he brightened, rode his bicycle over to the drugstore, and purchased a red, three-subject spiral notebook.

Inside this volume, a hardbound book with a red plaid cover, Joey's character sketches splay as though between glass slides, the embryonic remains of his short stories, long abandoned but still viewable. No manuscripts of his stories exist. Joey always sent them off to periodicals and publishers with only one safety copy left at home. After he received the published piece—out even that would go. I loved that Joey wasn't in love with his work. He loved people and saw his work as a tribute to humankind, not the other way around.

I set the book down for a spell, remembering my tote bag. In the bedroom, furnished with rugged furniture and decorated in shades of green and burgundy, I slip off all my clothes and stand naked and chilly. Yet I enjoy the feeling of nothingness, the sensation that only air clothes me and I am in much the same state I was at birth. I stand for several minutes, eyes closed, remembering my mother, remembering my baths and the way she'd dry me with a towel straight from the dryer, always singing "The Bear Went over the Mountain."

But enough. Who can go back? No one. Even God Himself can't go back. In fact, one of the few Sunday school lessons I ever heard only gave credit to God for making the sun stand still. Going back is an option for absolutely no one. I reach into the bag and pull out Joey's clothes from the hospital. I slide his boxers and his undershirt over my bare flesh, then slip into the plaid shirt, its softness gliding over the hair on my arms.

Noon already. I am hungry. I make myself a ham sandwich on rye with mustard, pour myself a cold root beer, and set my meal out on the deck. Dragging a lounger pad from the screened porch, I breathe through my nose, sucking in as much of the breeze as possible.

I throw the navy blue cushion on the redwood lounger and plop down on it.

The sandwich tastes good, bringing back memories of my mother, Valerie, who hailed from Baltimore city. She loved ham sandwiches. I eat them to remember her.

Joey loved her so much. "You have a good mother, Pearly." It was his idea that we care for her after she was diagnosed with lung cancer.

I raise my sandwich to Valerie Kaiser. Maybe she is with Joey right now. But I don't know. Mom wasn't attuned to spiritual things the way Joey was. I know little about any of this stuff, and to be honest, right now is not the time to worry about it. I just want to eat my sandwich, drink my root beer, smoke my cigarettes, and feel the breeze. I don't even want to cry right now. I just want to sit here in Joey's clothes and read about Joey's people.

5 January 1971. Havre de Grace.

I met a man named Chervil Williams today. He reminds me of a picket from a weathered beach fence. He said he forgot how old he was but remembers the Civil War because he had two older brothers who died. He sat down on the shore at the confluence of the Susquehanna and the Bay, near the lock house. Despite the cold, his old coat was opened and his shirt unbuttoned. Ribs showed above the neckline of his guinea undershirt. I asked him about this, and he said, "It's my secret to long life. Get a little cold air into the lungs whenever you can." He spent his life down in the shipyards in

Baltimore but moved out here with his daughter years ago. The daughter is long gone, but Chervil remains. He doesn't know why. I asked him what his story is. He said, "I don't have much of a story. I just try to survive each day without hurting anybody."

Down at the Chat 'n' Chew during breakfast, a young woman walked in wearing a torn denim jacket and a long velvet skirt. Army boots magnified her feet. Brilliant really, the whole getup. Already a story forms regarding this woman and Chervil. Perhaps Chervil will really be a spirit. But his message? Too soon to tell.

I run my fingertips over the dried ink. Joey's own handwriting. He touched this book. Is there a cell or two of Joey's that my fingerprint will sponge into one of its crevices? Please. I hold the notebook to my chest, then rub the binding up my neck and beside my ear, and there I rest it, allowing it to pillow my pain as the afternoon wanes and the sun slants its rays, further defining the yellowing leaves on the maple trees by the driveway.

I awaken beneath the stars. Something's eaten the crusts of my sandwich. I remember Pumpkin. Poor Pumpkin!

Inside, I call Maida on the kitchen phone.

"It's Pearly."

"Where *are* you?"

"I can't say. I need to be unreachable."

"Well, I can just push *77, Pearly."

"Okay. I'm at the cabin."

"I figured as much."

I'm so annoyingly predictable. I flip on the kitchen light, squinting as it illumines the tiny room. "Can you feed Pumpkin?"

"Of course. He's already over here."

"I should've figured as much."

There is a space of dead air.

"Burial or cremation?" Maida says suddenly.

"Burial."

"Where now? I didn't catch the location before."

"We have a plot in Churchville. Harford Memorial Gardens."

"I know it. I'll call to make arrangements. I take it you're not coming back for the funeral?"

". . ."

"You know, Pearly. Not seeing him dead, or in a coffin or anything funeral-like isn't going to make him any less gone."

". . ."

"I won't have a viewing, then. Just the graveside service. I'll call Father Charlie, and he can arrange things."

"Thank you, Maida."

She sighs. "I've got to tell you, Pearly, that I don't understand any of this. Not one bit."

"I don't either. But I can't face this. That's all I know."

"This isn't good. You're going against everything they say is healthy about grief."

"I know."

"I'd even venture to say it isn't right either."

"Joey's dead. He won't care either way."

76

"Oh, Joey knows, Pearly. I'd bet my job, my house, everything I own on that one."

Is Joey haunting our house? Oh my, I'd never even considered that!

"I'd better go call Father Charlie," she says.

"Thanks, Maida."

"I guess you'll want me to close up the house for the time being?"

"Please. Could you go by the post office and have my mail forwarded here? I'll have the phone turned off myself."

"What if I say I won't do it? I mean, the guidance counselor at school talks about this enabling business. That's what I'd be doing. Enabling you to run away from life."

That really describes it!

"You'll do it, Maida. You can't stand to see stuff undone."

"Well, that is true. But promise me you'll be in touch every so often."

"I will."

We hang up, and I pour myself a glass of wine. I down it in three swallows there at the kitchen sink. At this time I cannot possibly sip wine and act civilized. I pour another and another right there at the sink, eating oysters, smoking like crazy, silently, grimly cursing the night, yet begging it to never end.

I made it through full day number one. And I cannot pretend to understand it. The sun rose as expected, the morning breeze let up a bit by noon, and here I sit on my lounge chair once again looking at the water, flip-flopping between goose bumps and the sweats.

My hangover may have something to do with it. I haven't been hung over since Mom died.

Cheeta and Peta should be arriving home any minute. I parked my car around the other side of the house so they'd only see it if they decided to walk down to the water. I hope they won't notice; I'm still wearing Joey's clothing, and I haven't brushed my teeth since I left my house two mornings ago.

After pouring myself another cup of coffee, I settle into the lounger in the living room. My feet rest comfortably on the ottoman, and I look up at the beamed ceiling of our cabin. It's actually a one-bedroom A-frame with a sleeping loft. I berate myself for forgetting Pumpkin. He loves running along the beams up there.

A vicious knock vibrates the side screen door. "Hey, Pearly! You in there?" It's Peta.

"Back here in the living room!" I holler.

She swings into the room. Peta inherited most of her mother's Blackfoot genes. Her heavy salt-and-pepper hair is pulled back into a long braid. She wears suede sandals, wool socks, a western shirt, and a long, full denim skirt. She is a Libertarian, which really gets Cheeta's goat. I find all their politics incredibly funny, as I haven't voted in eons. "Well, I can't believe I had to read about it in the *Sunpaper* obits!" Hands on hips.

"Joey?"

"Of course, Joey!"

God bless Maida. I'm sure she placed the notice.

"And what in blazes are you doing here, Cousin? Go home!"

"Thanks for your sympathy, Peta."

She crosses herself, though to my knowledge, unless things have changed, Peta isn't Catholic. "He was a good man."

"Yes, he was."

"So you've got some explaining to do."

". . ."

"Not going to talk about it, huh? Well, that's fine. Just tell me when and where the funeral is."

Thank goodness Maida called me earlier. "Tomorrow, Harford Memorial Gardens in Churchville: 9:00 A.M."

"All right. We'll go."

She turns around and leaves.

Not two minutes go by until Cheeta arrives. "Thanks a lot, Pearly!"

Gold jewelry is Cheeta's vice. She wears at least seven bracelets, ten rings, and five necklaces of varying length that get caught in her ample décolletage. She is a sun goddess, and to be honest, the thought of counting *her* moles, freckles, and liver spots gives me the willies. What her hair looks like these days is anyone's guess, because she took to wearing turbans two decades ago. A committed Democrat, she's been a delegate to the national convention and everything.

"I'm sorry I didn't call you when Joey had the stroke. Besides, you all were away."

"That's beside the point. We're talking intentions here."

"Oh, brother."

"Don't 'oh, brother' me, Pearly. Now get ready, we're all going up to Havre de Grace."

"No we're not."

"Yes. We are."

"We are not."

Cheeta crosses her arms. "I'm not going to let you regret this for the rest of your life."

Oh, brother. "I'm not going, Cheeta. I can't."

"This is ridiculous."

". . ."

She crosses her arms the other way now and stares at me. "I'm not leaving until you tell me you'll go."

She won't either. "You're a stubborn old goat," I say.

"Ten years more stubborn than you, that's for sure."

She's right about that.

"I'm not going to the funeral. But I'll drive up with you."

"That's better. I'll leave you alone until we leave, then. We go at five tomorrow morning."

"Five?!"

"Yes, five. Period."

They drop me off at the house and head toward the cemetery. Maida's driveway lies barren. I notice as I walk past the school, a nice little hike, but hardly impossible, that the buses are gone and all the class-rooms sit empty, presumably everyone gone off to the funeral. The school sign says, "Good-bye, Dr. Laurel. We'll miss you." The downtown shopping area seems empty as well, a balloon with too little air.

I want to see the grave. I want to be there. But I can't.

I figure sitting at the lighthouse will be a somewhat tribute. After strolling by the abandoned, boarded-up lightkeeper's cottage, I cross the street toward the conical building. Concord Point Lighthouse squats small and spare, whitewashed to an Ultrabright gleam, its lantern room and roof painted a dull black. I've always loved it here, always felt at peace near this stone lady in her black bonnet. Today is no exception.

I asked Joey about lighthouses once. I said, "What is it about them, Joey? Why do people love lighthouses so much?"

"It's about finding your way, Pearly. It's purely metaphorical. Somewhere deep inside, we all know we'll never completely avoid the rocks on our own."

"You're my lighthouse, then," I told him that day as we sat on the very banks I sit upon right now. That was about ten years ago.

He didn't tell me I was his lighthouse, for that would have been a lie. He just pulled me close.

In truth, I've lived a charmed life. Good parents, farm upbringing, wonderful marriage to a charming, delightful man. Everything, even the deaths that I've been forced to bear until Joey's, has come along as it should, in the proper timing. So is it any wonder I feel the way I do right now?

So now what? *My* lighthouse has no automatic timer now that its lightkeeper has left. How can I find my way? Do I really care to?

Joey's thirty years old and he's done it. He's a Ph.D. now. We've done it together. Sure, I'd like to go back to school someday and get my degree, but I can't say I don't feel some sense of satisfaction at helping to support us while Joey went all the way. It's a kick being married to a Ph.D., too. Sexy, really. All that brain in there finding me attractive, needing me. I like that a lot. Man, I love it when Joey makes love to me. He's so intense and, well, so *there,* in tune with me. I feel like I am the most important thing in the world to him, like I am the Queen of Love and Beauty. Even though his schedule with school has been hectic, he finds time for me.

The school was wonderful about his degree program too, extending him loads of time to study and learn. I look at him across our breakfast table. "What do you think, Joey? Time to hunt for a house?"

He smiles. "There's one for sale up west of the park. It's not right on the water, but it's only one house back. Rachel Hughes—you remember, mathematics? Her mother lives there, and she's selling to move in with Rachel and her husband."

"Good price?"

"Very. Now it's small, but brilliant."

"I love small." I stand up, lean over, and kiss his mouth. "Maybe we can go over there today?"

"I'll call them and ask."

Of course, with house payments I'll have to keep my receptionist job at the local State Farm office, but that's okay.

I ask Joey if he'll make love to me before he heads off to school. I tell him I need him just now and I do. So we slip upstairs, back between the covers, and I tell him it's okay if it's quick, I know he needs to get to school. But he kisses my neck, and I know that he won't mind being late just this once.

I feel his hand slide across my stomach, and I remember the first time he ever did that. We were window-shopping down the streets of Annapolis on our first official date. There we stood in front of a jewelry store. I wore a pink sweater, and as he stood slightly behind me and to my right, I felt his right hand slip under the sweater and caress my bare stomach. His left arm encircled my left shoulder, the hand coming to rest on the opposite collarbone. Oh, my. Joey's hands. The magic trails they leave behind.

I am so very much loved.

We are young, and we are lovers. Lovers of more than just the body. Oh, that truly is the definition of a lover, isn't it? A true lover penetrates point by point, into more than the body, but into the mind, the heart, the soul. A true lover is all into all.

I am his and he is mine.

I figure it will be at least an hour before they come back, so I return to the house to bury my face in Joey's coats. To smell his smell and quite possibly take some of him into my lungs. I left his other clothes back at the cabin.

Sitting on the floor of his closet amid his shirts, I decide to let myself cry a bit. Cheeta finds me, how much later? I don't know.

"I should have figured as much. You would have done better to have shed those tears at the cemetery. It was a beautiful service. They had a memorial service at the school chapel beforehand, not that anyone told me about it." She twiddles her necklaces.

"I didn't know."

"Of course you didn't. This is the craziest thing, Pearly."

"That, I do know. What was everybody saying? What did you tell them?"

"I told them you were prostate with grief."

"Prostate? Not prostrate?" Somebody just shoot me now!

"They got the message. They send their prayers and condolences."

"I'm going to need them."

I am holding a fishing shirt of Joey's. Balled up in my hands, it is moist from slobber and tears.

"Let's go, Pearly. It's a three-hour drive."

I nod and climb to my feet with a groan, my joints wanting to spring into action but feeling no gumption for it. I loved seeing Joey in his fishing shirt, watching him as he left the house and walked across to Maida's. He loved so many things. What a shame he didn't live to fulfill that list.

"Some of these items are for you, Pearly," he told me just before the stroke. Would he want me to tackle that list alone? The answer is easy.

A feeling that I got what I came for eases me along to the car.

Peta makes me sit up front as she drives. She talks about her garden and sounds like Grandma. This comforts me.

"I've put up loads of pickled green tomatoes and cucumbers, of course. Green beans, squash, peaches, asparagus, limas too. So you want any vegetables this winter, go on down into the basement and get some, just put a little tick on the inventory paper tacked onto the freezer."

Inventory paper? What is this?

She points at me, her finger almost up my nose. "If you planned on starving yourself with grief, you came to the wrong place."

Cheeta leans forward. "If you ask me, she needs some fattening up."

I roll my eyes and keep looking forward at the boring landscape of Route 13—fields, produce stands, and old gas stations—humming by like a repeating pattern as we thread down the stitches of the highway.

Crushing the soft flannel of Joey's shirt to my nose, I breathe deeply. Peta sighs and sits back. Cheeta shakes her head and says, "Give me one of your cigarettes, Pearly. I'm dying here."

As if she knows what that really feels like.

I'm alone! Thank you. Thank you. Thank you.

It's 4:00 P.M. and raining. I slip into my slicker, grab a waterproof tarp from the storage closet, and wing down to the water's edge.

The platinum of the sky hushes the scene before me, the water now overlaid in pewter, the trees, wrought iron black, retreating quickly into mist at the far shore. A flock of geese rest to my left on a small, grassy peninsula.

Canadian geese mate for life.

Yeah, yeah, yeah.

I'm so sad for them.

Yes, the anger begins.

I sit here on the banks of the Bay and begin to ruminate on the contents of the list, its wishes and wonders queued one behind the other, glowing with halos of what could have been. Now I would have quite possibly titled the list *What I Would Like to Do Before I Die.* But not Joey. His title, *While I Live I Want To . . .* proclaims his natural optimism.

I smile. If Joey can't do these things, I really am the next best person to accomplish the tasks. I will do it. For Joey. To seal a lifetime of love with a gift. And I may just add a few things of my own.

31 October 1971: A Waffle House on I-85
somewhere in North Carolina.

Her name is Marla Perkins and she waited on Pearly and me this morning. Marla's sparse brown hair covers her head like a spider's web in a breeze, glistening, fluttering threads around her face. She's open about her faults. She has been married before, lived with many men. Is living with a guy named Jay right now in her grandma's old house near the highway. The Woman at the Waffle House! "Men don't give no nevermind about nothin'," *she said.* " 'Cept maybe for you, mister. You look like a real nice fella, you and your wife both." *I asked her what her story is and she said,* "Repeated mistakes. That's my story. Tell me,

86

mister, why don't I ever learn?"

We ask her to sit down with us during her break. She and Pearly smoke like stacks and laugh like crazy about the smallest things. True, I may be more sensitive, in the enlightened, artistic sense. But Pearly, she's a social chameleon, fitting right in wherever she goes. I sympathize with people, Pearly becomes them.

The list sits atop the opened journal. I read it once again, and excitement wells up within me.

1. Go whale watching in Alaska.

2. See the mysterious figures on the plains of Peru.

3. Climb a pyramid in South or Central America.

4. Walk the Appalachian Trail.

5. Spend a winter on a mountain.

6. Try every entrée at Haussner's.

7. Get a tattoo.

Yes, this is it. This is my purpose. And I decide something else. It will become the swan song of my life, my final chapter, the last stop on the line, and any other expression that I currently cannot think of. I cannot live without him. Not really live. Oh sure, I can inhabit his clothing and our cabin, I can drink wine, smoke cigarettes, and eat ham sandwiches. But I cannot live.

However, I do want to fulfill some of my own desires, so I add to the list some items of my own.

8. Go to a rock concert.

9. Learn to play the guitar.

10. Read War and Peace in its entirety.

11. Run a 10K race.

There, an even eleven. So neat and defined. So tidy.

Oh, brother. The items are not nearly as ambitious as Joey's, but I feel more relief than disappointment over that. I always envied Joey and his guitar. He did teach me how to play "Louie Louie," telling me, "You can play a lot of songs with just these three chords, Pearly."

But I didn't believe him. I forgot the chords the next day. Besides, hearing him play seemed a more prudent use of time. He improved as the years went by, practicing at school on his lunch hour, in the evenings at home.

So welcome to my lot. After returning from my travels and my triumphs, I will visit Joey's grave and join him. How will I complete the final, unwritten task on my list? That question deserves more thought than this moment affords me. But I definitely lean toward the overdose. Wouldn't you? So right now, I'll just sit here on the sunny deck and start on the copy of *War and Peace* that has wagged its finger at me here at the cabin for years and years. Years.

I open up the volume.

Oh, my! Why couldn't I have picked something by D. H. Lawrence or a shorter Dickens piece?

Besides, Joey hated Tolstoy.

I opt for some TV instead, snuggling within the confines of Joey's shirt and a blanket. Something mindless, something silly, yes. That's what I need. Ah, MTV. That meets both qualifications. Let's hope that a future civilization doesn't dig up tapes of that network and so judge our society by the likes of that Aguilera girl, or that Marilyn Manson thing. What kind of conclusion could they possibly draw?

Joey would laugh at the thought. Yes, I always could make Joey laugh.

Eleven o'clock. Sitting at the counter in the kitchen, thoughtfully, playfully adding points to my list, I raise my nightcap to Joey. He's laughing if he can see me, I can tell you that.

"Oh, Pearly," he'd say. "This *is* a funny one! You amuse me, you know that?" And then he'd kiss my temple and tell me he couldn't live without me.

And I'd say, "I can't live without you either." Only I'm trying and it's just as horrible as I imagined. I remember my mother telling me after Dad died that she felt as though she had lost her right shoe. Well, I feel as if my right *foot* is gone, nothing left but a bleeding stump that will never be able to support me.

Back to my list, including a new, lower portion now titled *Pearly Laurel's Fantasy Wish List.*

12. Streak across the campus at Johns Hopkins.

13. Snap a Pulitzer-winning photo.

14. Eat whatever I want, wherever and whenever and however much I want, without gaining an ounce! Yes, that really is fantasy!

15. Hold my own child in my arms.

The final item surprises me, my hand giving voice to my heart without bothering to consult my head first. I've convinced myself for years that nonmotherhood is just dandy. The older kids from the school communed around our table every Friday and Saturday night. I felt maternal around these orphans and foster children. I fed them, listened to their trials and triumphs. But it wasn't

89

the same, was it? It wasn't the same at all. How could it be?

I tear off the fantasy list, ball up the paper, and fling it away from me. After all, only one item really means anything, and that is impossible. It lands somewhere behind the flour and sugar canisters. Let it lie, I say to myself. Let it lie.

The people in my family sang and sang. Joey fit right in, even better than I, who can't carry a tune. Now my grandma, who wagged her finger at me and said, "I'll pray for your soul until the day I die, young lady," sang hymns. On sad days, Methodist hymns like "Rock of Ages" and "Nearer My God to Thee." On meadowy days, she married her humming to Baptists all over, singing "Beulah Land, Sweet Beulah Land" and "No, Not One."

"There's not a friend like the lowly Jesus. No, not one. No, not one."

Sometimes, on a summer night, when the moths rammed the screens of the house and the breeze smelled of honeysuckle and meadowsweet, when the moon hung as feminine and true as the ovary of a cherry, and the darkness hovered between her and the Bay, I'd hum a Grandma song in my mind. Softly, so as not to disturb Joey as he sat quietly in his study.

"Sweet hour of prayer! Sweet hour of prayer! that calls me from a world of care, and bids me at my Father's throne make all my wants and wishes known."

That tune, contemplative, haunting, and clean, became my nighttime theme. Many times I wanted to pray, but in Grandma's church I heard the preacher once say that God only listens to the prayers of His children. I suppose we are all God's children in the way that orphans are the children of a headmistress. But I do not regard God as my father, and therefore I don't expect a listening ear, much less a broad lap. I am not wounded or abused, and whether the life I live is one He's given me or one I gave myself or one I allowed to be created by Joey, I cannot say. But after I married, the maturing embryo that was Pearly Kaiser went dormant, and I suspect it has long since died.

Not that it matters now. For Joey's sake, however, I will make one change. In what little time I have left, I will bring my own music to my own life and not rely on someone else to do it for me. I figure that by the time the end arrives, I will have heard the voices of angels or something as close to that sound as any foundling can come.

That rock concert may not be a great first step in the right direction, but hey, it'll at least knock one item off the list. I wonder who's good these days. Of course, I'll be learning the guitar as well, but somehow, I doubt I will really sound all that hot! In fact, it might make me do the final deed that much sooner!

Believe it or not, an excitement fills me. Oh, Joey, look down, won't you? See what just may become of your Pearly Laurel.

August 1951, Long Pond, Jackman, Maine

I am a rock.

I told Pop that yesterday evening around the campfire and he laughed. "How so, son?"

I told him how I was sitting down on the shore in front of our cabin, right there where a large slab of rock flows right down into the lake, and as I looked over the water, still in the evening and reflecting the red sky, I had this thought.

"God created the world and everything in it, right?"

"That's what I taught you, son."

"After the sixth day, He rested and said, 'It is good,' right?"

"That's what it says in Genesis."

"Right. So, I'm a rock."

Pop threw a slender birch log into the flames, and I watched its skin curl and blacken and the smoke thicken for a spell. "I'm just a simple green grocer, son. I don't have your high thoughts. I believe they came from your mother. You need to give me a little more to go on with this rock notion, buddy."

I really love my dad. He's a good father, and since Mom died he's been my rock.

"Well, if God said 'It is good' it means He didn't add anything more to His creation."

"I'd say I'd agree with that. But how does that make you a rock?"

"That rock I was sitting on has been in existence, in one form or other, since God pronounced it good."

He gave a clap, caught his tie between his hands, then pointed at me. "I'm finally following you! You could say the same about yourself, right?"

"Right! Everything that forms me, all the stuff that

makes up me, has been around since the dawn of cre-
ation!"

"Makes sense to me." And then Pop reached over
and messed up my hair, smiling and shaking his head.
"Son, I'm proud of you. Your mother would be proud of
you and I'm sorry to admit I don't do these conversa-
tions justice the way she would have."

"But you don't mind having them, do you, Pop?" I
asked.

"Anything that comes out of your mouth is important
to me, Joseph."

I felt a little shy at that, so I went into the cabin to get
some marshmallows. Pop sat back in his camp chair,
folded his hands over his belt buckle and closed his
eyes. I'm sure my mother smiled behind those lids. Then
he lit up a cigarette and stared out over the lake. He
reminded me of pictures I see at the camps, old pictures
of gentleman anglers, men in ties and hats holding up
strings of seven-pounders. My dad may be a simple
green grocer down at Cross Street Market, but he is a
true gentleman, the kind they just don't make anymore.

I arise from my seat on the screened porch, set Joey's
diary aside, and inspect the gold of the evening sky.
Imagine thinking thoughts like that at fifteen years old!
Thoughts as beautiful and grand as an evening sky, full
of depth and wonder and golden linings that catch the
breath. I can honestly say that Joey's thoughts would
never occur to me on their own. First of all, the creation
story is full of holes big enough to drive a semi through.
Six days? Please. That always steals the poetry of it all

away from me. Although, I must admit I do love the picture: a hasty, divine creation summons, complete with soundtrack—the *Sabre Dance*. Can't you just picture the divine spirit prancing, light-footed yet sure on the steppingstones of substance that poke their heads through the currents of the river of time? A slow, violent shift from nothing to large, small, animate, inanimate, breathing, dead, however, has its own peculiar brand of drama. But no soundtrack. Who'd want to hear the same song playing for millions of years, shifting undetected from movement to movement? And let's face it, it would sound like Wagner at his most depressing.

I ration entries in Joey's journals now, for he wrote not every day of his life but in wonderful, lively bursts. Five pages a day. I found that his journals filled most of that bookshelf by his lounge chair, shelved in no particular order. Not surprising, Joey being the organic soul he was. Most of them, only half-filled, contain memories and mundane tellings of the day's occurrences, as well as emotional accounts. Already I have found the same occurrence written of twice. The day Joey's mother died. He was twelve.

August 15th, 1950

Pop and I buried Mom today.
I remember how I felt when I heard the news that Hitler had died in that fire. Mom and I danced around the kitchen table singing Spike Jones's "Der Fuhrer's Face" in the heavy German accent she'd kept even

after escaping the "cleansings." Those dirty thugs, those filthy beasts! Imagine calling my mother unclean. That's another story for another day, though, but I must write it down someday because I'll have children of my own and they'll need to know about their grandmother.

And now Rachel lies out at the cemetery, the only child of only children, the last of an entire line of Schwartzes.

We gave her a Christian burial, Episcopal, which is what she converted over to after she married Pop. She felt that the Jewish version of God let her people down time after time and that maybe He was only trying to get through to them about His Son. Or maybe He left them to their own devices, allowing the devil, who hates them more than he hates any other people, to reign. I think Satan is trying hard to undo God's covenants with His chosen people. You'd think he would get a clue that God's not going anywhere.

I am angry today.

Rachel grieved for her people to the end. They threw her out of the family, what few of them were left. Just some distant cousins and an aunt or two. Four days ago, some dirty thug threw a bottle of beer out of the car window, aiming at her, and hit her right on the head. He yelled, "Kike!"

I didn't recognize him, but I recognized a boy from my class, Johnny Mosmeller, pale-cheeked and bug-eyed in the backseat. I told the police. They got the driver and the guy who threw the bottle because Johnny was afraid not to say anything. They were thugs from down near Pittsburgh come to visit the Mosmellers.

"Shucks, Joey," Johnny said at the funeral today. "I'm awful sorry."

I told him it was okay, it wasn't his fault and I thanked him for coming. But the hollow thunk of the bottle hitting Mom's head, smashing her skull, doesn't stop ringing in my head. I see her head jerk wildly to the right, her dark hair swinging around her cheeks and jaw, the waves springing and jumping like a marionette, a happy motion. As I jump forward to catch her, I fall over a tar strip in the sidewalk, and I see her heels wobble to the right, I see the scuff on her gas pedal foot, the wearing away of the mild chocolate-colored leather to reveal the creamy center. I see the shoes leave the ground altogether as Mom falls, her head landing with another watermelon thud on the edge of Mrs. Bauer's bottom front step.

Blood pools quickly and she won't respond to my gentle shakes. I cry, "Mom!" But there is nothing but her pale face, waxy and still. And the blood. I hold her hand, limp and fair, the same hand that sometimes held onto the back of my neck as we would walk along Light Street, window shopping or stopping into Epstein's for some socks for me or a new blouse for her. I keep screaming "Help! Help us please." Somebody comes and gently removes me from her side.

Pop and I, and Pop's sister and brother, Stanley and Esther, stood crying as the casket was lowered into the ground. Johnny Mosmeller and his mom stood nearby. I could hear them shuffling in the grass. As we walked to the car she said to me, "I'm sorry, Joey. Honest-to-goodness I am. I hope they throw the book at those guys. *I was trying to help their Ma, you know. They were giving her fits. Thought I could maybe straighten them out. I guess it's true what they say about no good deed going unpunished."*

I wanted to respond, but all I could do was nod and raise one side of my mouth in what I hoped was taken for a smile.

"Come on, Johnny," she said, pulling him to her side. "Let's leave these poor folks to grieve."

I watched them walk down the street whole and together, and all I could do was swallow hard and follow my father's lead.

We ate a meal together at Haussner's afterwards. Dad had Wiener schnitzel and I ordered sauerbraten. Mom's two favorites.

Neither of us ate much.

He's gone to bed now and I'm still sitting at the kitchen table, marveling that the curtains at the window overlooking the alley are in exactly the same position as they were four days ago when Mom pushed them back to let in the morning sun.

I never knew Joey was half Jewish! Not that it would have mattered. So why didn't he tell me? And I didn't know Joey's mother was murdered by some skinhead. Not that they called them skinheads in those days. He'd always said, "She was killed in an accident. Massive head injury. She died on the way to the hospital."

I am irate on Joey's behalf. Then on my own. I now realize Joey probably kept many things from me, that he rationed out bits and pieces of himself like a mother in a small neighborhood rations out her children's Halloween candy to make it last until Thanksgiving. This, however, is not what angers me most right now. A black rage at the person who stole Joey's childhood, who stole pieces of Joey from me, stifles my breath.

I watched Looney Tunes this morning as I smoked my breakfast and drank my coffee. Bugs Bunny took on the form of a manicurist as he fooled the red "Heart Monster," as Joey and I called him.

"Monstahs must lead such innnnn-terestin' lives," Bugs said as he filed the yellow and black nails of the beast in Chuckie Taylor's.

Many definitions of monsters exist, I suppose. I just never knew they lived so vibrantly in Joey's memories. Yes, they must live very interesting lives. I hope God got those villains. And maybe Joey had faith enough to know that He would. Divine revenge suddenly seems like reason enough to believe in His existence.

March 25, 1995
Havre de Grace, Maryland

Been thinking about Mom lately. I went back into my old journal and read the account. Amazing how I'd forgotten that she'd hit her head on the stoop. I only remembered the beer bottle. Mom came to mind today when I walked home to a yard full of Pearly's daffodils. Pearly's garden fills me the way Mom's endearing motions did when I was a child. The way she'd swipe her hair aside as she peeled vegetables. The way she'd always make a toast at every meal. How I loved that woman. There could never be a woman more suited to motherhood than Rachel.

I am cheated.

For better for worse, richer or poorer.

I'm a little angry at Joey, too, now. I fire up a Marlboro Light, searching the innards of the fridge for some supper. November blew in a while ago, and all I feel like eating these days is cold cereal and milk. I've allowed myself the luxury of eating any kind of cereal I choose. With whole milk. With only three years left—I figure it will take me that long to complete the list—I don't have much time to eat a box of each. Right now, my cupboard holds Cinnamon Toast Crunch, Reese's Puffs, and Franken Berry. I pull down the Franken Berry. I bought the box on Halloween, accompanied by Count Chocula and Boo Berry. I saved the pink stuff for last. Pink milk delights me in much the same way as squirt cheese, Slim Jims, and maraschino cherries.

Joey's list still sits on my coffee table. I say, "Darn it all." Why do I feel the need to continue his life when I didn't know the half of it? Why raise a tribute to the unknown?

It's the sanest thought I've had since I wiped that Jell-O salad off Joey's face. After all, he not only hid the murder of his mother, he never told me about a fiancée that died, the miscarried sister, the fact that he had to repeat the eighth grade because he couldn't cope after his mother died. He actually had the audacity to write, *I should destroy these journals someday soon, but the way Pearly smokes, I can rea-*

99

sonably say I'll outlast her.

Of all the nerve!

And yet, my heart still belongs to him. I still ache for him, yearn to feel his body next to me, to feel him inside of me as he completes me. I'm nothing but an empty shell in a pair of old boxers and a T-shirt, a locust shell of a woman flying around nowhere in a flapping plaid shirt. I needed him so badly. Didn't he know?

With a fresh case of marital bliss in my pocket, I float on the breeze from my gown. I am Mrs. Joseph Laurel. I have a fresh case of marital bliss. I am basking in the love of my family and my girlfriends from college. Ready to begin forming the receiving line, I feel Joey's tap between my shoulder blades. He grabs my hands and pulls me around the side of the house.

"I have one more vow to make, Pearly."

I allow him to pull me close, I feel his lips on my ear, and I shiver at the touch of his breath. "What is it?"

"I vow to keep the 'worse' to a minimum."

I stare at him.

"I mean it, Pearly, I'll make a conscious effort to do that as long as you'll have me."

"I vow that too, then."

He grins. "This thing might work."

Oh my. So that's what he was doing? Keeping me from as much "worse" as possible? Or didn't he give me enough credit? Did Joey think me incapable of shouldering a sliver of the cross he was forced to carry?

No. He wanted to protect me. It had to be that. He loved me. If I doubt that now that he's gone, my whole life will have been wasted. Yes, I lived for love. The poets and lyricists of the world would applaud me even if Helen Gurley Brown would beg to differ.

Shrubby Cinquefoil knocks on my screen door the Wednesday before Thanksgiving.

"Oysters?"

I nod. "Always, Shrubby."

He hands me the bowl. "Makin' your oyster dressin' this year?"

I nod again. "Me and the girls are having the family dinner tomorrow as always. No sense in breaking tradition because Joe's gone." I always call Joey Joe to other men.

"That's good, Pearly."

"What're you doing this year, Shrubby?"

"Nothin' I guess. No invites from the exes!" He laughs. His fourth divorce came to a very unnatural conclusion only recently. All anybody knows is that it involved a cult, odd food, and the all-out brainwashing of his wife. Not that she wasn't an utter kook all on her own. For one thing, she changed her name from Nancy to Lynx. And if that wasn't enough, she tattooed *Save the Razorheads* just below the hollow of her neck. We're still not sure what that was supposed to mean. Shrubby's better off without her.

"Wanna come eat with us?" Shrubby would never ask on his own. "Really, Shrubby, they won't mind."

Shrubby hacks out a cough and raises his eyebrows.

"Okay, maybe they will," I say. "But if you don't care, I don't care."

"Shoot, I don't care 'bout much."

"Me either."

So that's settled.

I tried to tell Peta that I'd make homemade cranberry sauce, but she said, "We've always had it out of a can, Pearly. Why go changing things now? Now get on over here and help me peel these yams."

"They're sweet potatoes," Cheeta yells in from her tanning bed.

"Stuff it, sis!" Peta yells back.

I laugh and pull up the sleeves on my green wool sweater. "You two never change."

"And it's a good thing, too. You've done enough changing in your lifetime for everybody in this family."

What? "Oh come off it, Peta. I've lived the same life for the past thirty-five years."

She obviously doesn't hear me. "First in high school you go off to France for that exchange student non-sense, where you meet that French boy who gave you more of an education than was necessary."

"He wasn't French. He was an exchange student from Madrid."

"Oh, *pardonnez-moi!* Like that makes any differ-ence." She inhales. "Then you go off to college, lugging all that camera garbage, bent on seeing the world. Then barely a year passes and you're getting married to a graduate student. *Then* you quit school and devote your life to him."

"I always thought you liked Joey."

"I did. Best thing that ever happened to you, that man. Who knows where you would have ended up?"

I grab a potato and peel it as though it were Peta's head. "What's that supposed to mean?" This feels like a conversation that should have occurred years before now.

"Oh, don't take me for a blind fool, Pearly. I heard you sneaking out of the house all those nights, sneaking off with Shrubby or Marsh Cinquefoil. I knew you were off getting high and who knows what else."

"Why didn't you try and stop me?"

She smiles. "I did the same thing a decade before you. Only it wasn't the Cinquefoil brothers, it was the Purnell boys, and it wasn't marijuana, it was Southern Comfort."

Sure, I have regrets. We laugh though.

Peta runs her peeled potato under water, cleaning off the remainder of the dirt. "Yep, you weren't exclusive, that's for sure."

"You mean I was easy?"

"If the shoe fits."

"Joey knew and he didn't hold it against me."

"Oh really? Did you tell him the wide reach of your fishing net?"

"No. But he knew I wasn't a virgin when he married me."

"Well, we all have our secrets, then, don't we? Joey's was just a little less ugly than yours and that's really what makes you mad."

Leave it to Peta to take away my right to feel anger at

Joey. Not that I could be mad at him forever. Dead or alive, Joey's still Joey, my lovely Joey. Dead people have a kind of glow, don't they? It's actually nice.

"Well, if it makes you feel any better, Peta, I regret those times."

"Oh, shoot, we all have regrets."

"What are yours?" I finish up my potato, slip it beneath the stream of water and slide it into the bowl of cold water nearby.

Peta takes her time answering, and I immediately regret the question. Still, it's Thanksgiving Eve, gateway to the holiday season, and I can't help but be glad I'm back in Grandma's kitchen. They've changed nothing over the years except to add another coat of paint or two to the glass-front cabinets along one wall. So many layers of the stuff hugs the wood it's impossible to shut the doors all the way anymore. It is possible, however, to actually leave fingernail marks in the creamy surface if you press hard enough. Same porcelain sink, bleached yet stained. Same old gas range Grandma had installed new in the early '60s. Wood floors, soft pine, nicked and buckled, shine with wax. I love this house, which is why we built our cabin so close. Not to mention the view. I came to the right place to heal.

Heal?

Well, maybe "bide my time" would be more apropos. I will begin my crusade of the list come January the second, when I leave for the cabin I've rented on Massanutten Mountain in Virginia. Guitar lessons, as soon as I find a teacher down there, will begin, as well as endurance training for my walk along the Appalachian Trail next fall. I hope to get that 10K race out of the way this summer.

I'll have to start jogging.

My side stitches up just thinking about it.

And the cigarettes? Oh dear! This scares me, but hopefully I'll meet my ultimate deadline even sooner if I quit. Ironic, isn't it? If I only have to hang on in this state of suspended animation for two more years, I'll be grateful. I thought Joey's absence would feel fuzzier as time protracted, but it only sharpens, cutting me deeper each day I wake to an empty bed.

Peta pulls me out of my thoughts. "I guess I regret a lot of things. But the biggest is when Cheeta got ditched right before her wedding. Jerald was just scared. He loved her, I knew that. And when he came back with his tail between his legs, she sent him away because I convinced her it was the only thing to do."

"She didn't have to listen to you, Peta."

"No. But she always had, and I knew that, too. I just didn't want her to leave me. And now she's a dried-up old prune, wearing gold jewelry and low cleavage and looking, quite honestly, downright scary these days."

I laugh. "I wouldn't go quite that far, Peta."

"Me, I was made for the single, spinster life. Look at me, I'm hefty, strong, and secure. But Cheeta wasn't. I don't know what she's going to do after I'm gone."

I reach for another potato. "Well, who knows? You might outlive her."

Peta shakes her head. "My regret comes easy these days, honey. I've had cause to do a lot of thinking."

And then, I just know. "You're sick, aren't you?"

"Sort of."

"Is it cancer?" I set down my peeler. I do not touch Peta. It's an unspoken rule.

"No. It's polycystic kidney disease."

The same disease that killed our Grandma. "Oh, dear God." I almost see the toxins building up within her. Why didn't I notice the peculiar pallor of her complexion before this?

"They diagnosed me three years ago."

"Peta!"

She shrugs. "It's my business, Pearly."

"How close are you to dialysis?"

"I'm at a 5.5 on the creatinine levels. Seven is when they want you to start."

"People can live a long time on dialysis," I say.

"Not everybody takes to it."

Grandma didn't. She was dead within a year of starting it.

Peta shakes her head. "So, not only will Cheeta be left alone, she'll have to take care of me. Unless I just do myself in before it gets too bad."

I gasp. "You can't do that!"

"Oh, I could, but I don't know if I will. I think that would be worse on Cheeta than the decline."

I try to act normal. "Cheeta loves you, Cousin. She needs you more."

"That's what I was saying before. I sure did the wrong thing all those years ago."

"Don't kill yourself, Peta. You can't."

"I know. Although, when the dialysis comes, I may

decide to forgo. I probably won't. It's just a wish I have to cut this thing off at the knees." She turns away. "And while we're on the topic of wishes, what's this wish list you have on the coffee table in your living room?"

"How did you find that?" I'll let her change the topic.

"I went in when you went to town to buy groceries."

"Peta!"

She finishes rinsing the last potato and sets the bowl in the refrigerator. "Well, don't act so shocked, Miss Smarty-Pants. I'd never learn a thing if I didn't find out on my own."

"As if you can talk! Anyway, it's a list Joey made and kept in his pocket. I'd never seen it until just before he died."

"It's interesting, I can tell you that. I'd like to do some of those things myself before I go."

Hmm. "Like what?"

"Definitely the pyramid one, and the Alaska whale watching, too." She pulls out a bag of onions. "Here, get peeling. We might as well start on your stuffing."

I obey without question.

"I'll tell you a secret, Peta."

"Hold on while I catch my breath."

"Are you okay? Is it the—you know—?"

"Of course not, you ninny! I'm just in a state of shock you're actually deigning to take me into your confidence!"

"Oh."

"So? What's the big secret?"

"Well, it isn't a *big* secret, just a secret of my own." I set down the bag of onions, feeling my eyes brighten for the first time in heaven only knows how long. "I'm going to fulfill that list."

Peta's eyes spring to life as well. "No!"

"I sure am. In fact, I'm starting just after the new year."

Peta starts fingering the bottom of her braid, the way she's always done when nervous. I spare her the agony. "Wanna go on the Alaskan cruise with me?"

"What about Cheeta?"

"Maybe this will be a time for her to learn to be on her own a bit."

"Let me think about this."

"Okay. Just let me know before—"

"I'll do it!"

"That was fast."

"I don't have much quality time left, honey, I have to think quick these days. When do we leave?"

"May. Either this coming or the next. I'm not sure how long everything's going to take."

"Why then?"

"That's when you get to see the whales. It also gives me time to get a good hold on my guitar."

Peta smiles. "I've always wanted to learn the trombone myself. You don't think . . ."

"No way! Don't make us glad to see you go, dear."

Turkey, oyster dressing, sweet potatoes, mashed potatoes, green bean casserole, sauerkraut, rolls, butter, gravy, pickles, congealed salad, and Peta's canned cranberry sauce. Almost a meal fit for a king.

Peta scoops a huge spoonful of lime gelatin onto my

plate. "Eat hearty!" She winks.

I have to; it's Cheeta's only contribution to the meal. Be nice and that sort of thing. Oh, Cheeta looks positively wondrous this morning. Wearing all black, she mourns the loss of liberty with a toast of Scotch. "Well, here's to celebrating the government creating a day when we're supposed to pray and give thanks, clearly a violation of the separation of church and state." She displays her gold jewelry against a fresh dose of tanning-booth skin, creating quite a fetching appearance when added to the black, sleek turban that hugs her head.

Shrubby dressed up. He wears a blazer with his work clothes and a pair of loafers without socks. He heard that was preppy one time. When I let him in, he whispered, "I've got a tie in my pocket just in case."

"Just in case what?"

He just shrugged and handed me some fresh oysters for a half-shell appetizer.

Peta sits across from me at the table looking beautiful. I wonder if she thinks this is her last Thanksgiving and seeks to be remembered as lovely. I've never seen her like this, her long hair piled on top of her head, its own natural waves ebbing and flowing down around her temples. I think she borrowed some of her sister's lipstick, for her lips shine a soft plum. Probably one of Cheeta's castoff colors. She wears a new sweater she bought in Salisbury when she ventured up to find a good-sized turkey. Its mustard and bronze hues catch the Blackfoot in her skin. She is beautiful. I never realized Peta is such a classic beautiful woman.

I wear my death ensemble to honor the poor turkey. Black pants (bumblebee boxers underneath), black shirt (long-sleeved for the cold weather), and my mirrored shawl. I hang it over the back of my chair as Shrubby stands to his feet, glass of wine held out in front of him.

Shrubby makes us all do the thankful exercise.

"I'll go first," he tells us. "I'm thankful I don't have any wives to speak of, I found a previously unknown oyster bed, so drudgin's been good, and while I'm sorry Joe's dead, it's been nice seeing Pearly around these parts again."

Peta snickers. "You would say that, Shrubby."

"You're such a Casanova," says Cheeta.

I shrug. "You know they think we made it together when we were in high school, Shrub."

He laughs. "You and me?" He turns to the cousins. "Where in the world did you hear that one?"

Peta shakes her head. "You two snuck off together enough."

"Yeah. So I could be the lookout for her and my brother Marsh." He shudders as though sex with me would have been horrible. Well, he's probably right. I'm officially dubbing this the Sexual Therapy Thanksgiving. I hardly gave this stuff a thought for the past three decades, and they're rubbing my nose in it. Guess it's true that you can never go home again. Guess this kind of thing is why.

All in all, I admit to being thankful here in Grandma's kitchen, with Grandma's plates, cupboards, wineglasses, and even Grandma's disease if it makes Peta realize her full potential for however long. I raise my glass, the candle flame behind it turning the garnet wine to ruby. Inside, I toast Joey, promising him I'll never forget what a lucky woman he made me all those years ago, telling him that even I realize God gave me a gift in him, and I will always be thankful.

Good thing Joey didn't specify the altitude of a proper, winterable mountain. I'm sure he pictured something Alpish or Rocky, not the mildly undulating Blue Ridge. But while I'm capable of roughing it to some extent, this is not penance I'm doing. It's a final act of homage. So I made sure central heating and hot and cold running water came with the package. There's no TV, though. As well as I knew my husband, I know he wouldn't have wanted any such cultural intrusion upon the time.

I bought my own, new guitar, bright blue and shiny, a huge fake-it book with the chords charted above the lyrics, and a stack of CDs. Music winter begins. I will learn to play my way around simple songs and appreciate what I can afford to buy. And I'm going to quit smoking this winter in time to train for my 10K when spring comes. Lynchburg, Virginia, only a couple hours away, hosts the Virginia Ten-Miler. And I will be there in my shoes and shorts. I bought good, waterproof hiking boots to start hiking this winter. Climbing around the hills when there's no snow should help me get in shape, too.

I call Maida, just to see how things fare there. They must have hired a new headmaster by now. I don't really want to know who he is, but my curiosity does get the better of me. And I haven't found out what's going on with Shelby and Brock on *Loves, Lies, and Lifetimes* in months. And poor little Pumpkin? What's become of him?

"Hi, Maida, it's Pearly."

"Pearly Girlie! I don't recognize this number. 804? Where's that?"

"Virginia?"

"How come?"

I refuse to explain about the list. "Just thought it would be a nice place to winter. I'm near Luray, you know those caverns and all."

"Have you ever heard that stalacpipe organ?" she asks.

"No. I've never been to the caverns."

"Then I think it's high time you go."

"How's my little Pumpkin?"

"Fine. Gotten fat and lazy. I can't bear to let her roam outside the way you did. All those bugs out there. Ugh. Not to mention the winter cold."

"So tell me what's happening on your soap. Did Shelby and Brock ever make it back from ancient Egypt?"

"No. They're just about to get married. She gave up her throne for him—well, just deserted it really—and now the Phoenicians are after her, trying to make sure she's dead now that she's in such a vulnerable position."

"Were the Phoenicians around with the Egyptians, and were they enemies?"

"Who cares?" says Maida.

Joey would.

I think of Joey's wonderful stories, so acclaimed, so brilliant, so meticulously researched when called for. But Maida makes me wonder if that was all a needless bother. *Loves, Lies, and Lifetimes* is daytime television's biggest hit, faulty research and hackneyed, implausible plotlines or not. Maybe Joey was right. Maybe he should have just penned some sleazy bestseller, then taken the money and run.

He left me well enough off, so I can't complain.

"So what's happening at the school? Who's the new headmaster?"

"A woman, if you can believe it." Oh, the disapproval oozes out of the receiver!

"Really? What's her name?"

"Yvette Brown. A black woman."

"You sound doubtful about her."

"She sashayed into my kitchen on day one and informed me a nutritionist was in order. Miss High and Mighty Ph.D. 'This stuff has more fat in it than my grandma's Sunday dinners!' she said."

"Well, I think that's kind of funny."

"She was laughing when she said it, that's true. But it still wasn't very nice."

"How old is she?"

"Late forties, I'd guess. Has seven children of her own, and her husband works in Washington, D.C., of all places. Catches the Amtrak every day, if you can believe that."

"Maida, dear, she sounds lovely."

"How can you say that, when she replaced Joe? Joe was the perfect headmaster."

"Well, I won't argue with you on that count."

She is silent for a moment. "I put some flowers by his grave on Thanksgiving."

"Thank you, Maida."

"When will you be home, Pearly?"

"When I'm finished."

"Finished what? I'm taking care of your cat, I have a right to know."

A knock sounds on the door. "Gotta go, Maida. My guitar teacher is here."

I hang up before she can say anything. I yank open the door to find Matthew, one of the busboys over at the Mimlyn Inn. He plays acoustic sets at the new coffee shop on Main every so often as well.

The poor child's face churns with acne, but at sixteen, he is already a well-respected guitar player. "I love classical guitar, but if all you want to do is learn to strum some tunes, I could teach you that anytime, any day."

We'd struck up a conversation at the gas station near the Wal-Mart.

It's my first lesson. "Matthew!" I swing the door wide. "Come on in."

"Whoa, nice place. Yours?"

"Nah. I'm just renting it until March. It's kind of small."

I usher him in front of the fireplace, where I've already arranged two armless kitchen chairs. He sets down his guitar case, brown and worn. "It was my grandfather's. Notice how both front and back are rounded? You can literally drive a car over these puppies and the guitar will remain unscathed."

I thumb back at the kitchen. "Want something to drink?"

"No. I bought a soda on my way here."

"Must be nice to have your own car."

He grins. "Oh yeah. But I work hard enough for it."

"Yeah?"

"Uh-huh. I bus at the Mimlyn, work at Taco Bell, give guitar lessons, and I detail cars too. Your car need detailing?"

"It could use some freshening up inside."

"Oh yeah. And when the weather's nice, I power-wash anything people want power-washed."

"You're a regular entrepreneur."

"Well, I really want to go to college, but I'll have to pay my own way."

"Will your parents help you?"

"They can't. Dad just works at the Wrangler fac-tory—well, Vanity Fair owns it now, actually. It's hand-to-mouth around our place."

"Wow. That's a shame. What about your mom?"

He rolls his eyes. "Hopeless. But at least there's one thing I know. I'm not going to end up in their shoes. I'm going to make it big."

"In music?"

"Yes ma'am. Classical guitar. You'll see me playing with an orchestra behind me one day."

"Can you play me something?"

"It's your twenty bucks, Mrs. Laurel. If you want part of that to be a concert, I'm not going to argue."

But he blushes, acting sixteen again. "It's not that I won't play for free, or for the love of it, Mrs. Laurel.

But I have to go right from here to my own lessons."

I understand.

"Now you sit on the couch, close your eyes, and listen while I play, okay?"

"All right."

He flips open the latches on his case and removes an old guitar, nicked and worn. But it's polished, lovingly kept. "Was that your grandfather's as well?"

He shook his head. "This was my uncle's. He died a few years ago in a car accident. The only one in the bunch worth anything."

Now there's a statement that makes you want to know more and puts you off all in one fell swoop.

Matthew begins. The tones of the strings when he plucks them, picks them, strums them are like nothing I've ever heard before. Mint and chili pepper. Crystal and clay.

And I thought Joey knew his way around a fretboard.

So young and tender are his fingers, so young and tender is the melody. My heart stutters, falls and shatters on the floor of my soul, and I miss Joey in this moment more than I ever have before. Matthew's music embodies him somehow, curling its tempo into a Joey shape, its tune into a Joey sound, its rhythm into a Joey movement. I cry. I don't mean to, and Matthew doesn't notice until he lifts his head forty minutes later.

"Guess I got carried away."

I wipe my eyes.

"Are you okay, Mrs. Laurel?"

"I'm just sad. My husband died in September. Your tune made me miss him."

He sits down beside me on the paisley couch. "Did you like it?" Eagerness fills his eyes.

"Yes. It's perfect."

"I wrote that for my uncle. I wanted to tell him of my longing."

"You captured it exactly."

"You want to get started on your lesson?"

I shake my head. "No, just play for the rest of the hour. We'll call it inspiration for the next time you come."

Matthew complies, a Spanish hue warming the tones. I awaken later to a dark and quiet room, the fire on the hearth burned down to curious coals. The darkness settles around me, and I fumble toward the bedroom and my tote bag. I dreamed about the yellow socks, you see, and I wish to wear them here, right now. I lie down on the double bed.

Normally these days, sleep comes upon me when she wishes, but as the clock in the living room chimes nine, I take sleep for my own, refusing to say good-bye, praying that she guides me back to Joey, the now literal man of my dreams. At times he seems so real, as if he's not simply a dream, but that he inhabits one. I woke up laughing the other night, my voice warming the silence with a mirth only Joey could provide.

I close my eyes, seeking the peace once more.

It is eleven o'clock. No dreams. No sleep. As if I thought I could control something so arbitrary. I turn on the light, squash a square of nicotine gum against my molars, and pick up the latest journal of Joey's. About to read, I look outside at the stars over the pine treetops, and I actually think maybe God notices I'm here after all. I heard heaven earlier today, and it ushered me into a peaceful, unplanned sleep. Surely times like these do not happen by accident.

Then again, maybe they do.

May 15, 1966
JHU, Baltimore

I've never heard the name Pearly before. It suits her, the girl with the perfect skin and pale green eyes. She glows inwardly with kindness. I'm not sure how I became privy to this fact, but I recognized it from afar, even as she walked toward our group as we sat singing. Yet I know she is not one of us, has not fallen at the feet of the Redeemer, but I believe she bears the mark of someone set aside for future reference. Good heavens, reducing her to research terms. I must be overly involved with my thesis. I asked her out as I walked her over to Kashka's for some coffee. To my delight she said yes. We meet tomorrow after classes. Pearly and Joe. Good heavens, it sounds positively Salinger. Or even Steinbeck, main characters of course. Although Pearly would be the name of a man. Some man with dusty trousers and worn-out overshoes flapping in a summer rain in Monterey.

Funny, I love the English language, but tonight, despite the scent of Mom's old roses on the lot shifting in the breeze, an opaque, darkened city sky and the tender spring of the cushion beneath my head, the only bosom I've known for eleven years, I cannot think of a thing to write. Perhaps her name is enough for now. Pearly Anne Kaiser. What delights will she hold? And why does she make me so bold as to believe that I will be the one to grasp them for my own?

I'm on a three-year voyage through infested waters, truth be known. I dream of falling over the side of this new boat, bearing the shock of the chill fluid piercing my aches and pains, my swellings, my ischemic will to survive. I can tell you I've already nixed the idea of jumping off the Bay Bridge. See, with my terrible luck, I'd survive the fall and drown, which is suffocation, which I refuse to bring upon myself. Imagine: If fortune kissed me, my lungs would fill up, stifling the burning sensation caused by the lack of oxygen. But I have survived the fall. Luck has snubbed me once again, and my epiglottis has folded over my windpipe, banishing the water from my lungs. My legs, of course, hang broken, or my arms. Or all four appendages. Or one of each on the same side. Let's go with that. It's the worst-case scenario, as it would force me to swim in circles. So there I struggle in the Chesapeake Bay, cars whizzing like arrows overhead on the bridge. Under the water now, I can't hear the sounds of the sirens approaching for the rescue. Good, because in the time it takes for my air to be depleted, I'll recognize the glory of life, and they won't reach me in time. But see, that's just my survival instinct crying out against my sealed fate, not me.

No, not drowning. There's too much time to ponder while the clock ticks against you. There's got to be a better method. Something quick and decisive and easy to administer myself. I definitely won't allow someone else to do the dirty work for me. How selfish. Imagine!

I set down Joey's journal, swing my legs over the side of the bed, and reach into my tote bag. My fingers brush the box of green tea, and I smile.

Yes, green tea will do nicely.

Joey's watch glints in the lamplight. I slip it onto my wrist. The battery still powers the golden hands, moving them past the numbers again and again, the battery Joey changed and planned on changing again and again and again. It's so real, so connecting.

Desolation comes upon me, and I hold the watch to my ear, the ticking piercing my brain, stabbing my heart.

Goooooo-oooo-ooone. He's goooooo-ooone.

He's really gone.

Joey's never coming back.

I kiss the watch, feeling the absence of his body heat, and I wonder when this battery will lose its power, and I decide that truly this is all I have left of Joey. When it dies, I will too. List or no list.

Relief relaxes my muscles. One way or another, I can see an ending.

Making the tea now, I am renewed. Tomorrow I will walk the hills, and I will begin living the end with all the gusto and verve Joey would have lived his, had he known it was just around the bend.

"Pearly?"

"Yes ma'am?"

I am twelve years old today! The morning sun streams through the kitchen curtains Mom pulled back before she put on the percolator. She calls the morning light "nature's first jolt." She calls coffee "man's attempt at morning light."

She turns away from me as I sit down, and I know what's coming. After opening the icebox, she whips around with a bowl of chocolate ice cream! "Happy birthday, Pearly!"

And she sings the song, doing a little side-step with the bowl in one hand and a spoon from the good silver in the other. "Happy birthday to you!" She ends the song, with a ball-change, a shuffle, and a tap of her heel. She tap-danced on the radio once when she was a kid. And the final, silent beat is a kiss, right smack on the lips.

We rub the kisses in.

"Twelve years old." She sits down catty-corner from me and rests her forearms on the tabletop as I eat. She watches me, examines me, and any moment she'll say, "It seems like only yesterday . . ." and she'll tell me about the day I was born. "January is such a lovely month to begin a life . . ." Always the same. Five weeks early, but still six pounds one ounce; the way I held onto my own ear, ripping it partially on the way out; the big bandage, still a cutie-pie though; how I peed on Daddy the first time he held me. Always the same story, told the same way, ending with tears overflowing from a heart so filled with love and thankfulness I swear sometimes, on nights when Daddy forces her to let my brother cry himself to sleep, it will be her undoing.

Anyway, my mother should have been on Broadway. She has a certain wild devil-may-care attitude. This thirst for anything and everything possible. And sometimes impossible.

One night at dinner she told us she thought sure Vienna sausages in lime Jell-O would be a good combination. "Combines both the meat and dessert in one fell swoop."

We all gagged on the first bite, and she whisked it off the table, gagging too. "I don't know what I was thinking. Let's have ice cream for dinner instead."

I bet my father wonders whether he really imported a Martian and not a Baltimorean out here to the Eastern Shore. He loves her though, in his quiet way. He's out in his fields a lot, but that doesn't stop Mom. She takes his lunch out there to him, and they eat it together. Of course, Mom stopped the farm tradition of a big meal at lunchtime once I went off to first grade. She didn't have much of an upbringing, so having us all together for the day's big meal is important to her.

She sits there across from me, and she lights up one of her Lucky Strikes. Oh, she looks so classy and smart! Mom always pulls her hair back in a scarf, and she wears those cute pedal pushers with sleeveless blouses in the summer and sweater sets in the winter. Little flat shoes grace her slightly large feet. She is elegant yet somehow manages to fit in with the farm wives around here. I suspect it's because she's always asking them for advice. People like to feel smart and needed, and my mom knows how to make them feel that way. She's a genius.

There's also my Mongoloid brother, Harry, to consider. He's such a sweetie pie. I think folks feel sorry for her, burdened with a child she'll never get rid of. But Mom doesn't seem to mind. She says Harry is the way all humans were supposed to be before they got too big for their britches. I'm not sure when that exactly happened to mankind, and she says she's not either, but it was sometime after World War I when one group of people thought they had the right to play God and put their own wants and desires over another group of people. I don't want to tell her that's been going on for forever. Mom graduated eighth grade and never went to high school because her parents were so poor and needed the money she could make at one of the canneries over on the other side of the harbor. She says she barely listened—even in grammar school! But as I said, she's a genius. I mean, what other mother serves ice cream for a birthday breakfast? None that I know of. She's always telling me how rich we are, how she and her friend Ida Johnson would get old issues of Hollywood-type magazines from Ida's aunt's beauty parlor and they'd look at the pictures of the stars. "All I ever wanted, Pearly, was to have a few nice things. And your father gets them for me. I don't need much. Just a few nice things."

Dad's sure proud of Mom. Grandma loves her too, even though Mom's not a churchgoing type. I think she hoped Dad would pick a church girl, but Dad says he leaves that up to Grandma. So we get dressed up on Sundays after the morning chores are done, and we go for drives up to Salisbury or Princess Anne, or we even take the ferry out to the Island of Tangiers. She puts her arm in his and they strut, everything swinging in perfect rhythm. Harry stays with Grandma on Sundays. She takes him to church with her, and boy does he love Jesus the way she does! Dad's not so sure about all that. "How can that boy be making an educated decision about what religion he wants to be?"

"Let him have the comfort, Carl," Mom always says. "That's what religion's for anyway."

I used to go to church with Grandma too, but just when I was really getting interested in going to Sunday school, they took me out. It was a nice little white Methodist church. Grandma's told me lots of times about the revival meetings they had over here on the Eastern Shore when she was a girl. "People gettin' saved left and right, Pearly!" she'd say, eyes looking heavenly. But now I go with Mom and Dad, and we have us a good time.

I spoon more ice cream into my mouth. This is such a fun tradition. My mom's full of them.

Harry's guttural, "Mama!" sounds from the bedroom. He won't get out of bed until she gets him. Has always been that way. She pulls in one last drag on her cigarette and snuffs it out in an ashtray I made in first grade out of modeling clay. "Time to go get the boy!"

"What jammies did you put on him last night?" I ask.

"The race car ones."

"I love those!"

For some reason, it's become very important to us that Harry should wear a different pair of pj's every night of the week, and all cute. Well, actually, we know the reason. It's important to Harry. And we don't know why, but it's okay with us.

Dad walks in. "Happy birthday, Pearl the Squirrel!" And he kisses me softly on top of the head.

"Coffee's done, Dad!" I jump up and pour him a cup. "It's a cold day out there. What're you gonna do?"

"Feed animals. Wanna come?"

"Yep. I'm almost done with my ice cream." I pour his coffee, then hurry through the rest of my breakfast. "Will you wait until I change and get on my boots?"

He nods and sips his coffee. Harry lets out another odd sound from upstairs, and I see Dad shudder, and I see him try to hide his distaste. He smiles. "Hurry up, missy! Time's awastin'!"

Happy birthday to me! I run up the stairs, my bare feet thumping like a racing kitten across the wooden floor of the hallway.

By the time Matthew gets here, I've got the progression to "Louie Louie" down. A-A-D-D-E-E-D-D. Of course the tempo is dirgelike, but that's okay.

"This is the only thing I know on the guitar," I say. I don't tell him I used the chord chart that came with the guitar to remember what Joey taught me. Nor do I tell him it took me four hours to do so!

He laughs. "Oh, Mrs. Laurel, that's not as bad as you think. You can play a whole bunch of songs with those chords."

"That's what my husband told me."

"So he was pretty good on the guitar?"

I nod. "I didn't hear him play all that much. He

mostly used to practice on his lunch break."

"Now doesn't that make you mad?" He says this casually, because he can't know how true this is.

"Kind of selfish, I think," I answer.

"I mean, if you can't share music with the people you love . . ."

"You play much at home, Matthew?"

He nods. "I practice all the time."

Happy birthday to me!

I tromp through the hills breathing heavily, of course. Drat these dirty lungs. And my legs? Atrophy reigns. Yes, Happy birthday, Pearly Laurel, one year older chronologically, ten years older in every other way.

When Joey was alive, I'd daydream I was on assignment to some dangerous, war-torn land—Pearly Kaiser, renowned photojournalist, ready to risk life and limb and even her special Leica to capture the truth on celluloid. After a few years of marriage, I couldn't rightfully say what country I was even in, I'd removed myself so completely from world politics and unrest. I used to care so much about the world around me.

Oh, but . . .

I had found joy in loving someone. It was enough then. But it can't be now, or should it be? Yet I have a purpose now, a fulfilling one as I winter here in the Blue Ridge on this mountain.

I rest on an outcropping of rock that overlooks the south fork of the Shenandoah River. What loveliness. What a gentle hand painted this scene. What a sensitive ear engineered these sounds: this singing, jazzy winter breeze, the staccato slick of the branches as they respond in perfect rhythm. But the silence in between when the wind dies down fills me with wonder. How can so much be so still?

Dignity lives here. And I feel honored not only to observe but to be a living, breathing part of this immense moment. I am here, that is all, and it is large and wonderful.

Sean is something! I love sitting around and watching him rail against the government, bunch of pigs they are. Those poor children over in Vietnam. They're just slaughtering them. And for what? It's none of our business.

I watch his mouth, full bottom lip over teeth that are either naturally straight or were braced into perfection, speak passionately and with more conviction than most of these kids around here. He's talking about a sit-in here at JHU. I'm game. Exams are done, and I'll be leaving for Christmas break tomorrow. I'll just postpone my departure a day.

Oh, wow. He's looking right at me! Are his eyes lighting up? I think so! I could be mistaken, but I know men and their glances. He's uttering that phrase I keep hearing, "Make love, not war." And he's looking right at me!

I am in Sean's arms. He isn't my first and I'm under no delusion he'll be my last. I'm only a freshman, so there's lots of time left for me. Thank goodness Mom slipped me the Ortho-Novums a couple of years ago. I think briefly about Marsh Cinquefoil back home, our fumbling experiments. And I miss him.

It's 11:00 A.M. He's probably out on his dad's boat right now, cold wind curing his sweet face to someday match his father's. I love watermen.

Sean is more of the soft type compared to Marsh, but he'll do. I'm lonely, and I'll be going home, and Marsh and Betsy will be announcing their engagement. I told him he didn't have to wait for me while I was in college, but I didn't think he'd take me up on it.

Sean kisses me, and I make sure I respond like I mean it. He is one of the most popular guys here. I should be glad for the privilege, the adventure even. I want it all.

Matthew brought me a guitar strap today so I can learn to play without looking down at the strings, my guitar turned up like a platter. "That's plain unnatural, Mrs. Laurel."

It is February, and we are out on the deck overlooking the river. The branches of the trees clack, and the smell of a warm winter day clings in my nostrils, much like the buttery scent of cinnamon rolls or a good beef stew. The music of the mountain prompts awe, and we are about to add our own bit. Somewhat of a desecration really, at least on my part, for I haven't exactly made great strides in learning this instrument, but I'm trying, Joey, I'm trying.

Matthew attaches ties that look like shoelaces to the head of my instrument as he speaks. "The first time I ever played standing up, I thought I'd died and gone to heaven."

"Honestly?"

"Oh yeah. This is so much fun, Mrs. Laurel. Just wait and see."

Finishing the job in seconds, he hands me the guitar then grabs his own out of the opened case on the deck. "Okay, let's put them on."

"Do I have to do this, Matt?"

"Have I steered you in the right direction so far?"

"Well, yes."

"Okay, then trust me to know what I'm doing."

I must. He's the only teacher around that I know of, and besides, learning from a teenager cuts out all the pomp and importance. Matthew just makes it fun.

"If you say so." I cast him a glance dripping with doubt, or that's what I'm going for at least, and he laughs, swiveling himself through the strap on his Yamaha.

I mimic his movements, totally ripping out my pony-tail. "Ouch!"

He just laughs harder. So much for pity. But then sixteen-year-old boys aren't big on that sort of thing. I've observed enough of them to know.

"Okay, now. Grab the A chord. Ready?"

"Ready," I say.

"I'll do the intro, and you come in on the "Louie Lou-ay" part okay?"

I nod.

And he begins strumming the introduction, sounding exactly like the real song, only it's acoustic. His eyes light up as he hits the final D before I come in with him on the A.

We begin together. "A Louie-Lou-Ay!" And we sing

the entire song, him dancing around the deck with his guitar, looking like a trained monkey who's escaped the leash of the grinder, and me swaying from side to side, intent on the strings, afraid to move my feet even a millimeter.

But I'm exhilarated. I'm performing. I've never performed. I feel layers inside me, hardened crusts, split open, and something bubbles out, something young and reckless and lapping up abandon, something melodic, something harmonic.

When we finish the number, we throw back our heads and laugh, adding yet another layer of sound to a world that teems with song.

"Isn't it great, Mrs. Laurel?"

"Oh, my goodness!"

Matthew can't possibly know *how* great. Matthew can't possibly know what he's done for me.

"Maida?"

"Yep?"

"It's Pearly."

"Hey, Pearly Girlie."

"Just checking in."

"How's Virginia?"

"Wonderful. We got snow this week, which is a beautiful thing. And I even treated myself to dinner at the Mimlyn the other night. It's a fancy old inn, gracious Southern mansion-type place. Sure needs a coat of paint, though."

"You go alone?"

"Nope. I took my music teacher."

"That nice boy Matthew?"

"None other. You didn't think I was ready to start dating yet, did you?" She snorts. "I didn't think so, Maida. Believe me, I don't think I'll ever date again."

I know I won't. That wouldn't be fair. Establish a relationship, and then, *crick,* I'm dead. And with my luck, he'd find me and I'd scar him for life. That would be so terrible.

"Guess what?" Maida says. "Shelby is pregnant!"

"Past or present?"

"Both!"

"No! Wow. Is Brock the father?"

"Of course. But remember that Damien Le Coeur guy? That villain who runs some kind of international firm that's really a money-laundering operation?"

"Yes. Who could forget a guy like that?" Actually, the man is terribly sexy.

"Well. He's claiming to be the father."

"Is there a possibility?"

"That's the thing. Shelby got really drunk one night at Brock's club, and Damien found her wandering along the waterfront in a stupor, and he drove her home."

"Does she remember nothing?"

"Conveniently, no."

"Oh, wow."

We catch up on Pumpkin, the school, and Maida's latest home-improvement project: a new roof.

"I got all the shingles on special at that big roofing company in Northeast. What a deal. They're leftovers, of course."

"How many different colors?"

"At least twelve!"

I call the homestead next. "Peta?"

"No, it's Cheeta."

"Hey there! How you doing?"

"All right, I guess. Still mourning our new Republican governor."

The first in some thirty-odd years.

"Give him a chance, Cheet. You gave the Dems enough time to straighten things out, and the state's still a mess."

She snorts. "Easy for you to say."

"Face it, Cousin, I don't care about politics anymore. Not like the old days. How's the farm?"

"I don't know and I don't care. Ask Peta."

"She there?"

"Peta!" she yells. "See ya, hon. Enjoy the mountains."

"Thanks."

Peta's voice comes over the line. "Hi, Pearly. Didn't expect to hear from you."

"Yes, well. I just called to invite you down here for a bit. I need to go to a rock concert, and I thought you'd like to come with me."

"Sounds good, but I don't think I should leave Cheeta."

"Go! Go!" Cheeta yells in the background.

Peta says, "I've been telling her how jealous I am of you for the past month."

"Come on then, Peta. It'll do her good, and we both know why."

* * *

Peta arrives a few days later. Her appetite has dwindled, and her eyes look watery and lethargic despite her typical spunk in the attitude department. I let her sleep as much as she likes and try to make all her favorite meals. She tells me "no phosphates," which rules out all the dairy foods we both love. Protein is limited too. No wonder she doesn't want to live this way for very long. A life without cheese?

"And it'll be worse once I'm on dialysis," she tells me one night as we sit drinking brandy before a fire.

I want to tell her I'll take care of her when she worsens, but there's too much left to accomplish and I'll be dead long before she is.

Still, it fills me with regret to know I have discovered the wonderful light of my cousin only just as it's beginning to fade.

"The *Goo Goo Dolls*? What kind of name is that, Pearly?"

I just shrug. "According to Matthew, they're a great group."

"Why couldn't we have gone to see an oldies group, like Chicago or something?"

The landscape hugging I-66 whizzes by as we head to the MCI Center in D.C. "I wanted to go to a real rock concert again. If we go to an oldies concert, people like me will just sit there politely. I want lighters and body-surfing."

"You going to body-surf?"

"With the seats I got? Hardly."

Peta adjusts her seatbelt. "Nosebleed?"

"It was all they had left, unfortunately."

"Well, good. I don't think my eardrums can take anything right next to the speakers anymore."

"If they're anything like mine, they'd do better. I swear I'm lipreading half of what people say these days."

She smiles. "And you get it wrong half the time too."

"I do?"

"Just jerking your chain, Cousin."

Jerking my chain?

Good heavens.

My eyes tear up at the look of awe, life, and joy on Peta's face as the crowd erupts in applause after a song called "Slide." She claps so hard I fear her hands will burst, and how in the world will I get the blood out of my suede vest?

I clap too. Oh this lovely, wonderful noise all around. God bless Matthew for knowing!

Look at them all down there, their lives open before them like a six-lane strip of highway, so many choices, so many years left before the lanes dwindle, one by one, into a narrow, lonely path, with only smaller, dead-end side lanes to offer temporary diversion.

A haunting guitar begins to pick its way into a steady rhythm at the hands of the very good-looking lead singer.

"Baby's black balloon . . ." he begins.

I don't even pretend to comprehend the lyrics nowadays. I just allow my blood to flow and ooze along with

John Reznik's, for that is the boy's name. And when he closes his eyes, I do too.

Under the seat I stick a picture of Joey and me in London, right there in St. James's Park. Joey and me and all the birds.

June 2, 1997
Havre de Grace

A new student arrived at school today. LaJon Baker. He is fourteen and looks eight. His mother was killed by her pimp two years ago and he's been with an aunt ever since. She arranged his acceptance to Lafayette School. I talked with her myself and heard how much she loves the boy. "He's a genius, Dr. Laurel. I can't pry the books out of his hands even to come to the supper table!" He sat in my office with a stack of books on the table beside his chair. Eager. Bright. Scared. I cannot wait to see what LaJon accomplishes here. I hope I live long enough for him to return and visit me like Marvin Starling did today. I'd forgotten how much I missed Marvin until he came walking in the office, all six-foot-seven of him, looking like the moon was hung for him alone.

I sit by the fire as usual, reading today's journal allotment. Oh, Marvin Starling! What a wonderful boy. Could take anything apart and put it back together, too. He ended up at Virginia Tech and graduated with honors. Marvin dined at our house that evening after he visited the school. He told us of his young family and his new wealth—the result of an invention he'd dreamed up and manufactured, some sort of shoe-paging system for harried families. He told of a charity he'd begun that supplied coats and shoes to the needy. Joey glowed with pride and shook his head when Marvin said, "So thank you, Dr. Laurel. You deserve much of the credit just for loving this boy and believing I was worth something."

"No, no, no!" Joey held up his hand. "You did the hard work, Marvin, and God blessed you as He promised to do."

"Well, I can't argue with that. God's been good, that's for sure. And I've got more plans."

"No doubt!"

Marvin gushed about his dreams, all these years later, still bursting with trust in the person sitting across the table, knowing that his mentor, Dr. Joseph Laurel, would only, *could* only, believe the best for him.

I think maybe I'll give Marvin a call. He'll want to know that Joey died.

I sit down and list all the young men impacted by Joey. Yes, this is a bit overdue, but Joey deserves to have those who love him know he's gone. Definitely Richard King, our doctor. Certainly he knows, but I have to write just in case. Oh, yes. Dr. King. Another one of the Lafayette boys who grabs life by the heart.

I feel such triumph when I think of him. Men like him are what Lafayette, and Joey, were all about. Triumph. Victory. And life. And love. Such love.

My goodness! Two notebook pages filled with names. And those are only the boys I remember! I'm sure there are many more I cannot call to mind. I do believe the worst part of grief is that my mind has regressed from calculator to adding machine. Or perhaps even abacus. Nothing runs automatically anymore. I try to remember if I've eaten lunch—*click, click* go a couple of the beads upon the metal rod—well? And then I seem to recall a bowl of cereal, naturally, but what kind? I know I finished up the box of Froot Loops at breakfast, and I do believe I ate some Honey Bunches of Oats, and if that memory serves me correctly, then yes, I did eat lunch. I cannot even begin to think about anything important, and for the most part I simply make decisions on the fly.

I call the school to get phone numbers.

Joey's administrative assistant, Tanya Michaels, a young woman with a propensity for French braids and bridesmaid-looking dresses, answers the phone. "Mrs. Laurel? This is really you?"

"Yes, it's me."

"We've all heard you're taking Dr. Laurel's passing hard."

"Yes, well."

"You two were so close. I've never seen a couple so close like you were close."

"He would want the old boys to know he's gone, I think. Can I have a printout of the school's alumni list? I want to send them personal notes and let them know."

"Okay. Sure. But the news went out in the latest newsletter."

"That's okay. I still want to contact them personally."

I give her my address here at the cabin. "Thanks." And I hang up the phone with a quick good-bye before she can ask any questions.

Two days later the list arrives. I bought note cards yesterday in Luray. The front displays a shelf of books with lion bookends. Perfect for Joey. However, I forgot to buy a new ink cartridge for Joey's pen, so I'm on my way back into Luray to buy a pen and have lunch. I'm tired of cereal. I've made my way through three quarters of the top shelf at the grocery store. Variety, variety. Perhaps it's the milk. If I could eat it with juice instead, or even Sprite, it might help. There's a thought. That's pretty much all it is. Blech.

I pull my car along Main Street. There's the type I'm interested in, a real down-home looking place. Yolanda's Rib Room. In Luray? She must be a transplant from south Georgia, or Memphis. But the thought of those bones between my fingers bears up well.

This seems like a place that should have been on my list of things to do, so I walk in. Yes, I am the only pale-face in the establishment. Yes, I am met with distrust. But still I move to the only vacant table, a booth for two, formed from orange melamine, midway down the long, narrow restaurant. Working men dressed in varied garb—suits and ties, shirts and ties, uniforms, and factory clothing—sit at a counter lining the opposite wall.

"You want the lunch special?"

I turn my head a bit to the right and back, and there stands a chocolate-frosted crème donut of a woman wearing jeans and a T-shirt that says, "Yolanda's, Nothin' But Ribs . . . So Don't Ask for More."

"What's the special?" I ask.

"Half rack, greens, cornbread, and pinto beans."

"Sounds fine."

"Water?"

"You got Coke?"

She hesitates. "You *look* like a water person."

"Life's short."

She lifts half her mouth. "That's what my aunt used to say."

"Used to?"

"Uh-huh. Hardening of the arteries."

"Oh, great."

"Too many rib dinners." She turns and shouts the order to the woman behind the counter.

Now this woman is worthy of Joey's memoirs. She must have been in the back when I entered, because now the score for the palefaces stands at a whopping two. And yet, she's like no white woman I've ever seen. Everything about her shouts blackness except for her skin and her structure. I try to compute this. She wears an African-print shirt that wraps around her upper trunk, all sorts of animals traipsing in purple across yellow plains. Her draped purple pants remind me of that rapper who lost all his money. He had such a nice smile.

This woman's droopy pants, however, fall from a willow waist. Her thin brown hair, streaked with red and gold, is twisted into a mahogany comb at the back of her small head. Bracelets jangle on each thin arm. I don't believe I've ever seen a more beautiful woman before. Large hoops swing from earlobes drooping with overuse.

"Yolanda!" a cook yells from back in the kitchen.

She turns. "Yeah, Ray?"

Her accent is ebony. What a juxtaposition. Now Joey wouldn't hesitate to move his cutlery to the counter and start a conversation with this woman. Well, Dr. Laurel, watch this! And why not? Why not try my hand at pulling out a daisy of a story from the weed-sprouting garden most of us call our lives? I tap the face of the winding-down wristwatch.

"Something wrong with the booth?" Yolanda asks. She fiddles with one of the many rings on her left hand. She wears heavy, large gems that swirl around the bases of fingers whose knuckles are too big for their tiny girth. Size four. That's what I'm guessing.

"The booth is fine. I just enjoy the company of a counter."

"So do I! I stand behind here and talk to all sorts of folks. That's why I took over this place to begin with."

"Not to cook?"

"Oh, heavens no! I'm a vegetarian! Gave up meat for Lent one year on a whim and never looked back. I have a counseling degree. Just undergraduate. Couldn't afford to go on for the master's after my Grandmom Mabel died. I actually inherited this place. So here I am."

"Really? Why didn't you sell it and finance your schooling?"

"I figured all I wanted was to help people anyway, and I could do just as good a job at that here *and* not have to worry about malpractice or keeping up a license."

I screw up my mouth. "Not to mention the fact that some people would never lie down on a couch in a million years."

"Or they couldn't afford to even if they wanted to."

The waitress sets down my Coke and moves around the counter to take the order of a well-seasoned gentleman in coat, sweater vest, and tie. He shakes, every movement a tremolo of motion. He sits in the booth I deserted.

Yolanda nods in his direction. "That's Cerius Monroe. Too proud to see a doctor about anything. His wife's been gone a hundred years. No kids, no nothing. Comes here every day for lunch. Sits in that booth."

"Good thing I moved."

"Oh, he wouldn't make much of a fuss. It's downright sad."

"Order's up!" Ray hollers from the kitchen.

Yolanda hurries in and emerges a few seconds later beneath a loaded tray the size of a kiddie pool. "You get the special, honey?" she asks me after depositing all but one meal.

"Yes."

"Well all right then." She sets my plate down and puts the tray on a stand near the kitchen door. "Enjoy it. You look like you could use a decent meal. You been through a hard time lately?"

"You could say that."

"I can always tell." She rests her elbows on the counter, her face near mine. "You need an ear?"

I shake my head. "Maybe someday."

"I'll be here. Shoot, I'm always here."

"Do you have anybody you talk to?"

"Heavens, yes. My pastor!"

"Where do you go to church?"

"The Apostolic Church of Holy Joy."

About to stab my greens, I set down my fork instead. "Oh, my goodness. That's a mouthful!"

"I'm a deaconess there."

"How old are you?"

I've always pictured deaconesses as the human equivalent of a raisin, only swathed in a shroud, of stooped over and shuffling around with baskets of warm towels or baked goods, knocking on doors of sick people, showing up at just the right time.

"I'm thirty-seven."

"Kids?"

"Four. All in school, and I thank the Lord for that! You?"

"No kids."

"Married?"

"Widowed."

"Recently?"

"September."

"Oh, my dear Lord Jesus!"

I just nod.

"Well, no wonder you wandered in here! Not many older white women show up here in the Rib Room!"

142

"I guess I did feel a little bit drawn."

Did I? Sounded good.

"Well, just to entice you back, I'm going to send you home a big piece of my banana cream pie. Best in Luray, maybe even the entire state of Virginia."

"You don't want me back. You've got enough heartache on your shoulders."

She eyes me, looks at the ceiling, and nods. She locks her gaze into my own. "Oh, my shoulders aren't big enough for much. I just borrow the pair of the One who gives me marching orders."

There is no way I'm going to ask whose shoulders those are, because her being a deaconess assures me they're the same shoulders Joey always threw matters onto. I swear. It just goes to show. I manage not to roll my eyes.

"Well, I'd better tend to my customers. Please, come on in anytime. What's your name?"

"Pearly."

"That's a name I can remember. The pearly gates!"

I just smile. Oh, dear.

The ribs go down more smoothly than single malt whiskey. After months of cereal, the sloppy richness is intoxicating. Yolanda doesn't know what she's missing. I'll be back. Life's too short.

I'm drunk. I'm drunk. I'm stinkin' drunk. I've tried so hard to make it not come to this again, but here I am, alone in the chalet feeling so sorry for poor old me I can't stand it another second.

Boo-hoo, Pearly!

Actually, I'm sitting under the deck, and I'm stinkin' drunk.

I used to love margaritas, years ago, before Joey "got convicted" (whatever that means) and reduced our alcoholic consumption to red wine. I mean, they drank wine in the Bible, am I right or am I right? I remember Joey saying, "They try to say it's grape juice. Hah! These are the same people that say, 'When the plain sense makes no sense seek no other sense,' except when it's their thing."

I didn't know what he was talking about, and I still don't, really, but all I know is that we drank red wine from then on out. Shiraz, merlot, cabernet. Red, red. Red.

So I said, "Forget this" tonight. I went right down to the ABC store and bought myself a bottle of good tequila and some margarita mix. And I drank and drank and drank. Even put the salt on the rim for the first few drinks, then lost the salt, then lost the glass, and finally, lost the bottle.

But I am warm and wavy now, my head light and floating above me and my circumstances, and this seems good for now.

I'll just lay my head back a bit. Yep, that's it. Lie back and feel the merry-go-round spinning beneath me.

If the watch stopped last night, I deserve nothing less. When I bowed over the toilet bowl after I came in from the cold, I remembered that yes, there is indeed a God, because I was praying to Him to get me through this. A lot of people can't begin to understand the appeal of getting drunk. All they've heard about is the slurring and the barfing, the spinning and the barfing, the stumbling and the barfing. But for a while you feel good, and you feel so good you totally forget about the inevitable barfing.

Matthew comes today for guitar lessons. Poor boy. I have a feeling something concerto this way comes.

Matthew arrives at five as usual, but something about him has changed. The brightness around his eyes and mouth seems sanded down. His hair lies in greasy ropes, and the fabric of his pants drapes in softer folds, their normal, ironed crispness gone.

He walks in, refusing to look in my eyes. "Hey, Mrs. Laurel."

"Hi, Matthew."

He sets his guitar down by the hearth, clicks open the latches, and sighs.

Although my head has stopped throbbing, my stomach is still tidal. "How about a concert day today?" I ask.

He only nods and lifts his guitar out of the scarlet-lined case. Easing down into the dining room chair I bring out for each lesson, he leans over again and grabs his folding footstool. I meant to buy one in Luray, but naturally I forgot. I really do need to start writing things down.

He shifts his weight, and he hunches over the guitar, examining the strings, searching them for inspiration, I guess. I ache for him. Seeing him for the first time as the vulnerable teenager he is stabs my heart, and the maternal arms that I possess but rarely have the honor of using throb to reach out.

Several measures, tentative and shy, tumble into the air between us. And then, four violent, discordant strums that still sound better than anything I've ever played.

"I can't," he says. "I just don't feel like playing my guitar today."

How can this be? Matthew and the guitar are interchangeable.

I've seen many boys in this state before. Usually they're willing to talk; they just have to pretend for several minutes that they don't wish to.

"You seemed upset when you walked in."

"I'm okay."

I nod. "I feel like a cup of hot chocolate. Want one?"

Actually, the last thing I feel like drinking is a rich mug of cocoa, but it's all I can think of that's quick, easy, and enticing to a sixteen-year-old boy.

He shrugs. "That would be okay."

I jerk my head toward the door. "Come on back into the kitchen with me. Give an old lady some company."

"You're not an old lady."

"Compared to you I am!"

Showing mercy, I turn before he can respond, but I hear the squish of his sneakers on the wooden floor behind me. I decide to put him to use while I make the drinks. "Can you just bring in a bit more wood from the deck? I'm planning on keeping this fire going until bedtime."

He nods with enthusiasm. "Sure." He blows in relief as he turns.

I wish Joey stood here with me right now. Well, yes. Of course I do. But he knew how to handle situations like this. My job was to smile and set a plate of good food in front of them, provide fuel for the man-to-man discussion. Maybe he'll put in a good word for me up there, out there, or wherever heaven happens to be. I always liked to think heaven isn't really so. That we recycle ourselves or our eternal being creates some sort of personal, delight-filled reality that we bask in for the rest of our existence. Whether that be for eternity or not, who can really say?

But I don't feel that way now. I don't want that at all. I want Joey to still be Joey, to still be alive somewhere and happy and able to put in a good word for me.

I've been thinking a lot lately about where I'll go after I die. I've had my fair share of discussions about reincarnation over the years. Especially during college. Oh, my! You'd think we had all the answers to hear us talk. But I've noticed one thing over the years. When loved ones die, I don't care what the family left behind has believed about the soul's final destiny, they *always* say, "He's in a better place. She's in a better place."

Well, what if he's got some bad karma to work out? How can I say for sure he's in a better place? He might be a cockroach right now for all I know. A person can't ever know the true state of a person's heart and soul, whether he was truly enlightened or just faking it like the rest of bumbling humanity.

So yes, I'm hoping Joey can see me. I'm hoping there's a real God with real feelings who's listening to Joey saying, "Lord, can you lend a helping hand to

Pearly and Matthew down there?" Oh, let me tell you, Joey will ask if it's within heavenly protocol! That man never minded asking questions.

Matthew enters the kitchen just as I'm topping off the mugs with a couple of big marshmallows. No mini kind in my cupboards. Joey wouldn't have had that, and I agreed. "Cute only goes so far," he always said.

"All finished. Hey, I think I need to take a rain check on that drink."

"How come? We're not even close to the end of lesson time."

He curls his fingers around the mug handle. "You'll still pay me?"

"Sure."

"But I said—"

"Shoot, I don't want to play either! Let's call it student-teacher bonding!"

He grins and curls his fingers around the handle of the mug. "Okay." But the smile fades like the final note of a sad melody, hanging there slightly, almost painfully.

We sit down at the bar that separates the kitchen work area from the table. "You might as well tell me what's wrong. I'll get it out of you sooner or later."

"Just family stuff. It would be way too boring for you."

"Are you kidding me? I had a family once. Well, I still do have a brother. He's got Down's syndrome and lives in a home."

"Oh, wow."

"Yeah. My mom took care of him until she got sick,

then died. Dad had passed on by then, and I wanted to take him on, but I couldn't bring myself to do it. I couldn't face a life like that. Pretty sad, isn't it?"

"I don't know. That's a lot of work, isn't it?"

I shrug. "I don't know. He's pretty self-sufficient. I guess I just didn't want the . . . upheaval."

Upheaval? Where did that word come from? Joey, are you around?

Hah.

He grunts. "Upheaval. I can relate to that."

Hmm.

I don't say anything, I just wait. I'm scared if I utter a word it will break the spell that has suddenly formed.

"I mean, if you saw where I lived." He sips his cocoa with a loud slurp, skimming off the cool top layer.

Wonderful, he spoke! "Something happening at home?"

"It's what doesn't happen."

I wait.

"My parents are slobs, Mrs. Laurel. Absolute slobs. There's garbage everywhere. The kitchen counters are piled up with dirty dishes, and there are roaches and bugs everywhere. Maggots growing on the stuff at the bottom."

"Oh, my." The hangover reminds me it's still around. Don't lose it, Pearly.

"I tried to keep the house clean myself for years, but it's a losing battle, so why try?"

"I don't blame you."

"But I can't live like this."

"Are they . . . alcoholics or something?"

He shakes his head. "No. I can't understand it. It's depressing."

"I'm sure it is."

"I've got to get out of there, but I don't know how. Where could I go?"

I knew. "What are your grades like?"

"I'm not bragging or anything, but I'll get valedictorian next year if I don't screw up."

"Okay. Let me tell you about the school my husband used to be headmaster at."

We move into the living room for comfort.

We sit talking long after the lesson time expires. He leans farther forward on the sofa with each minute that passes, muttering, "Wow" and "You're kidding" as I speak.

"But what about music? Do they have a good music program?"

"It's getting better. It's like any school. They add more each year. And funding makes a difference too."

"Peabody Institute is in Baltimore," he says.

"That's right. About forty-five minutes from the school, I'd say, maybe an hour. And you have your own car."

He sinks back into the couch. "Wow."

"Do you think your parents would be open to it?"

He nods. "They know I can't stand it at home, but they're powerless to do anything. It's like it's gotten beyond them."

Boy, do I know how *that* feels. "Talk to them about it. If you can just hang on through spring and summer, maybe we can get you in for your senior year."

"I will." The sparkle returns. Oh, the resilience of youth! He looks at his watch. "I missed my own guitar lesson."

"Well, why don't you stay for dinner then? I'm making . . ." What am I making? "Cold cereal!"

He laughs. "What kind do you have?"

"Come and see."

I open up the cupboard door and display ten different boxes.

"Oh, wow."

I shake my head. "It's difficult to explain." I open the refrigerator and reach for the milk, the only item inside.

Matthew peers in then looks at me, crosses his arms. "Mrs. Laurel, no offense, but you need to get a life."

Richard King is the most stunning African American man in existence. Actually, he's the most stunning man, period. His eyes slant upward slightly, dark brown yet luminous, deeper in tone than his aged-oak colored skin. He's warm in appearance and in his bedside manner. In other words, he's just delicious, and I've always wondered if his wife sees his beauty the way I do. I do hope so. He deserves love in hearty portions.

He came to Lafayette School years and years ago out of a horribly abusive situation. Smart and kind and conscientious and even then wanting to be a doctor. He loves children.

He's the perfect man, though he assures me otherwise.

This note from him, offering, of course, to do anything he can, gladdens my heart. He loved Joey so

151

much. And the way he talks! So utterly beautiful. Joey tried to talk him into politics, you know, as a sideline to the doctoring. "With your talent for rhetoric, you could really change the world, Rich," Joey said many times.

But Richard would have none of it. "This is where I'm supposed to be, with my patients and my family. That's all the world-changing I need."

"Smart man," Joey would say.

I imagine he could give a rousing stump speech that even Cheeta might appreciate.

"Call me. Richard." His note ended that way. So I do.

"Ring Factory Family Health Center," a chipper voice answers. They're very chipper at the Ring Factory Family Health Center. I should know. I've been going there for years.

"Dr. King, please."

"He's with a patient. Can I tell him who's calling?"

"Pearly Laurel."

"Oh, hi, Mrs. Laurel. It's Gayle."

"Hey, Gayle."

"I know he'll want to know you're on the phone. By the way, we were so sad to hear about Dr. Laurel."

"Thank you."

"We'll miss him."

"Yes, well, he was the type of person to be missed."

"That's for sure. Hold on, I'll get Dr. King."

I wait for several minutes, and that's fine. I set my breakfast bowl in the dishwasher and wipe down the counter. It begins to snow. Oh, the luscious sound of falling snow. I heard yesterday in Luray we're in for the year's biggest storm.

"Miss Pearly!"

"Richie!"

"I'm so glad you called."

"I just got your note."

"Thanks for sending out your cards. But I want you to know I was at the funeral."

"I figured. How was it?"

"Tearful. A lot of the guys were there. We went down to the Chat 'n' Chew afterward and reminisced. We haven't all been together in years. Shame it took something like this."

"It always does. Did the school notify you of his passing?"

"No. We saw it in the *Aegis*. Nice long article too. Almost worthy of the man himself."

"I wonder why nobody told me about that?"

"Don't know."

"Richie, I just wanted to call and thank you for the offer."

"You need anything?"

"Not right now. But you never know."

He chuckles. "That's right."

"How's the family? The kids?"

"Well, Sheila's fine. And we're up to three now. All boys."

"Great!"

"It's been awhile since you've been in for a checkup."

"I know. I'm still down in Virginia. And guess what? I'm down to five cigarettes a day."

"Good for you. Too bad you didn't do that while Dr. Laurel was alive."

153

"You two. It's amazing you couldn't talk me into it."

"You're a stubborn old girl."

"Hey, watch that!"

"We've got a lot of years together, Miss Pearly. That entitles me to some affection."

I smile so broadly my cheeks tire right away. Oh, lovely. So lovely. "Well, Richie, I'll let you get back to your patients."

"All right. Remember, if you need anything. Anything."

"Will do."

January 1970
Conking Street, Baltimore

Something happened to me tonight. I was sitting in my kitchen chair, Pearly had long been asleep in bed, and a desire to breathe the cold night air beckoned me onto the porch. I left my coat hanging on the rack by the door and the chill breeze blew up my shirt sleeves, raced up my arms, over my shoulders, and down my chest to my stomach. But there I stood with expectation as though I was keeping some appointment. I'd been thinking a lot about Pearly, about what a blessing she is to me, but because of her outlook on life and faith and God, I cannot tell her even this. I grieve over this but I hope I hide this well. I try. I don't want to pressure her or make our home awkward for her. But I wonder if I am sinning by not being more overt about this aspect that is not only of importance to me, but truly, in the end, is of ulti-mate importance to her as well. Perhaps if I'd been raised a Baptist or a Pentecostal I never would have married her in the first place, but the whole "unequally yoked" portion of Scripture I came upon last year had never been stressed in my church. Shame on me for not knowing more of the Bible, I suppose, and yet, God is still able to take what man does either out of ignorance or evil and turn it into something wonderful. Like my marriage. It is truly a union of heart and mind. I can only pray a union of our souls will someday follow. But will I be held accountable on judgment day for Pearly's soul? I can picture the Lord saying, "You had all of those years with her and failed to press the issue even a little bit, Joe." I can only pray for God's mercy. But last night, standing on the porch overlooking Conking Street, the cold stones of Sacred Heart Church gleaming beneath the street lamps, I waited and it didn't take long. My heart was impressed with the words, "Leave her to Me, Joe. It's ultimately My job, not yours. I love her even more than you do." And I was comforted.

I went back inside, locked up for the night and heated up a cup of warm milk. The porcelain-covered pan my mother used to use comforted me further. And now, Dad's asleep upstairs in their old room, and Pearly sleeps in ours. The night is quiet and my heart is a silent symphony. I am blessed.

Joey wrote that years ago, shortly after he graduated from Hopkins with his master's when we still lived in his parents' old house on Conking Street.

I'm not sure why I've always resisted Joey's faith. I

155

abandoned so much of myself the day I married Joey. I left behind so many dreams and desires, so much freedom and, yes, even folly, I suppose. Joey truly knew God and walked with Him. Even I could sense the deep spirituality, the real relationship. But me, I'd only be doing it for Joey, and that smacked of someone who can't make her own decisions. He made all the decisions for our home. I at least would make all the decisions for my own soul.

But I'm beginning to see so much more value in the life I led, so much love and harmony. And I experience a great deal of satisfaction that Joey and I "got it right." How many people can say that? How much greatness would so many gladly trade for a bright warm hearth cared for by the tender hand of a loving spouse? I felt such happiness in his presence. Is it any wonder then, that his death has ravaged me down to the mere state of being, caused me to question why I gave it all up for him, why I lost myself? And will that same love bring me someday to the point where instead of asking why, I can honestly ask, "Why not?" Who would argue against the fact that a life lived for love and in love is a life lived for the greatest purpose of all?

I never knew how much I grieved him, though. There were times I wanted to ask him something or other about God or Jesus, but I always stopped myself. Joey was like a wrecking ball with ideas. Once you expressed an interest, he came at you with all the intellectual excitement he possessed, and there you'd be, splattered against his enthusiasm and flying up into the air with the force of it. Hey, he convinced me to marry him three weeks after we met. He overwhelmed me so much—not in a bad way, as his excitement always led to something wonderful—but I'm glad he kept this from me. I'm glad he didn't share his disappointment, or there I'd be, accompanying him to matins or prayers, pretending I cared.

"Hi, Maida."

"Pearly! I was wondering when you were going to call. It's been weeks."

The crocuses bloom now on the hillside. I'm down to three cigarettes a day and jogging two miles. I read a statistic that someone who smokes between one and nine cigarettes a day has only a .03 percent greater chance of getting lung cancer than a nonsmoker. This encourages me. Of course, with my luck . . .

I mailed in an application for the Virginia Ten-Miler. I can play "Louie Louie," "Cat's in the Cradle," "Leavin' on a Jet Plane," and "American Pie." I love the keys of D, G, and A, and the watch is still running. I look at it at least twenty times a day because I'm a little bit dismayed, even though I have yet to fulfill much of the list. However, I can play the guitar to my own lax standards, and I've wintered on a mountain. Not to mention having seen my new favorite band, The Goo Goo Dolls. Three down, eight to go.

I pull Joey's shirt tightly around my middle. "I've been busy, Maida."

"Well, I've got another stack of mail here for you from all over the country. I recognize some of the names from Joey's conversations. You want me to send these down too?"

The boys.

"No. I'll be up in two weeks. The cabin lease is up mid-March."

"You coming back to Havre de Grace?"

"Just passing through. I'll pick up the mail and then head back to the farm."

"Well, guess what's happening with Brock and Shelby?"

"They back from Egypt?"

"Oh, yes! They didn't really go back in time, we found out. They went into a past life regression together."

"Can you do that?"

"What? Find out about your past life?"

"No, do a simultaneous regression?"

"If you're soul mates, I guess so. I mean, you're going to the same point in time, right? So the other would naturally be there. Right?"

"I guess. So, did they learn anything while they were in their trances?"

"Just that they really were soul mates. And it's made all the difference. Their love is cemented now! Damien's baby and all!!"

"Oh, so it *is* Damien's!"

"Well, *I* think so."

I smile. Oh, boy.

"I'll bet you and Joey were soul mates."

"I'll bet we were."

"Which means it's just a matter of time before you're

together again." Her normally forceful voice slips into a silk sheath. "I mean, I'd never met a couple like you all. You were meant to be together for eternity."

"Maida? What's wrong with you? You sound positively drippy."

She whispers, "I think I'm in love."

"What?!" Oh, my goodness! "With who?"

"Shrubby Cinquefoil."

"Shrubby? How in the world do you know Shrubby Cinquefoil?"

"He's living in your house is how."

Oh, great. "Let me guess. My cousins." Probably Cheeta.

"Yep. Shrubby's having a hard time of it right now, Pearly. Since I couldn't get in touch with you, and he needed a place to stay, and with Cheeta's peculiar brand of persuasion—"

"Did she threaten to beat you up?"

"Almost! She's something! What a pip!"

"That's the truth."

"Anyway, Shrubby just needed to get away. I found him a job on a friend's fishing boat and he's doing better."

"Why did he need to get away?"

"His last ex-wife brought a lawsuit against him. Claimed he abused her son and sued for his property, which we both know is all he has. He got scared and gave it all to her without a fight. I'm sure it will all go to that cult too."

"No!"

"Of course he didn't do anything to the child. Not one

159

thing. But Shrubby's not a fighter."

"No, he's not."

"So when did you say you'd be here?"

"March 15."

"Okay. Come around lunchtime. Can we at least have a meal together?"

"Sure, Maida. That would be fine."

"I'll make sure there's plenty."

As if I doubted that.

Poor Shrubby! I'm so thankful for the marriage I had. I just wish it wasn't the only thing I had.

Good-bye, lovely little chalet. Good-bye, grand mountain. Good-bye, winter music.

Before locking the door, I lay a picture from my album in the back corner of the cabinet over the refrigerator. Joey and me in front of Graceland. The gates, with their musical motif, appear even more tacky out here in the middle of nature.

Finally, I close the door. My feet crunch down the pathway toward the car. I climb in and drive away.

I am flying over the plains of South America in a small Cessna. My pilot's named Juan. A former fighter pilot, utterly bored. He's seen these ancient figures etched into the landscape of Peru many times. They've become commonplace.

I, on the other hand, cannot keep my mouth from dropping open. We start out low, and I see only tan lines of dried earth. I know they form animals and people and geometric designs etched by aliens, or a race of giants, or who? No one can really say. Joey always wanted us to do this? But why? I'm glad, though, because this takes up much less time than wintering on a mountain or learning to play the guitar.

"Oh, my gosh! It's the spider!" I've seen pictures of this spider. The type is not indigenous to this area, the books say, but to me, it looks like a regular spider. I wouldn't be surprised if someday an arachnoid-type scientist discovers a new species around here that looks just like this guy. Or maybe not. I don't know why I even feel bound to form an opinion on this. I know nothing.

But I love a good mystery. Well, actually, before Joey died I loved reading mysteries, because the author is kind enough to solve it in the end with some parlor scene or a courtroom confessional. Not at all realistic according to Joey, but highly satisfying to me. This mystery, however, unsettles me a bit. And the higher the altitude the more I wonder who did this, and why? What grueling toil! Did some alien race carve some of these lines for spacecraft runways? Or a pre-Flood race of giants experience a large-scale creative urge? Maybe these document the ancient equivalent of a men's club, a place to get away from your mate, but instead of sitting around smoking cigars, they decided to make really big pictures that would keep them away from home most nights of the week. They probably blamed it all on some god, a deity demanding this of them. If you don't want fire to come down and consume you and the children, you'd better have supper on the table when I get in from the field, and a kiss on the cheek when I head out the door half an hour later.

Goodness, this altitude must be scrambling my brain.

We fly higher, and a canvas of earth and vegetation splays before me as though Jackson Pollock had thrown the forms forth from his bucket. I think of the adage, "Put a monkey in front of a typewriter, and sooner or later he'll type the Gettysburg Address," and I wonder if these figures are just some manner of chance. But I doubt that too.

I don't know much, and there's absolutely *no* doubt about that. Thank you, Joey. Thanks to you I soar above a true mystery.

The great monkey spirals its tail before me, the torso's spare underside almost kissing its top side, a singular line contouring its form, then moving on to form stairsteps, stepping across millennia and explanation. We skim the air above this tapestry. A condor, a hummingbird, a man in boots, trapezoids, parallel lines, a lizard with a tail bisected by a southerly highway. I could have only comprehended the mammoth scale of all this by viewing it myself. Yes, this experience is more than seeing. This qualifies as a state-of-being, of sight mingling with event to form . . . an epiphany! Yes, that's it. Only I'm not sure what it is yet, but I am part of this! I'm viewing something far bigger than myself at the vantage point from which it was made to be seen.

My eyes. My eyes. This glorious vision.

Oh, Joey, you knew. You knew how this would affect me. I want to close my eyes at the ecstasy, experience the thrill alone, but I cannot miss this moment, jealous even of the blinking of my eyelids.

* * *

Juan is still bored.

"How many times have you seen these?" I ask.

He shrugs. "Too many. Not so special now."

"That's sad."

"*Sí.* Sad when nothing makes you wonder."

I'd never thought about that before. I wonder about everything. Maybe I need to add an F-U-L to the end of that word, learn to see the marvelous mysteries and happenings that fill this amazing world. Maybe that's already happening.

"You ever hear of the Viracocha, ma'am?" Juan asks.

"No."

"Here in Peru, many many thousands of years ago, a stranger walked among the people, a great god. The creator and the civilizer. Some say our ruins were built five or six hundred years ago, and some of them were, but some"—he shakes his head—"they were built around the time of Viracocha."

"I've never heard of him."

"He tried to civilize the ancient people, but in the end, although he brought great change, he left us. He was spotted in Mexico."

"Before the Flood? The Noah Flood?"

He shrugs. "I think so. But then I'm Catholic." His voice lowers. "I'll tell you something really mysterious. This visitor was a white man with a beautiful beard and flowing white robes. He had something to do with snakes."

"Snakes?" Satan was a snake, right? Oh, Joey, where are you when I need you?

163

"Sí."

"That's odd. Are snakes bad things to these ancient civilizations, like in the Bible?"

"I don't know."

Who was this Viracocha? Immediately I think of Christ. Did he appear to these people before the Flood? Did he seek to bring them to God?

When the plane lands I deposit beneath the seat a photo of Joey and me on our trip to Nantucket. The Atlantic is gray, the sky matches, and our smiles warm the composition snapped by a mother walking her two-month-old baby in a battered stroller. I'm sure there's an entry about her somewhere in Joey's writings. Large, small, in-between, Joey saw the whole world as worthy of his honor. So much beauty. So much art.

I'm reading in Joey's Bible tonight about a snake that the Israelites lifted up on a pole. All who were afflicted by a great plague could look upon the bronze reptile and be healed. So snakes aren't all bad then, are they? Well.

Once again, this white god Viracocha stands at the front of my mind as I climb toward an ancient temple in Bolivia. My guide is more knowledgeable than the pilot. I hired him for this very reason. He is a priest. Or used to be, until he fell in love with a woman named Consuela Maria, a very large ex-prostitute whose soul Jorge sought to save from the oven of a mission down in Mexico City. She runs the guide service and offered me dinner, and because Joey would have said yes, I did too. It is easy to see why Jorge left the priesthood for her. Saucy yet kind. Impertinent yet giving. Arms as big as my thighs. A Winnie-the-Pooh T-shirt bridges the great chasm between her ten-gallon breasts. She broadcasts softness and welcome.

"You stay with us. Cheap and clean," she said. "We take good care of you."

So I packed up my bags, checked out of the flea-bitten inn where I had been staying, and walked a block down the dusty street and into a charming little home. Plain and clean, with lots of flowers growing, smooth tiles underfoot.

Jorge and I venture toward the temple area of a town that once stood on the shores of Lake Titicaca but now sits in ruin twelve miles away, the lake having "relocated" during "some cataclysmic event" according to the guidebook.

"Many have dated this temple to as late as the 1500s. But look at this stonework. This is the work of the Viracochas."

There's that name again. Only he's talking of a people, not a person. Interesting.

The wall beside me is a crazy quilt of stones, some many times taller than myself and Jorge, obviously weighing many tons. My fingers drift over the surface of the mammoth stones, seek out the seams where the great rocks fit together more perfectly than a set of spoons. How could anyone do this? Suddenly the plains of Peru seem almost infinite when compared to this precision, this ancient feat of engineering. Again, I meld with something far larger than myself, something I can touch, something real, warmed by the sun, smoothed by gritty winds of centuries, perhaps millennia, if Jorge's hunches are true.

I close my eyes, inching along as I drag my hand across the wall. I stop and tell Jorge what the pilot said regarding the ancient lore.

"How do you deal with this? The tales of this white god?" I ask. "As a former priest. You still believe in God, don't you?"

"More than I ever have. In Mexico they call him Quetzalcoatl. But more than anything, God is gracious, and this is true. Does it seem so impossible He sent prophets to help His creation?"

"Well, no. But does the Bible mention any of this?"

"No. But then, the Bible around this time period is limited to the Middle East. We can't assume God only dealt with people in that region, can we?"

"I wouldn't think so. How do you reconcile all of this, then? With your own faith?"

"There's nothing to reconcile. I simply trust in God, Mrs. Laurel. He is who He is regardless of what I believe. I don't have to fully understand Him to love Him."

"But don't you doubt?"

He shrugs. "At times. But what honest man does not admit to this? True, there are many mysteries in life. If it causes you to seek out the one true God, then I am glad. Honestly, mostly *people* make me doubt. Their cruelty, their selfishness. My own cruelty and selfishness. Not mysteries like this. This just further confirms the fact that nothing happens by accident."

I doubted he could ever be cruel. "My husband used to say, 'The supposed jewels in the crown of God's creation are the greatest cause of atheism.'"

"I have to agree."

I reach into my knapsack and pull out a photo of Joey writing at his typewriter, typing, most likely, a small tale swollen with meaning and filled with a childlike trust. I kiss his face. We climb down into the ruins of the temple, a large rectangular hole in the pavement, steps leading down amid the six-foot-high walls that lend it the air of a large swimming pool. A stone pillar towers in the middle. The white god himself, Jorge tells me. I lay the picture at his feet wondering if he was Christ, or a prophet or the devil.

"Did he come before the Flood?" I ask, running my fingers along the stonework.

"Some say yes. I would agree. Now you'll see ruins with typical stonework, nothing so miraculous as this. All the pyramids over here. All the lore. Very much like Egypt."

"I've heard that."

"There's even a Babel legend over here."

"As in the Tower of Babel?"

"*Sí*. Where God scattered the people because they began to know too much. He confused their language."

Good. A Bible story I actually knew. "It's almost too much to comprehend."

"*Sí*."

I just trust God, Mrs. Laurel.

Did Joey seek to confuse me? Or did he want me to realize that I can't know everything, that part of the charm of being human is recognizing that some mysteries are best left unsolved and serve only to be enjoyed, not thoroughly understood? For perhaps in the understanding, we would find we had lost the wonder as well.

I just trust God, Mrs. Laurel. I don't have to fully understand Him to love Him.

That night, we share the evening over glasses of wine. I reach into my pocket and pull out Joey's silver writing pen. "Here, Jorge, take this. I'd like this to be yours."

"But why, señora? This is too beautiful."

"It was my husband's, you see. And he trusted God too."

Back to Luray for a visit. Eat ribs with Matthew at Yolanda's Rib Room. After sucking every bit of meat from the bones and, subsequently, every bit of food from between my teeth, I stick in a nub of nicotine gum.

I've been telling them about my trip and my discoveries.

"Now why a white man?" Yolanda wants to know. "Why did God send a white man?"

"You're white," I say.

"On the outside."

Matthew sets down the napkin he's been ripping to shreds. "Maybe him being white would get their attention. You know, make them take notice."

Yolanda shrugs. "I guess it would."

I flick my hand. "It doesn't matter anyway, does it? We can't say for sure he was from God anyway."

"Everything matters, Pearly," Yolanda says.

Matthew nods as though looking at a coffin. Mr. Sober.

"So how come you two are in cahoots?" I say. "Good heavens, I introduce you two so that Yolanda can help you out, and you end up ganging up on me."

Matthew shrugs. "Then you have only yourself to blame."

Yolanda swats his arm. "Good one, boy."

Matthew stands to his feet. "It's time for my set."

"What?" I ask.

Yolanda rubs his arm. "We got us some live entertainment during the dinner hour on weekends now."

Matthew blushes. He's got a crush on Yolanda that's visible from three miles away. Marvelous! He leaves the table and lumbers to the corner where his guitar case leans against the wall. I lean forward. "How bad was it, Yolanda?"

She shudders. "I've never seen such squalor, Pearly. I'm glad you got in touch with me."

"They let you in?"

"Uh-huh. Nice people, personality-wise. They just got problems. Depression on the mom's part, I think. The father stays away as much as possible because of the condition of the house."

"So where is Matthew living now?"

"He's still there, but he stays in his room most of the time, comes here a *lot* now. Sometimes he sleeps on my couch. My kids love him."

"That's good."

"He's a good kid. We'll do right by him until he leaves for Lafayette School."

"Thank you, Yolanda."

"It's why I'm here. Like I told you that first day."

"You certainly have a magnetic quality."

"Oh, it's just the food."

I look into her eyes. "No, it isn't."

"I've just been given a job to do, and I try my best to do it with all my heart."

I tuck that away for later.

"So where you gallivanting off to next, Pearly?"

I look at Joey's watch strapped to my wrist. Still ticking, the pesky timepiece. "I'm running the Virginia Ten-Miler."

"Think you'll make it the whole way?"

"I'll crawl the last nine-and-a-half miles if I have to. But I think I'll do okay. I'm down to two cigarettes a day now. One after breakfast and one after dinner."

Her brown eyes crinkle. "Good for you, girl."

"Yep. Good for me." My smile feels smug, but a second later it turns false. Good for me? Why? Why do I think I am so "all that," as Yolanda would say?

I want to die. Six miles in and I want to die, die, die! I'm in the back of the pack of geezers. My lungs are killing me, but I'll be darned if I quit. Not after all the cigarettes I've deprived myself of and the fact that I want to tick this off my list so badly I feel it in my throat. That watch won't go on forever. I've got to get through all this as quickly as possible now. Eight months have passed since Joey died. I've trained, somewhat, for this.

Oh my knees! My muscles. I am so old and tattered.

I must look like an idiot out here. Why this race, Pearly? Why not some bike race or even some "walk for the cure" type of thing? I am dying.

And would that be such a bad thing?

I pick up my pace. Hey! Now that's a thought. What would it feel like to die from running too hard? What would happen? Would I have a heart attack? And if I keep on going, pushing myself through the pain, would it take on steadily more massive proportions? Would I even be able to keep running once it began? Drat this low cholesterol. But I do have years of cigarette smoking in my favor. Still, dying here in Lynchburg, Virginia, among a throng of people in great shape, doesn't seem like the best way to go. On the other hand, no telltale signs I was purposely killing myself would remain. Brilliant! Cheeta and Peta will say, "Well, at least she went on her feet." And Shrubby will bring over some oysters, ones he had to buy at the grocery store since he's abandoned ship, and they'd slurp down the little suckers with some spicy cocktail sauce made from my mother's recipe and they'd talk about me, and they'd talk about Joey, and they'd say, "Isn't this fitting, though? Less than a year later she goes. They always did do things together."

I slow down a bit and gather more air. No, I won't give them the satisfaction. I hope that watch lasts at least until this coming October. Only six items left now. Drat, I wish I knew when he changed this blasted battery! I'm trying, Joey. I'm really trying.

I ran the Ten-Miler in, well, quite a bit more than record

time and bought a pack of cigarettes on the drive home. The general shape of the mountain before me brought back my stay in Mexico.

Standing at the top of the ziggurat pyramid at Chichén Itzá in Mexico (I had no idea Joey was so fixated on those ancient Indian cultures), I wondered about jumping to my death. It seems like a good way, especially if you dive and smash your head against the base of wherever it is you're diving off of. But on second thought, I would want something that ensured death—a jump from the Eiffel Tower, or into the Grand Canyon, or perhaps even a skydive—not some awkward fall that might render me a quadriplegic with no wherewithal to take my own life afterward. I'd have to rely on, God help me, Dr. Kevorkian, which means I may have to meet that obnoxious, shaggy-haired lawyer of his who always makes my teeth hurt with his emotional rhetoric and sloppy ties. No, not the pyramid. That would definitely be injurious, but not certain. Anyway, with my luck, I'd have slipped on the way down, and there would go all my plans for finishing the list.

Lately I've grown comfortable with this sense of purpose. Hopefully one sense of purpose won't lead to another, though. Ah, but the watch! The watch assures me this will not happen.

But I made it safely back down, having deposited a picture of Joey and me at his graduation from JHU with his M.A. degree.

It is June. Shrubby's still living in my house, and he and

Maida are quite the number. He got a job at the school—said working on the water was too painful—as a janitor and they take all their breaks together. Pumpkin ran away but returned three months later looking fat and happy. That tomcat.

I'm spending the month here in Luray reading *War and Peace*. Halfway through. I can't tell you what's going on; I'm just determined to finish the rotten thing. So I rock on the porch of the Mimlyn Inn where I'm staying, drink coffee, smoke, and read. If I realize my mind has been wandering and not one word of the last few pages has sunk in, I don't go back. The watch still runs, and I don't have time to read *War and Peace* five times just to get through it once. Silly, yes. Just plain silly. But I will meet this goal, for in having done so, I'll be more than halfway through.

The phone rings, waking me from my afternoon nap. I push myself up to answer it. It is Matthew.

"Can you come get me?"

"Of course. You at home?"

"Uh-huh." His voice shakes.

"Are you all right?"

He sobs once. "I've got to get out of here before I kill myself."

Oh no! "Hang on, I'll be right there. Hang on!"

I hang up and realize I have no idea where Matthew actually lives. I speed over to the Rib Room. "Yolanda!" I yell as I push open the door.

"Yeah?!" she hollers from the kitchen.

"It's Matthew! He wants us to come get him. He says

he's got to get out of there."

She appears, brow plastered flat, eyes wide.

"I don't know where he lives," I say. "Car's running outside."

"Come on! I'll go with you. Ray! I'll be gone a while. Hold things down for me!"

"You got it!" the cook yells back.

We hurry out the door. "I'll drive," she says.

We buckle in, and she throws my car into first, peeling away from the curb.

"He says he needs to get away before he kills himself," I tell her.

"Mmm. I thought he was falling into a depression."

"Is it any wonder? Living that way?"

"Not at all."

She heads down Main Street.

"Just prepare yourself, is all I can say, Pearly."

"That bad?"

"Probably like nothing you've ever seen before."

Nothing grows in Matthew's yard. Not really. It's more a collection of various weeds and wildflowers without much bloom. One large clump of daffodils sprouts right next to the sidewalk, obviously planted many years before. Perhaps Matthew dug the hole himself (with a spoon because houses like this don't keep trowels handy), having made a bulb arrangement for his mother in school, knowing it would die where it sat atop the refrigerator next to a pile of five-year-old bills, two rotted stuffed animals, and three boxes of long-expired cereal, not to mention a ball of yarn, a box of tooth-

174

picks, and an old black soft-foam sponge, cracked long ago and crumbling. A can of silver spray paint too.

Maybe. It's what I picture, although judging by what Yolanda says, mine might be a bit too antiseptic. The rotting sponge is a nice touch though.

I'm a little nervous about ringing the bell, but Yolanda steps right up onto the small cement pad and knocks five quick hard raps of the knuckles on the back of her hand.

My breath comes quickly now.

"Don't be scared, Pearly. They're all right. They won't hurt you."

The door opens. Matthew. He's been crying. "Thanks for coming. Hi, Yolanda."

"You okay?"

He shakes his head. "I gotta get outta here."

"I know, baby." Yolanda rubs his arm. "Your mama home?"

He nods. "Mom! Can you come talk to Mrs. Laurel and Yolanda?"

"Tell them to come on in!"

He reddens. Oh, Matthew. He pulls the door wider. "Oh well, I guess you'll have to see for yourself sooner or later."

Boxes stack up in the entryway and on into the dim living room, towering in front of the windows. Only little rat trails run in between, and those are covered with papers, disposable plates and cups, crumbs, flattened and creased clothing, and Kleenex. Cats lounge everywhere. There must be ten of them in plain view. The stench grabs my stomach.

"I'm back here in the kitchen!"

"Keep following that trail there," Matthew says. "I'll go grab my duffels."

He picks his way carefully up the stairs.

I turn to Yolanda. "How did he try to keep this neat before?"

"Beats me."

It's so dark and dusty and such a wide variety of items is strewn throughout this place: playthings large and small, furniture, car parts, large cans of ketchup and the like, evening gowns, shoes, hats, appliances. "Do they go to yard sales a lot?" I ask.

"All the time, Pearly. At least that's what Matthew says."

"Good heavens. Pack rat disease."

"Yes."

Dirt and grime and grease lacquer the kitchen. The faucet drips, the refrigerator door stands slightly ajar, and Matthew's mother sits at a table piled with bowls, papers, mail, and craft items: yarn, pipe cleaners, pom-poms, googly eyes, silk flowers, glue, and only the Lord knows what else. A Big Gulp cup sits in front of her, filled with soda. Another large plastic cup, this one bright red and sporting a NASCAR logo, overflows with smelly cigarette butts. She's smoking and reading a joke book. *10,000 of the Funniest Jokes EVER*. It's obvious she's been laughing.

She appears neither heavy nor thin and her house-dress, five sizes too large, twists around her middle, highlighting a small potbelly. Her graying hair is scraped into a frizzy ponytail.

"So you've come to take Matthew for a while?" she asks after we've said our hellos and such.

"With your permission," says Yolanda. She reaches for a green pipe cleaner and begins to bend it around her index finger.

"Oh, you've got that. He's been unhappy for a long time now. He blames this place." She looks down. "I guess I can see his point. I think they make fun of him in school."

"He can come stay with me for the summer," I say, "and then I'll take him up to Lafayette School for the term."

"Go ahead. I think he'll be glad for it. He's been so down in the mouth lately. But what can you do?"

I shrug, tongue-tied, then I nod, to add an extra bit of concern. But I don't understand. I'd have given anything for the chance to raise a child like Matthew, a boy that came from this unproductive body I've been given.

August 26, 1995, Ocean City, Maryland

I believe I could observe enough people to provide a lifetime of fodder right from this bench at Trimper's.

I saw the monster first. Oh God, how did Your creation fall so far? Oh God, why this sort of thing? Why let Lucifer have this much victory in one situation?

Some sort of palsy afflicted the boy. A boy? I suppose. His handicaps shuttered his age from the accidental voyeur. Eyes averted quickly as he pumped his palsied legs up the asphalt incline that led from the Middle Eastern Delights fun house into the building

177

housing the kiddie rides and the bumper cars.

"Bad boy! Bad boy!" a haggard man dressed in work khakis, a black T-shirt, and a tight denim jacket hollered, practically driving the child forward. Large warts covered the poor thing's head, hair sprouting like onion grass in wild profusion from around the lumps. Dear God, they reminded me of giant, flesh-colored ticks, burrowing into his damaged brain, sucking what little intelligence lay therein.

This human being bleated, its garbled speech neither human nor animal. Bile filled my throat. Pearly looked the other way, watching the children on the balloon ride. I couldn't call her attention to the scene as the man grabbed the boy's arm and yanked. "Come on! Bad boy! Bad boy!"

The boy bleated again and moved backward, resisting his father's intentions.

Oh Jesus, I cried. I don't think I'll ever forget this. Indeed, I know this is one of those moments I'll hold on to forever, a moment I can pull forth when I need to feel the pain of the world, to coax some life into myself, some sense of justice and mercy when I've become numb by the newspaper, the movies, the way things have become.

"Bad boy! Bad boy!" the father yelled again. The boy pranced his palsied gait further up the slope, advanced in his crablike ambulation, hands curving in and down, head painfully askew, large and addled.

Somebody obviously needed a miracle here, and one hadn't come.

I always remembered Trimper's as a collection of amusements, rides, games, a mirrored funhouse, an antique carousel inside. Apparently Joey's view encompassed much more there in Ocean City, right in the spot where we moldered almost every Friday night during the summer.

Joey didn't realize I saw that boy. I'm sure he was actually in his late twenties or thirties, but truly, it was hard to tell. I felt sorry for the child. Personally, I felt sorry for the father, too, wondering what being saddled with that kind of macabre responsibility for the indefinite future must be like. Made me thankful for Harry that day, I can tell you. I remember thinking this was just a mess-up of nature, a big stinker in the genetic doings of the human race. But not Joey, obviously. Joey always made everything so deep and so big. And he always assumed I shared the same feelings, tucked way inside me.

I am a bit ashamed of myself, I guess. I just accept these pops and jerks of human genetics as a statistical thing. I mean, the odds are things will get messed up every once in a while. Who knew what happened to that boy? Did his mom take some kind of medication during the pregnancy? Did inbreeding, drug usage, or a fall play into it somehow? Did the doctor use forceps? So much can go wrong not only when a baby is being formed but during birth and childhood, it's a wonder so many of us turn out relatively normal. Maybe a miracle even. Had Joey comforted himself with that thought after he finished questioning God? Did God draw him outside again and say, "Look around you, Joey, there's more right than there is wrong." And did Joey agree? I'd have to say I would agree. But then I've always been more of an optimist than anything else.

Oh brother! Did I really just say that?

Why I let Richie talk me into this full-body scan, I don't know. It's annoying to say the least, and honestly, I don't want to know what's wrong with me. What's the use? Our good Dr. King just sounded so excited about the new technology that, as usual, I couldn't refuse. He sounded so much like Joey. So here I sit at Johns Hopkins, waiting. I'm thinking of the exact words I'm going to use when I give Richie King a piece of my mind.

Gene Shalit never changes. I mean, they talk about Dick Clark, but he's *finally* starting to show his mortality like the rest of us. But Gene Shalit quite possibly knew Moses, and he probably hasn't changed since!

I click off the morning show having no idea which movie he just reviewed. I've never been much of a moviegoer anyway. And, at the risk of sounding like a curmudgeon, they just don't make them like they used to. Sex equals romance these days. Joey always said that the screenwriters are just being lazy in that regard, plugging in a false emotional bond, a quick joining of hearts, so that they can move the plot forward at a rapid pace. He said, "Pearly, I fell in love with you like lightning without that." Sex or cancer, that's what they rely on these days, he always said. He'd have had a field day with his own death and what it's done to my life!

I pick up Richie King's note and call the number at the bottom. They patch me through right away.

"So you've only got one working kidney, Miss Pearly!"

"Isn't that a kick?"

"But it's fine. No polycystic kidney disease."

"That's good. My cousin has developed hers."

"That's a shame. It's not an easy illness."

"I know."

"Other than that you look great. Nothing in the lungs. Yet."

"I don't know how."

"Neither do I. You still cutting back?"

"Yes. Two a day."

"Good for you."

"It's been a nightmare."

He laughs. "I'm sure. But you hang in there."

"Oh, I will. That's something I somehow always end up doing whether I want to or not."

I've postponed the Alaska cruise until next May. I've got Matthew to think of now, which means more to me than seeing some whale's tail crash into the sea.

"Are you sure you want to spend the money on this?" Matthew asks me. He fingers the fretboard of a travel guitar.

"It's really not that much. And we'll make good use of it on the trail."

"It's going to be hot. And buggy."

"I know, Matthew. I've got bug spray. And did you

see those crazy citronella bracelets? They're a hoot."

Now Joey wished to walk the entire Appalachian Trail. Fat chance of that! I mean, having loved the man so dearly, I'm trying my best to fulfill these wishes, but the entire Appalachian Trail? Well, enough is enough! Not to mention that wristwatch ticking away. Why I factored that little timepiece into this mix is a wonder. It seemed like such a good idea when I thought of it, but now—well, I hate the pressure. Maybe without the annoying thing, I'd actually complete the entire trail.

Or maybe not.

"How long does it take to hike the whole trail?" I ask Matthew.

Matthew's been reading guidebooks for the past two weeks since he moved in with me at the Mimlyn. "Depends how fast you walk. If it was us, it would take months and months."

"That's what I thought."

"You know, though, people do phases at a time. Year by year."

"That's interesting."

"We could take two weeks every year, Mrs. Laurel. And someday we'd finish."

Oh, I'll be finished long before that. I least I hope so. I've only got four more things to do.

"That sounds like a nice plan."

I'm careful to agree to nothing.

We are on our way up to Havre de Grace to gather a few things from the house before we begin our two-week hike. We're starting at the northern end of the trail, up in Maine. I told Matthew that hot isn't an option. I can stand almost anything if I'm not sweating profusely and panting like a dog. Matthew's a little chunky, so he naturally agreed.

We set the guitar on the counter at Beverly's Music. A smiling, young blonde hippie girl says, "Get everything you need, darlin'?"

"Uh-huh." Matthew blushes, his eyes staring at a large rock wrapped with silver wire suspended just above her breasts. Her skin shines like sunsoaked buttermilk.

I smile and feel a bit of Joey right then. There's so much beauty in the world. Music, youth, infatuation. So many small, everyday triumphs. God is winning. Isn't He?

Nothing compares to the feel of your furry old cat purring in your arms. Pumpkin returned to Maida's from another foray only yesterday, looking fatter than ever. Matthew scoops him up with ease as we negotiate Maida's front walk. "Boy, did you give him the right name, Mrs. Laurel. He's almost as fat as a pumpkin."

"You're telling me."

"He's a purr machine."

"It's nice, isn't it?"

Matthew scratches Pumpkin around his ears. I've always thought that must feel so good if you're a cat. "Some of Mom's cats are aloof, but we have our share of nice ones too. Although I tried not to let any of them into my room."

I saw Matthew's room that day. Neater than a dry martini, air-freshening devices hanging, sitting, or stuck to various horizontal and vertical planes. The smell still encroached, however, infesting the otherwise perfect chamber like lice.

He shrugs. "Except for one. A little cat named Billie. Little black female. I named her after Billie Holiday."

"That's a whole lot more creative than Pumpkin."

He lifts the corner of his mouth. "But Pumpkin fits."

Poor Matthew. Where does he fit right now? This must be horrible for him.

"Let's see Maida," I say.

I climb the stoop and rap on her door. When she answers, her eyes swell and her cheeks redden. "Pearly! What a surprise!"

My radar tells me something's going on. Especially since she clutches at her bathrobe like a virgin priestess caught in hanky-panky with a palace servant, à la Brock and Shelby.

"So . . . Shrubby in there?" I ask.

She nods. Sighs. "You might as well come on in."

Shrubby's sitting at the kitchen table, the blond wood, tile-top design Wal-Mart always has on special. "Pearly!" He begins to rise.

"Don't get up, Shrub." I open the cupboard and grab myself a mug. "Just point me to the coffeepot."

"Right there by the fridge."

"Well, sir, you know this place pretty well already, don't you?"

He smiles. "A man can get lonely, Pearly."

"And you've never had anything but a well-oiled zipper." I pour the coffee into a mug that says, "America: Love It or Leave It." "Wow, Maida. How

184

long have you had this mug?"

"Yearzzz."

I turn to Matthew. "Let this be a lesson to you. Fornication isn't a good idea to begin with for various reasons I won't go into, as I am not your mother, but look at these two. At their age, it's downright seedy."

Maida slaps my arm. "Well, Miss Morals, it just so happens that Shrubby and I eloped a month ago. So get down off your high horse, thank you very much."

"You're kidding! You actually *married* him? This is his fifth time!"

"I'm fifty years old, Pearly. Time's awastin'. It's not like I can be choosy at my age."

Shrubby rubs his morning stubble. "Not sure I like where this conversation is going."

Maida gives him a peck on the cheek. "He may not be much, but he's all mine!"

"Oh, dear heavens," I say. "Well, does this mean I can stay over at the house tonight, then?"

"You're actually going to sleep over there?"

"Yep." That sounded brave.

"Sure. Shrubby's brought his stuff over here anyway. It's back to being all yours."

Shrubby's eyes met Maida's.

This is very, very good. Just lovely, in fact.

"The tent's in the shed around back," I tell Matthew as I unlock the kitchen door of my house. "It's in an orange drawstring bag. Get the two sleeping bags, too, and lay them over the clothesline right there by the pine trees to air out."

Matthew salutes. Charming. The boy is absolutely charming. If he lost weight, he could make it in popular music, I bet. I hope he keeps to classical though. Seems a safer world, that.

But then again, what do I know?

I gather up our camper's kit. Two plates, cups, bowls, knives, and forks. A tin fry pan and a pot. "We'll stop at Sunny's for the rest!" I holler out the kitchen window I opened upon entering the house. "Do you like tea?"

"Yeah!" Matthew heaves my bag over the line. It's red. Joey's is blue, and it hangs there, sucking in fresh air. Hardly fair.

I grab that box of green tea again, still sitting in my tote bag, staler than ever, but the price is right. I reach into the counter under the sink for canteens. I feel a surge of wonder hit me. I'm actually going hiking along the Appalachian Trail. I didn't ever picture this. I mean, camping on the beach is one thing, but this is a completely different level of outdoorsiness.

Matthew enters the kitchen with a gust of air. "This is going to be great. I can't believe I get to do something so cool."

What if the watch stops tonight?

Matthew's sweet face, smooth and open, smiles. His eyes glow. "Fix yourself a glass of water," I say, and I turn toward the steps. "I'll be right back."

Obviously Shrubby didn't sleep in our bedroom. It's just as I left it.

Oh goodness.

My heart drags itself through its motions, tumbling through grit and dirt and rocks. I steady myself with a hand against the doorjamb. My blood pressure plummets, and orange and purple checkerboards spiral and twist in front of my eyes, small explosions of violet pulsating as though pushed through a colander.

I throw myself on the bed as the nausea takes over. I will it to stop. "Matthew!"

"Yeah?"

"I'm going to take a little nap. Go ahead and watch TV or something. Is that okay?"

"Sure. I may do a little fishing. If that's all right. I saw the gear in the shed."

"Go ahead. Use Maida's dock."

I burrow beneath the covers, close my eyes, and sleep in my bed for the first time in more than nine months. The last time I slept here, Joey did too.

What would happen if Matthew just found me dead? Dear God, just let me die and let Maida find me.

I'm awake again. Pulse still present. I had an idea I'd react like this. Why else would I stay away so long?

I must choose which book of Joey's to take on the trail. There's one of the journals, naturally. Or his people notes. I am torn.

I throw back the covers on our bed, flutter back into Joey's shirt, and descend the stairs.

"Matthew?"

No answer. I look out the living room window toward the Bay. He's casting with one of Joey's fly rods at the end of Maida's dock. Has a nice rhythm going too. Not surprising. I watch the fly flick and settle, flick and settle, near the marsh grasses.

On to the den. I settle onto my haunches in front of Joey's little bookcase. There are so many clothbound and leather-covered volumes. All small. I knew my husband loved words, but I never knew to what degree writing consumed him. Truly a lifetime of collected observations stand in display before me like mysterious fruit in some Middle Eastern market stall. Begging to be chosen? I don't know. Perhaps. Joey left them in plain sight. He never told me they were private. In fact, sometimes he'd leave one open, face up. But I respected him too much to peek, for I've always suspected writers are very private people. They're also nosy. At least Joey was. There wasn't a detail too small for him to find some fascination in it. I asked him about that once, how life could so utterly intrigue him.

"Why, Pearly, imagine how God felt when He created the first blade of grass."

No other explanation was needed, he gathered, for he said nothing else.

I slide from my haunches down into a cross-legged position. Slide? Hardly. Sliding presumes some measure of control. And I'm going to hike for two weeks up and down mountains? Needless to say, I've done no running or hiking since that marathon. I have read *War and Peace* in its entirety and cannot relate one concrete idea or occurrence. But I did it. I am so easily satisfied I even have to wonder about myself. All my items are completed, and I don't feel all that accomplished. In fact I'm a little disappointed, but what's done is done. I met a goal really, so hey, why not pat myself on the back for once? Joey would. He'd be downright proud of me.

A volume covered in floral chintz catches my eye. Floral chintz? What possessed him to pick that out? I can picture Joey in Barnes & Noble, standing before the blank-book rack and thinking, "Well, isn't that lovely?" And he'd walk right up and pay for it without even the first blush of embarrassment.

My hands shake. Dealing with his absence was all much easier away from home. A pinky-peach ribbon ties the book shut, and with trembling fingers I pull one strand, feeling the tug of fabric, the soft release, the complete surrender of the knot. I am Joey for just a moment, reveling in the microscopic, the smell, the sight. The ranuncula and stephanotis on the cover caress my eyes, and I think of weddings and babies and satin shoes. Why this volume? Why this lovely cover with its transporting ribbons?

I open the page, the woody scent of handmade paper surprising me.

I inhale and turn the first page, blank, and read the words, scribbled in Joey's atrocious handwriting: *A Book of Psalms.*

I weep once more, and I don't know why. We will not stay the night here in this house. I must run. I must stay the course. Finish the journey.

I scramble to my feet, march to the kitchen, shove the volume in my backpack, and put the collection of people observations in as well. I just can't choose between the two, and so I won't. The watch ticks, and I'll simply take two books with me if I choose.

189

"Matthew!" I yell out the front door. "Let's get packed up. We'll be leaving in a couple of hours!"

He turns, nods, and begins gathering up the fishing gear. Now why is this? Why do some of the most unparently parents get obedient children? I find that more unjust than the boy we saw at Trimper's. You see parents doing their best, attending all the soccer games, all the art shows, every parent-teacher night, and the children treat them like the plate of hardened liver and cold mashed potatoes they refused to consume the night before. Then there are parents who do absolutely nothing—believe me, I saw both kinds at Lafayette School—and they produce children with such drive. This bothers me. And yet I'm happy for children like Matthew who instinctively rise above their parents' apathy, who possess intelligence and common sense. Now if Joey had been having this conversation with a table full of students here in our kitchen, he would have raised his index finger and said, "Ah, therein lies the grace."

I'd shake my head at the counter where I chopped up celery and carrots and think, *Goodness, Joey, how in the world do you bring everything around to God?*

But the more I read of his thoughts, the more I begin to understand. I still think, however, that spirituality is an almost genetic quality, which would account for Joey's ears hearing the voice of God with such acuteness and me just accepting things the way they are and not trying to attach a greater significance to them than they deserve. I've begun to fear that Joey thought I despised that side of him. But the truth is, how can one despise what she doesn't even want to understand? No. That isn't the truth. I was jealous of God. Jealous that although Joey was my greatest love, my only love, I was hardly his. And how can a woman compete with that?

Maida's lips curl down, and she shakes her head, clicking her tongue as if I'm four. If she waggles her finger at me one more time, I'm going to bite it off!

"Running away again, Pearly."

"Oh be quiet, Maida."

"I'm only calling it like I see it."

"Well, since you don't know the half of it, I'd say you're only making a half-good call."

She raises her eyebrows.

"Really, Maida."

"Really, Maida," she mimics.

Oh, great.

She's actually got me rolling my eyes. "You know, Maida, you shouldn't make it so obvious that you work around schoolchildren all day."

"Whatever, Pearly."

"Now you sound like a middle-schooler."

Her mouth sets into a hard line.

"See?" I say. "It's not so much fun when the shoe is on the other foot."

"Oh well. It was worth a try. I thought I might embarrass you into staying."

Shrubby enters their kitchen. "Car's loaded up, Pearl."

"Thanks."

"That Matt's a good kid. This is a real nice thing you're doing for him."

I just smile. "Well, when school starts, I'll be depending on you all to do right by him."

"Oh, we will," Maida says. "That won't be a hardship at all. It'll be good to have a young person around the house when he deigns to come into the presence of us old fogies every once in a while."

I nod. "We sure had our share of them in the old days."

In the old days? Oh, God, please let that watch stop soon. I deserve it.

"I'll let you know what's happening on *Loves, Lies, and Lifetimes.* Right now Brock and Shelby are in a good stage. She's almost ready to give birth to their first child. And they found out it couldn't be Damien's. He's as sterile as Tom Cruise in a pair of latex gloves."

"Are you sure it's Brock's child and not some spawn of Satan or something?"

"Well, there is a little room for doubt. See, Shelby had this strange dream where the ghost of this sea captain, a pirate really, came in and ravished her. Right around the time she had been ovulating—"

Shrubby winces.

Maida bats him. "It's all right, Shrubby. 'Ovulating' is a perfectly acceptable word. Anyway, she wonders whether it was really a dream, but she hasn't told Brock. In fact, the only person she's told is Eduardo."

"Who's Eduardo?"

"This voodoo practitioner."

"What?!"

"Yep."

"Oh, goodness, Maida. This is getting to be too much."

"That's what makes it fun, Pearly. If it was like everyday life . . . well, I get enough of that on my own!"

"Ain't that the durn truth," Shrubby mumbles. He pushes off from where he stands at the counter and leaves the room.

Matthew begins to strum the travel guitar outside.

"He's a special boy," Maida says.

"Yep, he is."

"God's got plans for that one."

Oh, great. Maida too.

God, God, God. You'd think He was everywhere or something.

I call Yolanda from our hotel room in Lowell, Massachusetts. We arrived last night around 9:00 P.M. and ate a late dinner in a place called Four Seasons. Don't let the name fool you. It's a glorified bar with Portuguese food. Now I've never eaten Portuguese food, but the clams and potato dish that slid across my palate deserved an entire page in *Gourmet* magazine. I kept thinking of that old song "Brandy, You're a Fine Girl," and I saw Brandy in our waitress's eyes and wondered if she would be a good wife, or if she was already. Goodness, I sound like Joey. Lord, help me if I start writing this stuff down!

"Hello?"

"Yolanda, it's Pearly."

"Pearly Everlasting!"

Okay. Not sure what that was supposed to mean. Don't want to ask. "It's me. We're leaving in just a few minutes for Maine."

"You getting on the trail today?"

"Nope. Lobster in Freeport tonight."

"Oh, you roughin' it!"

I love the warmth of Yolanda's voice. "Well, who goes to Maine and doesn't eat lobster?"

"A fool?"

"Precisely."

That warmed syrup chuckle stirs my heart over the phone.

"How's my boy?" Yolanda asks.

"Great."

"I saw his mother at church last Sunday."

"Oh, yeah?"

"I brought her myself."

"Yolanda, you don't let any grass grow under your feet."

"Nope. Something wrong in that family that only Jesus can fix."

Here we go again.

"Well, He sure can't hurt." That's the biggest commitment I can make at this time. Saying the name "Jesus" fills me with discomfort, and the holy pronoun isn't much easier.

Time to change the subject. "Yolanda, I know you have children, but I never hear you talk about a husband." I've been wanting to know this, but until now I haven't had enough of a reason to ask. I hate to pry. But really, this is a case of self-defense.

"I've never been married."

"Oh." Goodness, I should have kept my mouth shut.

"They're all adopted."

I sighed.

"Whew!" she blew. "I hear that relief. I was kind. I could have kept this one going for a long time, Pearly."

"I know it. Thank you."

"Pearly, one day you're going to meet Jesus face to face, and you just better hope you're alive when you do. Because if you're not, well, there'll be nothing I can do for you then."

"I don't even know what you mean, Yolanda."

"That's a fact."

I shake my head and grip the phone. "I've sure been meeting a lot of people like Joey lately."

"What do you mean?"

"Joey was a man of great faith. In Christ."

"Oh. Well that explains a few things."

"As usual, I don't understand."

"He prayed for you all his life, I'll bet. Well, at least since he's known you. Was he saved when you met him?"

"Saved? You mean like the 'save your soul' stuff?"

"Uh-huh."

"He never really called it that."

"What'd he call it, then?"

"Coming to faith."

"Same thing. Just different words. Well?"

"Yes. The first time I laid eyes on Joey, he was playing guitar and singing a hymn."

"Good. So, this is the thing, Pearly. The Bible says,

195

'The fervent prayer of a righteous man availeth much.' Was Joey righteous?"

"I never met a better man in my life."

"Well, then there's a lot of availing going on right now, I'd say. Prayers being answered and all."

"It would be nice for God to let me know, if that's what's really going on."

"Oh, it is. Believe me. I've seen it all. You a walking target for the Holy Spirit, which means the faithful will pop up all over the place."

There she goes again. The Holy Spirit. Talk about a spooky mystery to an outsider. But hey, I've always liked mysteries.

"I've got to go," I say. "We're going to head on out."

"Be safe, honey."

"I will."

"And keep me posted. Call me when you get off the trail in a couple of weeks so I don't worry."

I smile. "That's a nice thing to say, Yolanda."

"Everybody needs to know someone worries about her."

A Month of Psalms

Day One

I am a young man, but I love a God so ancient, so full of grace and mercy and a desire to give to those who seek Him a heart of wisdom.

Do my eyes witness pain and suffering for which God cannot provide a healing balm?

Do my eyes witness grief that the Spirit of the Lord

cannot turn to joy with the softest wind of His breath?

Do my ears hear cries of anguish and distress that the Savior of mankind does not hear and for which He does not ready a blanket of peace?

No. My eye has not seen, nor has my ear heard a single moment of sorrow that the Savior is not waiting to release, in one way or another, for those that ask Him.

I read the words in my head. Then I read the words to Matthew. "Do you believe all that?" I ask him.

He nods. "He sent you to me just when I thought I couldn't go on any longer. You're living proof of that psalm, Mrs. Laurel."

My goodness.

Did God really use me? Aren't peace and healing just things that suddenly come upon you, a rather magical gift, if they're from God? Why in the world would God use me when I don't really know if I want all that much to do with Him?

Well anyway, we're spending our second night on the trail, and I'll use the words of my dear mother and say, "This camping stuff is for the birds!" Only birds don't need to set up tents every night. I hate this.

Joey, why you wanted to do this, I do not know. I mean, yes, we camped in our time. One site, one setup, one teardown.

I hate this.

But here I sit in a clearing of oak and maple trees, looking down into a ravine. The sun sets and all the trees sway in silhouette, stick figures clasping their hands overhead, and Matthew plays the guitar. Something soft and, yes, Spanish, and soon the sky will darken and stars will appear, and perhaps I'll get a glimpse of something that lets me know I am not alone.

I suppose that is the only thing that makes me want to believe in God. I do not want to be totally alone. We are all alone in some way, each of us encapsulated within our own frame, within our own mind, our own feelings. No person truly penetrates another person. Not even Joey and me, for I was not his one and only, and I knew it. Perhaps those in situations of abuse and slavery feel they do not own themselves, do not travel like a bullet among bullets. But if there is a God, then He must surround all. And I would be inside His creation, His plan, and His movements. I would be part of something bigger, not some lone little ship in a sea of not much really.

I breathe in the scent of hills and trees, dirt and water and flame. I take it inside me.

Matthew still plucks, and the stars swim in the depths of night. The question is not whether I am glad to be here but whether I will last twelve more days. Still, I revel in the knowledge that here only the atmosphere separates me from Joey.

How I can be sure of this, I do not know. Matthew is playing a song Yolanda always hums, "Open the eyes of my heart, Lord." Matthew has spiritual eyes, open eyes. So why does he ask this of God?

Now for me, this would definitely be a prayer worth praying.

The watch still keeps time, although I suspect it's a little slow. This does not bode well. I'm actually a little angry at the pesky thing. I extended it way too much authority. Now what kind of idiot gives that much responsibility to a watch, an inanimate object, a completely objective measuring device? At the least, I should have extended this sort of lordship to something or someone I could manipulate in some way. But a battery? It does its own thing. That is the point.

We've been at the same campsite for a week now. I cannot bring myself to leave. Matthew doesn't mind. We hike. We fish. We eat the fish. We play the guitar, and we sleep. Matthew sings me to sleep each night. I stink under my arms—all over, in fact—and I am ready to go home. Sorry, Joey.

But oh, I've breathed and I've breathed. I've relished the smallest of scents: the grass crushed beneath our boots, the sweet aroma of maiden's bower, old leaves and newly grown.

I'm thinking of doing a little research on famous suicide victims. What drove them to live? What convinced them life wasn't worth it after all? How did they accomplish their goal? What fallout occurred afterward?

Yesterday, I left a picture of Joey beneath a fallen log. I took the picture one day as we sat on the lawn at JHU. Oh, wow, I can remember the day so well. I'd been focusing my 35mm on him and other subjects for an hour at least. Just framing shots, viewing my world through a lens, getting more comfortable with such a limited scope. Finally Joey pointed at me and cried, "Good grief, girl! Take the picture!"

I snapped that shot. Oh, it's glorious. He's so young and virile. Eyebrows knit, eyes intense. Joey snapped so rarely that I enjoyed it, though I hate to admit that. In fact, it rather turned me on to see him lose control every once in a while, to watch him fall off the pedestal. During those times I would reach for him, kiss him passionately, and welcome him to my world. During those times, I would make love to him and not the other way around.

I've returned to the cabin on the Bay. Matthew, firmly entrenched at Lafayette, has already formed a trio consisting of his guitar, some light percussion, and a bass. They perform Friday nights at The Crazy Swede, and all the diners love their breezy renditions of show tunes and standards. He visits one weekend a month, and how I look forward to that. I'm taking him back to Luray for Thanksgiving. Yolanda's hosting all of us.

Before I drove off, leaving him standing there at the curb all alone, I gave him Joey's wallet, stuffed with five fifty-dollar bills. He's one of Joey's boys now. Every boy who enters those halls will somehow belong to the man who made that school into what it's become.

His eyes misted when I told him it belonged to my husband. He promised never to lose it, told me he never thought he'd own an heirloom.

"It's just a wallet, Matthew."

"No, it isn't, Mrs. Laurel."

What a kid.

But right now it's Halloween. My jack-o'-lantern glows out there on the deck, and there are no trick-or-treaters here by the Bay, but I'm ready just in case. If nobody wants the full-size Snickers, I'll just have to eat them myself. I threw out all the cereal boxes when I came back here after that stab at the Appalachian Trail. Matthew and I ate like real people. A meat, two vegetables, and a starch for dinner each night. It felt good to cook like that again, and I owed it to him. He's dropped a few pounds eating real food instead of all the junk that must have been the daily fare in his house.

I'm writing down everything I know about my parents. I have no one to pass these details down to. I regret having no children more than I ever have before, and it's selfish, because I just want to have one for me right now. Why didn't we adopt? What had I been thinking not to force this issue?

Joey and I were just too stinkin' polite, I guess.

Sylvia Plath. I just had to find out more about her due to the suicide and all. Unfortunately, I don't see any similarities between this poet and myself. I'm in no ways a genius and have no mental illness to speak of, so I can't blame my yearning on those things. She couldn't have possibly felt as though she had lost her reason for being Sylvia, could she? She had too much going for her. Unlike me. Of course, her mental illness may have confused her a bit.

I should have given myself the gift of self-prescribed purpose years ago. But now it's too late for that. And anyway, I'm quite comfortable now with having lived for love. The clock ticks, and even if I wanted a new purpose, I have no idea what it might be. I'm too old to start all over again. Surely I am.

I am reading *The Bell Jar*, trying desperately to feel some sort of kinship with Sylvia, but I cannot. I thought maybe her time in the mental institution might set off an inner chord, but it only alienated me more. In fact, it's left me wondering if I am even qualified to commit suicide. Underqualified to off myself? That is indeed an extremely sad state of affairs.

"Moron!"

"Retard!"

"Dumbbell!"

My fists curl and rise. "Harry, just stand here by that tree."

Harry sweetly smiles and nods. And I am in for the fight of my life, but I don't care. I look around the schoolyard for Shrubby and Marsh, but they must be in the bathroom. They'd help me. They like Harry.

I've always hated this group of kids. Margie Phelps, Donnie Lindquist, Phillip Stark, and Terrence McHugh. The Three Stooges and My Little Margie. They're so stupid.

"So, Pearly Hurly," Terrence sneers from between his blubbery, pale pink lips, "you gonna do something with those fists or not?"

"You gonna take up for that half-wit brother of yours?" Margie sneers. I swear I've never known such a blinding hate before now. I hate her utterly. She is throw-up; she is dog poop. I watch as my fist smashes

202

her face. Even as the three boys charge, one lifting me, then slamming me down on the parking lot, one holding my arms, one my legs as Margie comes forward and begins to punch my face, I imagine Harry smiling and my mother and father nodding in pride. I am a good big sister. I am doing the right thing.

A Month of Psalms

Day 13
I've heard men cry that You are a trickster, that You send Your bolts of lightning or fling buzzing burrs our way so that You can sit in Your heavens and laugh.

But You are not a cosmic comedian, chuckling at our struggles and our humanity. You count every tear that falls, saving them for the day when we cry no more, when all of our painful memories are enveloped in Your love and Your light.

Wait, my yearning soul. The day will come when only love and the embrace of Divine light will rule my heart forever.

I'm glad Matthew accompanied me on the Appalachian Trail. I might have put feet to my thoughts and wandered far enough into the wilderness not to make it back alive. Of course, I thought of bears. Now yes, I really don't relish the thought of living much longer, but I think I'd live to five hundred if death could come only by mauling. I'm sorry, but life has got to be better than that.

Thanksgiving arrives the day after tomorrow, and I

can't believe the watch still runs. I'm quite angry at it but, at the same time, a bit relieved. I'm running out of palatable ways to do myself in and need more time to think about it.

I'm picking Matthew up at school, and then we're heading down to the Mimlyn. Yolanda will serve up a big dinner at her house, and she's invited Matthew's family and probably all her relatives and lonely hearts from the Rib Room. I'm looking forward to meeting this family of hers, these people that took a pale, skinny white baby in and made her their own. But before I pick up Matthew, I have another item to tick off my list.

How does one choose something she'll have to live with for the rest of her life, no matter how short that life may be?

Let me say up front that I cannot believe I'm sitting here at On Yours! Tattoo and Piercing Parlor. Why in the world did Joey include this one? Surely he could have done this at any point in his sixty-some years of life. I'm just now wondering if this decision I made to finish Joey's life for him was sound. Surely not! But "sound" is a bit too watered down. I *should* be doubting my own sanity at this point. It's been a year. I haven't "moved on" one iota. No, I'm still going from deed to deed and finding my life once again encased within someone else's dreams.

"I'm going off to find myself." Remember that one?

I always thought of that as a load of nonsense. Some indefinable act or ambition. Some excuse for inaction or indecision. Some inane sixties-speak buzz phrase for those who don't know their rear end from a hole in the ground.

Now I know differently. And I'm still vain enough to think that my years-ago compadres were just making excuses for the fact they had no real discipline or any real belief in any real cause—other than belligerence. I saw too many casualties of that mindset at Lafayette School. Thank God Joey dedicated his life to them.

Even so, it's true: I don't know who Pearly Kaiser is anymore. I look down at the gold band Joey slid onto my finger all those years ago, I see all the hopes and plans dancing in a circle around my flesh, and I almost lose myself in the grief. Yes, I lived for love, and now it's gone, and so am I.

But there I am in that gold, a tiny reflection of myself stretched out long and thin and distorted. And I know what my tattoo shall be.

I take off the ring. "Can you tattoo a ring onto a finger?"

The tattoo artist, an aging biker type with very thick brown hair pulled into a braid, nods. "Sure ma'am. I've even got some band designs." He reaches behind him, the denim of his jacket creasing into a topographic map of the Blue Ridge, pulls out another book, and turns to a page filled with delicate borders. But I already know what I want.

"Can you do a sunset between two mountains?"

"Sure. You want color?"

"Yes. A bright red sun and purple mountains. Maybe a greenish tree line."

"Your husband gonna be okay with this?"

"Yes. I know he will."

"No prob. I'll see what I can come up with. I make no guarantees if it's not something I can trace."

"I'll trust your artistic talents."

He rumbles a smoker's laugh, a lower volume than mine as I join him. Certainly laughter is the only thing we have in common here. I look around me at this shack of a place and am the only—what would you say—typical person in here.

The cars file by on Route 40, an alternative way out of the city during rush hour. I sniff, breathing in the aroma of many smoking substances. The smell sure takes me back.

He slides a paper in front of me, scenic band sketched just as I described.

"Perfect!"

He turns the paper back toward him. "Think so?"

"Yes. I like it."

A satisfied grin accompanies a nod. "Let's go then. I have to warn you, though. You've chosen to get a tattoo in one of the more painful places." He takes my hand into his.

Oh great. I feel my heart speed up at his touch. I haven't felt another man's touch in years. Yes, you shake hands and have brief physical contact with men all the time when you're married, but when you're not married, well, it's different. It's been so long.

". . . chosen your shoulder or something, it would be another story, a lot easier."

He's examining my finger. "I don't mind," I hear myself say. "I have a high pain threshold."

Using deodorant as a transfer medium, he transfers the design around my finger with a thin marker. "You right-handed or left?"

"Right."

"Good. Because, I'll tell you this, you won't be able to do much with this hand for a few days."

"Will it be that sore?"

"Maybe, but I'm thinking about the salve and the bandaging."

"Salve? Bandaging?"

"Oh, sure. This thing will bleed for a while too."

"I never knew!"

"No offense, but you don't look like the type that would."

After donning rubber gloves, he reaches for the tool of his trade and turns on the needle. This contraption looks like it's literally held together with rubber bands! Oh dear.

Beginning to draw the line, he looks up. "You okay?"

I nod. It feels as though he's running a razorblade across my skin.

"The outlining's the worst," he says. "The color is a piece of cake compared to this."

I just grit my teeth and let him continue. I mean, at this rate, it will only take about ten minutes for the outlining. A woman can stand anything for ten minutes. Ask any mother out there.

"So, what do I need to do to ward off infection?"

"Be faithful with the salve and wash your hands before touching it."

Well, I'm not going to do any of it and cross my hopefully infected fingers for bad luck! Maybe I'll get some big all-over infection, and it'll be too late by the time Peta gets me to the hospital, and there I'll go! Off into the wild blue yonder, me and my new tattoo.

"If you don't," he continues, "you'll scab over, and when the scab comes off, so does the color."

Oh, dear. I surely can't have that.

Foiled yet again.

Joey takes my hands. We sit on the banks of the Bay. Our small sailboat docked at the pier near Shrubby's bobs, and the thin waves pat the sides. "I think you need to set up your studio again."

"And photograph who?"

"Whoever you want to. Maybe you could do children. People love to have pictures of their children."

I picture teddy bears, little chairs, baskets, a miniature wicker settee, and corny backgrounds.

"My dreams weren't about photography, Joey. They were about recording history, about danger and relevance."

"Then maybe you need to finish up your degree, get on with the *Sunpaper* or the *Post* or even freelance."

I say nothing.

"Or you could take some courses at Harford Community College to keep up on the current methods."

Didn't he hear me? "It's not about the photography, Joey."

I love the way my husband's eyes soften when he looks at me this way. I feel as if I'm a precious toy a man has found in a box he hasn't opened since childhood.

"I only want to be your wife right now," I say. "It's enough. I'm finding great satisfaction in making a home the boys can come to."

He pushes one brow up toward his hairline. "Are you positive, Pearly?"

I am. I take his hand. "It's like this, Joey. I may not take pictures of historical significance, but I do make a difference to the future. Maybe that's more important. Maybe it isn't, but I'm content."

He begins picking at the long grass that cushions us. "Only if you're sure. I'd hate for you to look at me someday when we're old and resent me."

"I won't. I promise I won't."

Yolanda crosses her arms over her ample bosom, the only ample section of her wiry body. "Well, you have only yourself to blame, Pearly Everlasting!"

"What did I do?" I drum the fingers of my left hand on the comforter of my bed. I love my sunset tattoo ring. Although I wish the bleeding would stop. The nausea begins again, but I shove it down where it belongs.

" 'Oysters, Yolanda,' " she mimics me, " 'Thanksgiving isn't Thanksgiving without oysters.' "

"Well it isn't."

"But now you're sick, eating those bad oysters."

"They weren't bad!"

"How can you be so sure? You're the only one puking."

"I ate too many of them is all, Yo."

I consider veering into a description of the absolutely

most horrific vomit imaginable, but I like Yolanda too much to do that to her. And I don't know if I can handle it either. "How's Matthew?" His parents arrived too late to sit down with the family. Lucky for me I'd already puked the first time and was laid out here in Yolanda's bedroom.

"Fine. He and his parents are sitting in the kitchen having their pie. It's too noisy in the family room to talk."

I believe that. Yolanda's four children had been painting pumpkins and gluing Indian corn onto panty-hose cardboards. Next on the agenda: paper chains for the soon-coming Christmas tree. All this while watching videos that include *A Charlie Brown Thanksgiving* and *The Mouse on the Mayflower.* I didn't know any copies of *The Mouse on the Mayflower* still existed. I'm glad, though. It deserves to live a good long life.

"Where's your big family?" I ask.

"What big family?"

"You know, cousins and sisters and all, the people who adopted you?"

"Oh, Pearly. There was only Grandmom Mable, who left me the restaurant. She was a spinster."

I feel let down. "I thought you were part of a big clan."

"Nope. Just me and Mable. And her sister, Yvette, who's long gone too."

"I'm sorry."

"Oh, Pearly, I have my church family. I've been with them since before I can remember, and they love me, not to mention my kids."

"But holidays must be terrible."

"Does it look terrible around here? Truth is, I turned down three invitations for dinner elsewhere because I wanted to spend today with you."

I've already made a nice memory to tuck away.

I think I'll take a little nap. It feels good to close my eyes and think about a sleep that doesn't end.

What is heaven like? Is it like a never-ending Thanksgiving Day without bad oysters? Is it whatever a soul desires it to be? Lord, I hope not. I have enough trouble making up my mind as it is.

"Go to sleep, Pearly Everlasting."

Yolanda awakens me at six. "Hey, it's time for your pie now. You haven't had any yet."

Pie? Good heavens.

"You feelin' better?"

I purposely keep my eyes shut. Maybe she'll go away.

"Come on and answer me Pearly, I know you're awake."

"How?"

"The way your eyelids are moving around."

"I could be in REM sleep."

"Nah, that's not spooky looking." She sits on the bed. "Look, I've been raising children long enough to know when one is faking sleep."

I suddenly feel like one of Yolanda's kids. Lucky them.

"Okay." I open my eyes. "But I still don't think I can handle pie."

"Then come sit."

"I don't even want to smell it."

"You have to face Matthew's mother."

"I can't. I'm tired, Yo. And I still feel sick. I really do."

She softens as she so often does. "Still want to sleep, Pearly Girl?"

"If that's all right with you." Might as well offer something up to her.

"Oh, I guess it will have to be. Mighty convenient time to feel ill, now that my kitchen looks like Matthew's mother's kitchen."

"If you go ahead and do the dishes without waiting a bit for me to feel better, well, then, you have only yourself to blame."

She smiles. "That sounds like something someone quite brilliant has recently said."

"Yes, it certainly does."

Matthew is gone when I awaken. I look everywhere for him, but I cannot find him.

"Where is he?" I ask Yolanda. She sits on a stool in the kitchen watching a small color television that hangs beneath the cabinets as she sews a pair of pajamas for one of the kids. She wears reading glasses and looks great in them.

"He went home."

I am stabbed.

"She is his mother, Pearly. He loves her."

"But that place."

"Don't worry. He'll be back by tomorrow. I'd bet my life on it."

"Oh, don't do that. You're too important," I say.

She looks up and smiles. I catch my breath. I've seen beautiful sights lately in my travels, but none as beautiful as Yolanda's smile.

She is woman. And she doesn't roar, she sweetens, like an ever-expanding puddle of honey pooling around people's ankles and refusing to recede, demanding everybody just expand with her, sweetening their friends, neighbors, families, even the crusty old filling-station owner on the scary side of town.

"Have a seat at the table, Pearly. You want that pie now?"

"No thanks. Just a cup of tea. I'll make it."

"Suit yourself."

As I go about fixing the tea, I examine Yolanda from the corner of my eye. How do people like her get that way anyway?

I heat the water in the microwave.

"If you do it on the stove, it'll stay warm longer," Yolanda says with a mouthful of pins.

"I'm into instant gratification these days."

The machine whirrs, and the small light of the sewing machine draws me with its homey warmth. Tea and sewing and reading glasses. This is living. Even when she is alone, Yolanda is surrounded by the love of those she loves.

Love is something I've always doled out very carefully. Not the kind of love one feels for acquaintances or students or Shrubby Cinquefoils and crazy cousins. That all-inclusive, starshine love that seems unconditional but most probably isn't because, honestly, you'd

213

take it back if the recipient ever just totally turned his back, and in a mean way, like putting up a billboard on the Jones Falls Expressway saying PEARLY LAUREL IS A BIMBO. And it would include a picture of me, a horrible picture of me with a fake mustache drawn on or big ugly breasts. But the only person who could have done that and made me even care about it would have been Joey.

I guess it isn't full-bodied love if it's not somehow at risk of total ruination.

"What would happen to you if you ever lost one of your children, Yo?"

My tea is cooling.

She looks up, paling. "I try not to think about it."

"I need to love like that again."

I need to tell her about my purpose, my need to live greatly, to experience wonderful things, and to die. But she'll only say, "Then what, Pearly Everlasting?" And I won't know what to say.

They're all asleep. Matthew's back, and my heart puffs up like warm pastry. He said, "I love the idea of parents, and I thought maybe going in there would be different now that I don't live there."

I just nod and start breathing through my mouth.

He eats a second piece of pie, but he's lost some weight at Lafayette School. Even so, what's the difference? It's Thanksgiving. The night has darkened, the lamps are warm, and we all relax, satisfied and thankful here in a house still aromatic. I'd say another piece of pie is actually warranted, so I cut one for myself. It's a

shame my appetite has come into such a lovely existence. All my life food was just a means to an end. But
now—well, I can taste things as never before. And with
that blasted 10K behind me, I'm going to live it up. I
don't have long anyway. Why not enjoy it?

Hey, what if I eat myself to death? Can one do that?
How long would it take? Maybe I'll research that one.
I'll bet it would take longer than the watch battery will
last.

I look down at my wrist: 10:00 P.M.

Yolanda snips the thread attaching a sleeve to her
sewing machine. "So what are you thankful for today,
Pearly?"

"You first, Yo."

"I could go on into the night. You go first, and
besides, I asked the question."

Grade-schooler.

Matthew picks up the end crust of his pie and takes a
bite. "I'll go!"

"Okay," I say.

"Well, first and foremost, I'm thankful for a lady who
came to me for guitar lessons last year."

Yolanda nods. "I heard that. I'll add my thanks for
Pearly too."

"Well, I'm thankful for you two."

Matthew says, "And I'm thankful for the way God
takes care of us."

"Amen to that!" Yolanda nods twice this time.

I say nothing. Joey took care of me, and I've done a
good job of taking care of myself since he died. I will
say that it's odd that the watch keeps going. Maybe

215

that's one of those divine interventions of care and concern. I'm not about to say that, though.

I roll my eyes. Not again.

"I told you, Joey, Christmas Eve. It's all the church-going you'll get from me."

"But it's a special ceremony, Pearly. I'll never be ordained again."

"Lots of people get ordained. And why do you want to be ordained anyway? It's not like you'll ever be a preacher or anything."

"The town jail needs a chaplain."

We sit by our pool. Steaks are cooking on the grill, sailboats skim the Bay, summer fades in the colorless August sky.

Joey runs a rough hand through his hair. "What was I thinking, Pearly? You? The wife of a minister? Hah!" He storms inside.

I'm hurting him, but I don't know any other way to get this through his thick head. Maybe I need to put it on a billboard or something. But I hurry inside and pull him into my arms. I will make it up to him.

February 2, 1975
Lafayette School

Did Mom and Pop have talks about God? Yes, I know they did because I heard them. Oh, Pearly, Pearly. How I long to share this with you, to gather your spirit unto mine like a hen gathers her chicks beneath her wings, but you will not come.

216

I'd do anything for Pearly. Why will she not do this one thing? Do the scabs of living grow thick upon her heart so that she is afraid to pull them off and bleed that freshness of warm blood? Does she refuse to taste of her own pain and feed on the possibilities therein? Why is she so shut off and unable to open a vein?

I grieve for her, I grieve that she will not allow herself to experience humanity in its most exquisite state.

I'm mad at Joey again. The more I read his writings concerning me, the angrier I become.

Unwilling to open a vein? As if the man could talk, never once telling me how horribly his mother was killed!

No wonder Joey and I hardly ever fought. Obviously we rarely said much worth a disagreement.

All these years I thought I had a soul mate, only to find out now that I didn't know the man at all.

I sit out on my deck at the cabin on the Bay, snuggled into my long down coat from the seventies, and I feel for the thin scar down my temple, the one awarded to me at yet another fight in the schoolyard for Harry's dignity.

So why did God make Harry like He did? And why was I the one who had to fight for him?

Open a vein? How's this, Joey?

The little imbecile ruined my childhood. I might as well admit it. He turned me from Pearly Kaiser to "You know. Pearly. That retard's sister." He gave me a job I never asked for.

So boo-hoo again, Pearly. I just feel so sorry for you.

What's happening to me? I ask the stars. I can't keep a thought. I can't focus. I can't reason past anything. All I can do is feel and want to love and expand and be large and lively. But no one is around anymore. I love no one anymore. Not really. Right?

The cold waters of the Bay signal to me. I should check Joey's watch today. Maybe it stopped. Maybe I should just throw the pesky thing into the Bay and head after it, right into the frigid waters, right over my head to meet my fate with Shrubby's oysters. That, most certainly, would be a fitting end: to swim out farther than I can swim back. Yes, apropos. Something I've never done before, literally or figuratively. Pearly always finds a way back. I am hardened and crusty, and I can go on like this no longer.

Will I need to leave a note? The sad thing is, I realize I don't. Oh, they'll be sad at first, even frantic. But soon enough, life will return to the exact state it was in before I pushed my way into their lives through no fault of their own.

In the moonlight I examine the second hand as it stutters along the watch's face like an eighty-year-old's caress upon the face of her husband. It's time.

The pun almost rips me in two with laughter. Three shots of J.D. help too.

Do I leave my coat on? It is goose down and may cause me to float, which is fine because I'll need it for the swim out, I'll need to be able to keep going as long as possible. The flip side is that it could fill with water and drag me down, and I'd drown that way. That, actually, would be better, quicker and all. I like it.

I make sure the coffee maker is unplugged and the refrigerator is still humming, and I decide to scribble a quick note to Peta so they don't have to go looking all over kingdom come for me.

Let's just hope they never find my body. Or that they do before it becomes bloated and black and picked at by crabs and fish.

Oh dear.

I lock up the cabin and head down to the water. I'm ready. Ticking watch and unfinished list notwithstanding, I am unbelievably ready for this. Sorry, whales. Sorry, Haussner's!

I kick off my duck shoes, snap my coat up to my chin and step into the water.

Oh. My. Goodness.

I've never felt anything so cold.

I hurl the watch as far as I can into the Bay. It flips and twists as gracefully as an Olympic diver. The moon catches its face, a tiny, single explosion of light suspended in space. Then it plummets.

It is gone.

Dear God! What did I do? It was my reason for going on, it was my hope beyond the list, my sure ticket out.

I want to dive in after it. Wait, that was the plan anyway, wasn't it? I cannot think straight. And I step forward, the water swallowing my shins. Another step and my knees disappear. Dear Lord, it's so cold. I cannot go further. But I must. My feet will not move, and my eyes fixate on the watch's point of entry into the black water. I can only stand here, my mind still, my body beginning to quake inside the cold.

But I wait. I breathe. I expect a miracle maybe? Something supernatural? For a warm Joey-breeze to tell me I'm doing the wrong thing?

Nothing happens.

I breathe in. Yes, inhale the smells, the sights, the sounds.

Wait.

Nothing happens again.

I am alone with only myself. "Oh, what a redundancy, Pearly," I chide in a whisper. "You deserve to die for even thinking such a thing."

It's up to me now, only me. No list. No watch. Just a few more steps forward, a few minutes of waiting, trying to do that whole mind-over-matter business they used to show on programs like *That's Incredible!* where men would poke bicycle spokes through their skin. Go, go! Come *on!*

But I can't go forward. Strength would sure come in handy right now, some extra help, a leg up from an unseen hand. Yet too many faces come to mind. Not that Peta and Matthew and Yolanda would miss me all that much. I think *I'm* the one not ready to lose them.

Coward, Pearly.

But it's too soon! I hadn't planned on doing this so soon. Yes, that is it. It's just too soon. I need to gear myself up more. Drowning in frigid waters is nothing I had considered anyway! Now slitting my wrists, that's a more viable option.

I'm so cold.

I turn around. The cabin and the farmhouse stand like

black hulks against the indigo sky, shadows that move forward somehow.

I'm so cold.

I step toward the shore. My knees reappear, then my shins, then my ankles. I am out. I lean down, pick up my shoes, and think about a cup of tea and a foot bath.

How about sleeping pills?

Yes, that suits me even better than opening veins.

I am a coward.

When did this happen? I used to be so brave.

There's a fine line in loving, I realize as I drive toward Salisbury. I didn't bother to make a list since there's only one item, and once I ingest those, I sure as sunshine won't need anything else the grocery store has to offer.

But back to love.

There are people like me who don't know the meaning of it. Then there are people that just luv everybody. Luv, luv, luv. Love can be squandered, and maybe that's what I was afraid of doing in my life. Then one can be miserly, and I don't know if I went to that extreme. But why is it that right now there's no one in my life to really love? I mean, visit-every-day, woven-lives kind of love? I am all alone.

Boo-hoo, Pearly. You big baby.

But how do I regain this lifestyle of significance? How do I invest in just anybody at this point? Matthew already has parents. Yolanda considers me her project. Where do I go from here? Do I run down the streets of Salisbury and ask for someone to let me love them? Do

I go to some halfway house and pick someone out like one does a sad looking puppy at the animal shelter? What in heaven's name do I do?

I park in front of the Rite Aid and hurry in, heading straight back to the pharmacy. "What's the strongest nonprescription sleep aid you've got?" I ask the balding pharmacist.

"SleepRightTight," he says and points to an aisle to his left.

"Okay, thanks."

I find it with ease. In fact the box practically jumps into my hands when someone pushes an item too far in from the opposite side of the shelf. Surely a sign!

Peta waits for me in the cabin. She looks so gray these days.

"Pearly."

Oh dear.

"I just got word from Hollowell."

Harry's boarding house.

I place my bag of pills on the counter. "What is it?"

"Harry's got pneumonia. They called in the doctor. It's pretty bad."

"Why didn't they call sooner?"

She pours boiling water from my kettle into two mugs with tea bag tags hanging over their lips. "It all happened quickly. It seemed like a bad cold just yesterday morning."

"Most things do happen quickly."

"Yes. I'll drive. I'll go get ready. Drink your tea before we get going. I'll be back over in half an hour."

I feel the need to call Yolanda.

"Rib Room!"

"Yo."

"Pearly!"

"Hi."

"What's wrong?"

I pour milk into my tea, watching as the brown liquid rejects it at first, then capitulates. "Have I ever told you about my brother, Harry?"

"No."

"Do you have a few minutes?"

"Of course. Hang on. Ray!" she yells. "Tell Oleta to come man the front for a few! Okay, I'm heading back to my office." She yells a few more orders. I hear her ancient wooden desk chair creak as she sits down. "Okay, so tell me about Harry."

I tell her about his blond hair and how soft it felt despite its coarseness, about how it seemed like the only normal part of his head. I tell her about the winter I suggested my mother buy him a ski mask and how she slapped me, then immediately grasped me against her breasts and cried a silent wail. I described his first school shoes, their rubber soles and black licorice laces. And when she says, "You must really love your brother, Pearly," I tell her that I haven't visited him since before Joey died, so is that love? Hardly.

"Why do you want to tell me this?" she asks.

"Harry's got pneumonia. I'm on the way over to see him in a few minutes."

"Are you afraid he's going to die?"

"No. I'm afraid that he's not."

223

And there's the truth of it. Perhaps Harry's why I can't seem to grab a steak knife and butcher my wrists. And if Harry goes, I have one less reason to live.

I hate myself.

"Bye, Yo."

She says nothing as I slowly replace the receiver.

Harry looks so tiny lying in the bed. The air frays with each breath. Oxygen cools his nostrils. He sleeps.

"Should we take him to the hospital, Peta?"

"I don't know. That has to be your call."

The doctor told me earlier that Harry may pull through, but things like this can turn in an instant. The hospital would be safer, and the staff here at the home isn't equipped to handle medical problems. It's not that kind of facility.

"Peta, what do you think about death? Do you think you go when it's your time?"

She nods.

"What about things like suicide or murder or something?"

"That's different. Especially suicide. That's playing God."

"You've never seemed the type to give God a job."

She places her hand atop Harry's blanket. He looks old now. It's amazing he's actually lived this long. "Let's just say I'm getting a healthier respect for the Almighty the higher my creatinine numbers go. Dialysis is around the corner, you know. Fact is, Pearly, if you don't give Harry a fighting chance, you'll always wonder. And let's face it, it's his life anyway, not yours."

"Maybe he'd rather die."

"Nah. Last week he got employee of the month at the Food Lion. They've got his picture up in a frame and everything. Harry's not like us, Pearly. He's happy and not much else."

"Joey always said he thought Harry was closer to the pre-Fall Adam than the rest of us."

"I believe it."

"Does he still talk about Jesus?"

Peta smiles. "More than ever. I think he's got some kind of in, you know?"

Exactly. "Joey was like that in some ways too."

"But Joey noticed everything, Pearly. Joey internalized too much, looked at everything through a microscope. That much info going into one person has to wear him down. And yet Joey's faith made the unbearable bearable. Harry simply loves Jesus, and it makes him happy."

I squeeze Peta's hand and go to find Flo, the lady who owns the home and runs it with her family. She isn't in her office, but I know where to find her, out back on what she calls the smoking deck. It's actually the pad where the trash cans sit when not curbside.

I walk down the cement steps. "Hi, Flo."

She turns. Flo's getting old too. We're all getting old. "Pearly. Come on and have a smoke with me."

I reach into my bag and light one up. "I just saw Harry."

"Yeah. Poor Harry. I think he needs to be under more watchful care, Pearl. You know we can't be with him every second, much as we wish we could."

"I know." I inhale deeply.

"I've always liked Harry. I'd hate for this to take him down. He's a good resident here. Always has been."

Harry likes to help vacuum and do dishes. "I know. I'm going to call the doctor's office and tell them to send an ambulance over."

"That's a good idea. Make sure he comes back here to us. He's family after all these years."

We finish our smokes in silence, occasionally mentioning folks we know, each name eventually resonating into the quiet.

Harry doesn't cry. He sits and smiles there on a sofa catty-corner to my father's casket. Mom is pale, but her lipstick glows a deep garnet. She greets everyone as they enter to pay their respects. Lots of farmers and watermen hold their caps in their hands and nod gravely. The casket is closed. The accident tore Dad in half. Tractor trailer on Route 50 lost control. The medical examiner said he never knew what hit him.

I think Harry knew Dad never could completely accept him. I think that's why he clung to Mom and me so much.

Peta and Cheeta are going to move into the farmhouse. Mom invited them because Dad always liked them and she needs the help with the farm and Harry. Somebody needs to drive him to the grocery store for work.

The preacher doesn't say much really. Dad never set foot in a church once he got married, and this minister isn't the type to go on and on about God, but he does talk about Dad's love for life, his great number of friends, and his involvement with the VFW.

I'm not numb at all, but I don't feel like crying either. I feel more sorrow for my mother now, who has not only lost her mate but her compadre. She'll bear the loss at its most extreme. I'll go back home with Joey and resume my life.

March, 1997, Havre de Grace

If Pearly realized I am discussing issues of faith with her mother she'd have a fit. But although I am trying to respect her wishes in regards to her own faith, I cannot turn away from this dying soul. Not much time remains between Valerie's time here on earth and her time in eternity. She deserves to know that God loves her. She deserves to know that Christ sacrificed His life on her behalf. And she brought the topic up herself. I am surprised at how much she knows. But then her mother loved the Lord. She sees her life as wasted, but I told her that everyone's path to Christ is different. And surely, taking care of Harry, raising her children, working her garden were all noble pursuits. Not wasted at all.

She said more than ever she was ready to take the final step, and so we prayed together last night while Pearly slept after an exhausting day of running around to doctors and pharmacies and health-food stores.

Valerie said she enjoys the peacefulness of our home. "This is a good place to die, Joe," she told me. "Thank you."

I sat by her chair for a long time, then. We took in an old Jimmy Stewart movie called Harvey. When it ended and I helped her into the bed, she said, "I guess I always thought of Jesus as the Christian's Harvey. Now I know He's real. Maybe I always did but just didn't want to be one of the crazies."

I laughed and kissed her cheek. She is still a beautiful woman.

Harry pulled through. Thank God. I really mean that. He took a turn for the worse, and I called Yolanda and asked her to pray, then called Matthew and asked him to pray. Maida even volunteered to do that, even though I wasn't about to ask her. So Harry's staying with me at the cabin. Christmas is only a week away, and we've been making all sorts of crafts for the guests coming down for the holiday. Yo and her crew, Matthew and Maida and Shrubby.

Get this. You can actually put potpourri and a string of lights in a big Mason jar. A little while after you plug it in, the gentle heat stirs the perfumes in the dried petals and sends it right up into the air. We've been smelling pine and bayberry and cinnamon all day, and I keep wondering if these things are fire hazards. Harry paints little Christmas trees on the glass.

"I never knew you could paint like that, Harry. It's beautiful."

He smiles. Well, actually, he's never stopped. The grin just broadens, and I realize he needs to see a dentist. "I like to paint, Pearly."

I can't say the trees are exactly childlike. They're

free-form, expressive and honest. An honest Christmas tree? Well, yes.

"Can you do one for me with the Holy Family on it?" I ask him.

"Yep."

I have a feeling I could ask him to paint a small replica of the Sistine Chapel on one of the jars, and he'd say, "Yep." And he'd do it, in his own style and manner, but like it or not, it would be the Sistine Chapel. I yearn for that kind of bravado.

I've been realizing my own cowardice even more of late, and I'm ashamed I was almost willing to let Harry die. Maybe Harry would be better off here with me. Maybe we could spend the rest of our lives making crafts together and selling them at the local fairs in elementary schools or at church ham 'n' oyster suppers and bazaars.

I feel so comfortable with my brother now. But it is more than that. I admire him and wish that somehow I could be the wonderful human being he is. And yet would I be satisfied wearing such blinders? Still, I'd sure like to give it a try.

Would it be exchanging one set of blinders for another? Did you think of that, Pearly? Maybe you've been wearing blinders for years.

Flo the Boarding House Lady

Flo grew up at her grandmother's house, left school in the fifth grade to help run the boarding house. Flo got married to one of the boarders at the age of fifteen. She goes through life like a nail into a wall.

But every once in a while Flo dreams about being an actress, a singer, an executive, or the First Lady. She told me this last night as Pearly visited Harry. She even shed a tear as she did so. Pearly probably wouldn't believe it. She'd probably say something like, "Well, we all have our dreams, Joe."

Harry's asleep up in the loft. He loves it up there. He has his little books and a nightlight and his favorite blanket, and with that, he's content.

I'm parked out on the deck, wrapped up in one of those snuggly things that remind me of a sleeping bag with feet and armholes. I walk all over the place in this thing. I'm sitting out here smoking a cigarette and drinking a cup of hot chocolate. I'm thinking about bravery tonight. Coupled with faith. To be truthful, I'm tired of thinking about faith, tired that it has been taking up my thoughts since Joey died, sick of its unwanted presence in my mind. But I can't seem to help it. With the watch gone, all I have is the list, and I can't go on the Alaska cruise until spring, so I'm at a standstill. There's no way I can eat all the entrées at Haussner's, and I'm not going to try.

Why is it that people of faith are popping up in my life like prairie dogs? It's hard to believe, and I have to wonder if God really is sending me a message. Maybe I should go to church one of these days and see what all the fuss is about. But, then, maybe God is choosing to reveal Himself in alternative ways. I don't know.

What I do know is that the people He's sent into my

life are very courageous people. Yolanda and her Rib Room, her children, her church work, and the way she constantly seeks to drag people into a quiet redemption. Matthew, leaving home to better himself in an unknown place, mature enough to realize when a situation is finally beyond him. That counts as courage too. Peta, who's been reading her Bible and is looking forward to Yolanda's visit because she says she has a lot of questions she wished she'd had for the asking when Joey was alive. Even Harry, who is mentally handicapped but smiles all the time and sings "Jesus Loves Me" as he corrals the carts on the chilly parking lot of the Food Lion.

These people challenge me every day.

I take a drag on my cigarette and look out over the water, wondering if Joey's watch is buried in sludge yet. Probably.

Well, there's more work to be done inside. More crafts to be made. I know Yolanda will love one of those lighted Mason jars, but I want to do something else for her, in gratitude for showing me how it's done. Maybe I should drag my camera out. Oh, yeah, it's in Havre de Grace. What a relief.

"Peta! Why do you keep bringing all these jars over? We've got enough for Christmas presents for the next ten years!"

Peta, while still gray and watery, looks like a new woman. Cheeta took her shopping down at White Flint Mall near D.C., and despite her escort, Peta managed to come home with some tasteful outfits. They almost got thrown out of Saks Fifth Avenue for arguing over a pair of mules with gold coins on them.

Today she wears black slacks, a red turtleneck sweater, and a wonderful pair of chunky-heeled black boots that would actually go well with the gold corduroy skirt I have on. Peta plans on cutting her braid off after the new year, but in the meantime, she rolls it up into a sleek bun. I told her she might want to reconsider the haircut, she looks so good like this. She just informed me I should mind my own business, which, if she only knew, I'm much too good at to begin with.

She plucks jars from inside a cardboard box. "I found these in the cellar and washed them up. They're ready to go."

"What am I going to do with all these?"

"Let Harry paint them."

"And then what?"

Peta's face widens. "You really don't get it, do you, Pearly?"

"I guess not."

"It doesn't matter what the heck's done with the jars!" Her gray face turns pink. "Goodness gracious and a loaf of bread, Pearl! Must everything come to some glorious, world-saving conclusion? Isn't the action itself ever enough? Isn't that purpose enough? Doesn't the expression of a human being possess a dignity found beyond salability or some wider purpose? Does everything have to be overblown or not at all?"

I feel the heat rising with each sentence. "Okay, then, Miss Smarty-Pants. Give me one good example."

"Your picture-taking."

"Photojournalism, Peta."

"See? That's exactly what I mean! Because you couldn't fulfill that photojournalism thing to the letter, you gave it up entirely. You could be an awesome photographer by now, Pearly. Who knows what kind of pictures you might have taken, the places Joey would have escorted you to if you'd shown the interest? You blew it!"

I blew it.

"I think you'd better go now, Peta."

"I'm sorry, Pearly."

"I know."

"Someone has to tell it to you like it is."

"You've always been rather good at that."

"I'm dying, cousin. I've got some inside information about what it feels like for it to be too late."

Is it too late for me? Is there is a reason I so desperately want to end things but so desperately can't?

What needs to happen? I am pregnant with something, but have no idea what grows inside me and if the birth will be still and quiet or clamorous and large. Or if I will die in childbirth.

Dear God. And I mean exactly that.

So now I know. The Norwalk virus. I always heard a woman could get cervical cancer from promiscuity, but now I know why. Of course, they didn't know all this when I got it. A virus. A sexually transmitted virus stole my children from me. It seems so easy, the sex thing. Those women told me to take control of my own body, to enjoy sex like men do, to satisfy a natural appetite without making a big to-do about petty things like commitment and love. So here I am, mid-fifties, no kids, no life, no courage, and a portion of that which makes me a woman gouged out by a scalpel's blade.

Oh, yeah! They had *all* the answers! They thought they had it sewed up with more stitches than a man's business suit. They spoke with compassion and authority. They spoke as if it wasn't really in the stages of a grand experiment. They spoke as if it was time-tested fact.

The wenches.

The Norwalk virus.

A virus! Not some sort of genetic, predestined occurrence. Something I elected to contract when I elected to believe someone I placed in authority over me.

"Question Authority"?

Remember that one? Well, who is anyone to tell anyone else to question authority? Now, if the saying was "How About Questioning Authority?" or "A Suggestion: Question Authority," *that* would have made sense. But by telling someone to question authority, you immediately set yourself up as an authority to be questioned.

What a messed-up bunch of kids we were. What we really were saying was that we were our own authority. To which I now say, "Big Deal!" So I made my decisions, lived by my own creed. Now I am thick into middle age, alone and drifting like a piece of ice on a river, and because I set myself up as my own authority, I have no one to blame but me.

And I can't even kill myself now. I've no strength for either living or dying. I'm stuck in this limbo. I want to crack open, peel away this turgid scab that has entombed my spirit like some crusty brown sarcophagus. I never did like to pick scabs. That first lift was too painful, and no place ever looked good enough to begin.

I don't know where to begin.

Yolanda and Peta have taken over. I'm stuck out here with the kids. How did it come to this? We're celebrating at the farmhouse; the cabin just can't take this much humanity at one time.

"Okay, what do you guys want to do? Do you have any Christmas Eve traditions?"

Yolanda's four children sit in a row along the old floral sofa. The oldest, a very dark thirteen-year-old girl named LeeLee, says, "We like to watch a Christmas movie. But usually that's after church. We going to church?"

"Well, normally I don't."

The next in line, an eleven-year-old named Ireland, says, "Not even on Christmas Eve?"

"Well, yes. On Christmas Eve. But that's about it."

"Only on Christmas Eve! And you weren't even going to do it this year?" LeeLee again. The third child, a little girl named Kate, says nothing. She's too busy hugging Pumpkin, who came down with Maida and Shrubby. Yolanda's six-year-old son, Clay, the only white one in the bunch, stomps around in cowboy boots, clicking his tongue more loudly than any human being should.

"I guess I just forgot to plan." I feel silly apologizing like this to a teenager.

"Mom!" Ireland, not as dark as her sister and a bit more stocky, stands to her feet. "What about church?"

"What about it?" Yolanda yells back.

"We going tonight?"

"Ask Pearly!"

"I did. She's noncommittal."

Noncommittal? Where'd she get a word like that?

Yolanda appears dressed in an ivory caftan and head scarf. "Where's the nearest church?"

Harry rocks back and forth a bit and starts singing "Jesus Loves Me."

"Down the road. A United Methodist," I say.

Peta yells, "They're practically all United Methodist around these parts."

"We'll go there," Yolanda says and turns toward Maida, Peta, and Cheeta, who are working at various kitchen tasks. "How about it, girls, you game?"

"Not me!" says Cheeta. "I doubt Peta is either."

"Oh, I'm game, and I'll thank you not to speak for me, Cheeta."

"All right, all right. Maida and I will hold down the fort. We'll clean up the dishes while you all go and do your church thing."

Peta walks through the doorway into the living room, grimacing. "Gee, you make it sound so attractive."

"Something's burning!" Maida yells.

"My beans!" Yolanda spins around and heads back in.

236

The kids start looking through the video bin.

Peta sits on the arm of my lounge chair. "I'm tired."

"Why don't you stay home and rest?"

"No. Could be my last chance to go to a Christmas Eve service. Lord knows I missed enough of them."

"Don't say that."

"Can't help it. I'm going on dialysis in three weeks. It's hard on the heart, you know."

"I didn't know that."

"Well it is. I could die from heart failure before the disease kills me."

I don't want to hear this. I don't want Peta to leave me.

"You coming to church?" she asks.

"I guess I might as well."

"Don't sound so thrilled."

"Suffice it to say . . ."

The chefs clatter and joke in the kitchen, Shrubby and Matthew mumble man-talk out in the dining room where they and their checkers game are soon to be shooed away, and the children have narrowed it down to *A Charlie Brown Christmas* and *The Little Drummer Boy.*

"Look around, Pearly. A dozen people gathered here because they love you. I'd say Christmas has come to you with bells on, and you can't even go to church to say thank you?"

"Peta, I liked you better before you got God. What's with this anyway? Where are you getting this faith from? Who have you been talking to?"

She shrugs. "Harry. He's the most innocent source

I'm gonna get it from. But I've been going to church Sunday mornings. If you got up early enough, you'd see me leave for the first service."

". . ."

She sighs. "I'm not going to get angry with you, Pearly. It's your soul, and if you want to throw it away like you've been doing all these years—"

"Oh yeah right, Peta. You find a little faith to see you through your illness after having ignored God all your life, and you think you have a right to tell me anything?"

"Yes, I do."

"I'd like to know why."

"Because I love you."

Oh.

"You know, Pearly, Joey was a gentleman and played by different rules than most of us do. Joey was in love with you. Your love was even more important to him than you were."

"Thanks, Peta."

"It's true. We both know Joey was a man of great faith, and he was a man of great expression. He allowed you to squelch those things when it came to your marriage. Well, I'm not married to you. I'm family, and I'm not going to let you go on like this, smoking yourself to death, moping around—"

"I don't mope!"

"Oh yes you do. You sit out on that deck all day long now. You weren't doing anything until Harry got sick and came back to recuperate. What are you going to do with him after the New Year?"

"I don't know."

"Figures."

"Stop it, Peta. I don't answer to you."

"You don't answer to anybody, Pearly, and maybe that's your biggest problem."

"Who are you to tell me anything?"

My home in Havre de Grace is looking better and better these days.

"Nobody. That's the point. I'm a big fat nobody who's done nothing much with her life."

I can see where this is going. "Okay, I'll go to church."

"Good." She heads back into the kitchen.

Shoot, I thought she'd say something like "I don't want you to go if it's just to keep me quiet." Joey would have said that, but then, Peta doesn't play by Joey's rules. She's not a gentleman at all.

Each sill displays a burning candle surrounded by greens. The contrasting temperatures of inside and out breathe condensation onto the window panes. They're calling for snow, but it would be just too perfect for the sky to drop flakes on Christmas Eve.

The lights dim, the church now lit only by the gauzy strips of candlelight, soft in the hushed sanctuary. We collectively catch our breath at the beauty of it all, and silence stills us further, for at least a minute, as expectation rises. I've heard Christmas Eve called the holiest night of the year.

A flute breaks the quiet, the clear melody line of "Once in Royal David's City" floating down from the rear balcony. A young child's voice blends in from beside the wooden baptistery.

And I cry.

Oh, Joey.

Yolanda holds one hand, Peta the other, as the service continues and a story like no other is told. Something stands out to me this time, though, as the young preacher talks about the courage of the Christ, the Savior born to die.

Shepherds quake at the sight.

Glory streams from heaven afar.

Sleep in heavenly peace.

I sit still while the others partake in communion. As the service closes, the choir sings "Silent Night," and we light the slender tapers in our hands. I remember the way Joey's face would shine with anticipation at this moment.

"Behold, I am the light of the world," the pastor says. "May we shine the love of Christ into the darkness. Go in peace."

Go in peace.

"Thanks be to God."

"Go in peace. I am the light of the world."

The others file into the farmhouse, but Harry and I continue our trek to the cabin.

"Sleep in heavenly peace," he sings.

"Sleep in heavenly peace," I say, and I kiss my brother on the cheek before he climbs into his loft.

So I do love people. I've come to this conclusion with the holidays now ended. This is all about the courage to go on. It's about a reason to go on. It's about building a new life.

I just don't know how to go about it. But I'll find a way. I'll find a purpose, and it may not be grand or important, but it will be my own.

I'm glad I threw that watch into the Bay, because most likely it would have stopped by now, and I would have felt compelled to down all those sleeping pills in my cabinet.

Harry's back at the boarding house, and Peta, her home dialysis machine, and I are on board a Norwegian cruise ship bound for Alaska. I can't believe we're well into the month of May.

No whales yet.

I'm executing the two-minute scrub just in case Peta needs help hooking herself up to the unit. Sometimes she has a hard time piercing the solution bag with the pointed end of the tubing. They claim this home method is much easier on the heart, and this comforts me. It's eight o'clock. We'll take her off tomorrow morning at eight and go have a nice breakfast. Oh, the food on these ships. I think I've already gained back all the weight I've lost and then some. But what lovely hips I'm getting. Very womanly. Very maternal.

Peta tries to open the Baxter solution box. I swear, you'd think these medical supply people who send these perforated cardboard boxes would include their own Arnold Schwarzenegger!

"Pearly, I just don't have the strength tonight. Can you do it?"

"Of course." I guess I'll have to do another two-minute scrub after opening the box. After several months of these scrubs, my hands are drying out like crazy. If you judged me by my hands, you'd peg me for a ninety-year-old. And wouldn't you know it, I forgot my hand cream? The samples on the ship actually pour out of the bottle.

Peta asked me to take the lessons with her so that I can learn the machine. Cheeta wanted nothing to do with it. It frightens her, I know. And it ties me down, but how could I say no? Family is family, both my parents always said.

I dry my hands and grab the opening on the box. I pull. Oh great, this is a tough one. So I lift the box with a sudden jerk, the cardboard gives way, and the box tumbles onto the bed. "There."

Peta shakes her head. "You'd think, wouldn't you?"

"There's got to be a better way than these boxes."

"I guess they'd have thought of it by now if there was."

"Well, I wonder how many people who work for this company actually have to do this every night?"

Yes, this is Pearly Laurel's newest pet peeve.

I place one bag of dialysis solution on the unit's heater bed and another on the side table. It'll be a while before it reaches her body temperature, so I sit next to Peta, who has removed the tubing from its bags. She snaps opens the blue clip she needs to keep the fluid from flowing into her peritoneal cavity until it's time.

"So, what are you going to do tonight, Pearly?"

"Go hear some music, I guess. Get a glass of wine."

"That sounds nice."

"You got your books ready?"

"Yep. And the remote."

"Good thing the bathroom's so close."

She nods. "I hate being so dependent on this thing. But I do have to admit, I feel a little better now that I'm on it."

"I'll give you your shot tomorrow." I should have given her the Procrit today, but we were having such a lovely time on deck we forgot, and Peta, not much good with needles, never wants a shot right before bed.

"Let's do it before breakfast," she says. "Get it over with first thing."

"All right."

Back to the two-minute scrub. I look over her dialysis log. Every night and morning she jots down her weight, her blood pressure, whether or not she's holding water, how the exit site looks. She's slowly but surely losing weight. "How does your catheter feel?"

She flops the end of the rubber tubing protruding from her abdomen. "Fine." She lifts her nightgown and examines the exit site. It's pink and healthy. No crust.

"Looks good."

"Yeah. I hate this thing, Pearly. It grosses me out so much, I don't know what it must do to you."

"Don't begin to think that. It's not that way at all. Really, Peta."

I scrub my hands a minute later, sit back down next to her, making sure I touch *absolutely nothing*. "Think we'll see a whale tomorrow?"

"I sure hope so. I'd hate to think we went to all this trouble, and no whales."

In bed that night, I listen to Peta's soft breathing, hear the machine click as the old solution drains into a bag in a tub on the floor. The fresh solution fills her cavity, ready to suck out the impurities in her system via the peritoneal lining. I remember her words. It would be a bummer to go through all this trouble and see no whales.

And I realize that's life. Imagine going through all this trouble to survive, and not only just survive but do so graciously, with love and kindness and perseverance, and see no whales.

I am convinced. This life is about more than just the face value. It has to be. There have to be whales at the end.

A wild cheer erupts from all the people gathered on the deck.

"There it is, Pearly! There's our whale!" More color suffuses Peta's cheeks than I've seen in many months. "Oh, Pearly! It's . . ."

"Magnificent." Oh God, yes.

"Yes, that's it exactly."

The whale surfaces, its bumpy skin glistening in the Alaska sunshine. It spins, showing off its flippers, rolling in the Pacific soup, white belly gleaming.

"Do you think it will jump?" she asks. "Do you think it will jump and show us its big tail and flap it down on the water?"

"Yes, Peta. I know it will."

I am sure of this! I am sure without any reason but faith.

I watch with full expectation, ready for the tail, for the accompanying splash.

"Take a picture, Pearly, when it happens. Please."

I lift the heavy body of my old camera. I center the viewfinder in front of my eye, and I wait, afraid to breathe. Oh yes, God. Please. Please.

Half a minute later, the whale breaches. I follow his movement. I press the button. And I press again as he descends, his giant cloven tail directly in front of us, pounding the cold water. And we stand with the spray from his gigantic mass dotting our faces, hair, and parkas.

I caught it all on film. The first pictures I've taken on this camera in years.

"Oh, Cousin! Did you see?"

"Wonderful!"

"Did you get the picture?"

"I did, Peta. I really did."

She hugs me. I return the embrace so hard I fear we both may break.

The next day I throw a picture of Joey and me, taken in front of our cabin by my mother after it was built, right into the sea. Our faces swim on the waves for several seconds, then we go under, the water distorting the focus as it washes over the photo. Finally, nothing remains but the dark blue-green of the ocean. And I stand alone, moving forward into waters I've never navigated.

I've fulfilled the list. Except for Haussner's, and I've got plans for that! I can hardly believe it. We are flying back East, and I'm writing a new list. Things I want to accomplish while I'm still living. Sell the Havre de Grace house for starters. My life is elsewhere now. *My* life. Goodness, that sounds positively wild, doesn't it?

We land at BWI. Cheeta isn't there.

"Let's get a cup of coffee while we wait," I say.

"Okay. Decaf for me."

Hours go by. We call the farm. The phone rings and rings.

Peta looks pale again.

"Let's get a cab."

She raises her brow. "That will be expensive, Pearly."

"Let's go. You can't miss your dialysis."

Cheeta lies there looking more peaceful than she ever did in life. We decided, and rightly so, to bury her with her jewelry and her turban. Her hair, completely white, had thinned to a ghoulish sparseness. We found her in her bed.

The coroner said she'd been dead for at least five days. And I thought I was alone. Poor Cheeta, kept the world at arm's length, always playing the part of the angry young woman.

Peta weeps, grasping my hand as we stand looking down at the body. "I really thought I'd be the first to go. In fact, I was counting on it."

All Cheeta's Democrat friends gather with us at the funeral home. They're sad to see one of their warriors gone from the fray. Peta knows only a few of them. "I never liked Cheeta's friends," she says, then laughs. "Of course, that wasn't anything Cheeta didn't know."

"I don't think Cheeta really liked them much either."

We smile into each other's eyes.

"Life has really changed for us, Cousin," I say.

She nods and cries some more.

On the way home from the burial she tells me, "All I've got is you, Pearly."

"And I've got lots of others. We'll all make it through. Somehow."

"There's a lot to this life, isn't there, Cousin?"

"More than we ever bargain for, that's for sure."

"So, I guess, in the end, it's worth it . . . What are we doing for my birthday, Pearly?"

"Let's have everyone over. Yo and the kids, Matthew, Maida, and Shrubby. Just everyone."

"It's going to be the best birthday ever, don't you think?"

"I really do, Peta."

"You know people can live for years on dialysis."

"We'll break some records. I can tell you that."

The whale splashes his tail, and we feel the spray on our faces, and we hold hands, confident the mist will never dry.

I've begun a new hobby. An old-lady hobby. I started identifying wildflowers this past spring. Peta and I are spending two weeks at a cabin in Maine. Who knows, maybe it's near the spot where Joey and his father summered all those years ago.

I run down to the shore of the lake where Peta sits in the sun reading a book called *Surprised by Joy*. She looks up at me, and the sun turns her eyes from chocolate to caramel.

I plop onto the beach chair and open up my wildflower field guide. "Look here."

She examines the flower on which my thumb is placed. "Pearly Everlasting."

"Yes. It's a lovely flower, isn't it?"

I pull out the specimen I found by the pathway near the lodge. Its flower, tightly knit white petals, reminds me of a large pinhead. The stems and leaves are downy and silver-green. I hand it to her.

She runs a finger tenderly across the blossoms, down the stems and over the leaves. "A hardy looking plant."

"Yes, extremely so. I always wondered why Yolanda calls me that."

"Guess she pegged you from the beginning."

I guess she did.

A bank of dark clouds slides in from the east. "Looks like a storm is coming in, Cousin," I say.

She takes my hand. "Nothing that you, me, and God can't handle."

I laugh. "That's the truth."

"Yep." She gazes across the waters of the lake. "That's exactly right."

It's a good day to live. Last night I took out those sleeping pills and crushed them one by one. Joey smiled at that, I'll bet.

"We building a campfire tonight, Pearly?"

"Of course."

"Take some pictures of it, won't you?"

"Sure."

My darkroom is backed up for months, and that's okay. Will I sell my photos? Probably not. I might just pin them all up around my potpourri Mason jars and pronounce them good simply because they are.

And that will be enough. Not because it has to be.

Lord, make me an instrument of your peace,
Where there is hatred, let me sow love;
. . . where there is injury, pardon;
. . . where there is doubt, faith;
. . . where there is despair, hope;
. . . where there is darkness, light;
. . . where there is sadness, joy;

O Divine Master, grant that I may not so much seek
. . . to be consoled as to console;
. . . to be understood as to understand;
. . . to be loved as to love.

For it is in giving that we receive;
. . . it is in pardoning that we are pardoned;
. . . and it is in dying that we are born to eternal life.

I seek to live up to the prayer of Saint Francis of Assisi.
I fail every day and I wonder if it's so far from the
nature of the normal male as to be unattainable. No, I
do not wonder, I know. And it stands to reason that the
man deserved sainthood to even think up the prayer in

first place. I've been reading about the Christian mystics and their experiences of God. I yearn, but I am too attached to this world, I fear.

I can't shake the look that filled Peta's face after we saw the whale. It lasted for two days, this shining peace. She talked about it constantly, excited to view the photos later on. But honestly, the way she described everything about that whale in such detail, I knew her mind captured the whole thing more completely than my camera ever could. The pictures, however, are thrilling. And beautifully done, if I do say so myself.

Peta deserves to live. Peta deserves life more than ever, now that she's awakened to the world around her and the Holy Spirit that Joey talked about so much. Cheeta, God love her, did nothing but drag her sister down. I have to wonder about her death. I have to wonder whether it really was just a sudden occurrence.

I feel terrible for even thinking that. But some people are just too much work on the world. Not at all like Saint Francis.

I found the book Joey had been reading on the mystics. While I am now pursuing an understanding of faith, realizing this is important, an ingrained part of being human, I'm even farther from Saint Francis's ideal than my husband ever was. I have cast aside forever the idea of suicide. My search has become paramount; and I'd like to just fall head first into love with Christ as Joey did, but I know so little as of yet. Who was He really? Why did God need to sacrifice Him for the sins of the world? It all seems a little strange to me, maybe because I grew up with very little training. I read Joey's writings voraciously now, and I see Christ's fingerprints on each page, even as I hear Him in each note of Matthew's music and each gleam in Peta's and Harry's eyes.

"Greater love has no man than this, than he would lay down his life for his friends." Now that I can understand.

I remember again the look on Peta's face. She deserves to live, and I am ready to make the sacrifice. I am able to do this. I can do this. It's not suicide if you really don't want to die, is it?

"This is ridiculous, Pearly," Peta says. She shakes her head, her signature smirk attached.

"I don't think so at all. The least we can do is see if we're a match for a transplant. We're family, so there's a better chance."

"Just when I got used to dialysis."

So Peta and I are a match. Now comes the hard part: finding a surgeon who will do this for us. Of course, Peta can know nothing about the present state of my kidneys or the whole matter will crumble. I have a feeling we'll have to go overseas for this, to Holland or some country that allows assisted suicide and the like. Yes, there are definite moral implications to this, I know. I'm dealing with them day by day, as they surface. Is it moral for a healthy person to die for the sick and suffering?

Jesus did.

But . . . but . . .

I hear all the arguments against this. First of all, I'm not Jesus. I can provide no mass redemption. I am fully aware that only the actual death is what I would have in common.

Second of all, if this became common practice, we would all be in a mess. I admit that, too.

But my heart tells me this is right. I love Peta. I love her more than anyone else here on earth now, and she'll do more with her life and health than I ever will. Even now, I still have no real purpose. At least my dying would serve the greater good. And what a great way to go! They put you under the anesthesia, and then, *poof,* you're gone. No pain. No suffering. Nothing.

"I have the power to lay down my life, and I have the power to take it back up again."

And there's the difference between me and the Lord on this matter.

Richard King is going to have a fit, but he said if there was anything he could do . . .

"Miss Pearly, this is ridiculous! You can't do this."

"Yes, I can."

"Not with my help."

"So my life is more important than Peta's?"

"Not in the grand scheme of things, but to me, yes."

We're sitting over coffee at the Greek Family Restaurant. Richie requested the nonsmoking section. I guess I'll forgive him.

He reaches out and takes my hand. "Miss Pearly, are you actually considering this? I mean, for real? This isn't one of your plots?"

"One of my plots? When have I ever had a plot in my entire life?"

He shakes his head. "No time that I can think of really, but no one is ever too old to start."

"I guess I'm living proof of that."

He is silent. He removes his hand and takes a sip of his coffee. "You've got a lot to live for."

"Name one thing."

". . ."

"See? You can't think of anything. Not now that Joey's dead."

"Oh, surely Dr. Laurel wasn't your whole life!"

". . ."

"This is craziness!"

"I know. I've always been a little crazy."

"No you haven't. So don't even go there."

He must be upset, using vernacular and all. Good. I'm glad he realizes I'm serious.

"Have you thought about this from all angles?" he asks.

"I believe so."

"Have you thought what this will do to Peta?"

"Yes. She'll go on. Peta always does."

"What if she doesn't?"

"She has to."

"No, Miss Pearly. Nobody has to. You're living proof of that with this scheme."

"Seems I'm just the living proof of a lot of things. But Peta still deserves this. I do know that."

"Maybe. But she's on the list for donation, right?"

"Yes. But she's almost seventy, Richie. I imagine she's pretty far down. And I'm a perfect match."

"Would you do this for anybody else?"

"Probably. Anybody's life is worth more than mine."

"See there?" He flat-hands the table. "You're depressed. If I get you on Lexapro or Paxil, I bet you'd change your mind as soon as the medication kicks in."

"I don't think so."

"Will you give it a try? For me?"

"I think you're wrong."

"Then you can go on with your scheme. Just give it a try."

I look up at the ceiling, wondering if he's right. Is it depression that's leading me to even consider something like this? What could it hurt? Peta's fine on the dialysis for now. We do have a little time. "Okay. I'll try it."

He blows a sigh of relief. "Good. I'm calling the prescription in and having it delivered, so you have no excuses. Eckerd's. Right?"

"Yes." I roll my eyes. "You're still a piece of work, Richie King. You still don't know how to take no for an answer, do you?"

"Never have."

This time I reach for his hand. "I do love you, Richie."

"Then show me you do by abandoning this plan."

"I can't do that. I love Peta more."

Well, I traded in my old Escort for a sporty little MG. Mustard yellow. I figure with the limited time remaining I'll live it up. Joey would approve.

I pick up Matthew at Lafayette. The school year is over. Oh, his graduation stirred us all. Peta and I, Maida, Shrubby, and Yolanda sat there and cried together.

"I've decided to have a big yard sale next month," I tell Matthew as we zip down Route 13. "I have so much stuff I'm not using. Then I'm going to sell the house in Havre de Grace."

"Staying at the cabin for good, then?"

"Yep."

"Great. That's where your life is anyway."

"I know."

What he doesn't know is that I'm leaving everything to him, for his education. I'll die much better knowing Matthew's all set.

"So," I say, "you want to stay at the cabin all summer? You're more than welcome to."

"I think so. I'll need to visit Luray a couple of times, but I really need a job. I gotta make some bucks for school."

"I wanted to talk to you about that. I want to pay your tuition for this year."

"Mrs. Laurel! Really?"

"Yes. I find myself feeling awfully responsible for your welfare."

He grins. "Well, thanks. That'll make it a lot easier. Now I'll only have to make enough for room and board."

He's going to Towson State to major in music. I told him to try for Juilliard or something, but he refused. I wish he possessed more confidence, but he still sees himself as the boy living in a hovel. Hopefully the confidence will come.

"So what's on for tonight?" he asks.

"Dinner with Peta and Harry."

"Cool."

The wind ruffles our hair. "There's a little present for you right there in my tote bag."

He reaches into the compartment at the back and pulls out the small, gift-wrapped box.

"It's not your graduation present, mind you. It's more of a welcome-to-summer present."

"You're too much, Mrs. Laurel."

"I try."

He pulls open the paper, opens the hinged box. "Sunglasses! Wow, these are cool."

"The guy at the mall assured me they're the latest thing."

"They're great!" He slips them on and looks at me. "What do you think?"

"Fabulous. I couldn't have you tooling around with me in the MG without cool shades."

"I never thought I'd own a pair like this."

"Well, life can surprise you sometimes."

"Tell me about it!"

It's Yolanda. It's almost midnight.

"Hi, Yo!"

"Pearly Everlasting!"

"How did you know I'd be up this late?"

She laughs. "Because you always are?"

"Well, besides that."

"Just got an urging of the Spirit to call you."

"Well, then I'm glad you did."

She hesitates. "Are you all right?"

"Very."

"Okay. You just usually hate hearing about the Spirit and all."

"Well, life's too short, Yo. Besides, I'm beginning to see that the Spirit is alive and well on planet Earth."

"Hallelujah!"

"Don't get overly excited. I'm still on the journey. I'm not there yet."

"Who is?"

Hmm.

"Saint Francis of Assisi?"

"Well, he was a *saint,* Pearly. He doesn't count."

"Maybe not. But at least he's a good example. As are you."

She snorts. "Oh, please. I've got so far to go it isn't even funny. Just the other day, I got so mad at Clay I thought I would kill him!"

"What did he do?"

"He went into his sock drawer and cut off all the toes of his socks. I didn't even know he could use the scissors so well, and I don't know how he got to them! I keep them way up in one of the kitchen closets."

"One of the girls?"

"If it was, they aren't saying."

"Can you blame them?"

"Of course not! Oh, Pearly, it's good to talk to you."

"Likewise."

"When you coming down to Luray?"

"Soon. Matthew wants to visit. He has the weekends off."

"What's he doing?"

"He's working on one of the boats. Pulling up crab pots and all that sort of thing. Leaves the house at 4:00 A.M. every day."

"Must be beat."

"You know how it is with the young."

"I hear you. So anyway, back to my message from the Spirit . . ."

"Let me have it."

"I don't know what this means, but the message is, 'There's another way.' "

Whoa.

"Does that make sense, Pearly?"

"I think so."

"Want to talk about it?"

"Nope."

She chuckles. "I didn't think so."

"You know me."

"Yeah, I sure do. I'd better go. It's late."

"Thanks for calling, Yolanda."

"Can't wait to see you. The kids will be excited to know you're coming. We'll have us a big supper to celebrate."

"As if I expected any less."

"You know me."

"I sure do."

It's a beautiful summer night. The earth soaks in the warmth. All the creatures do, including me.

"Miss Pearly?"

"Richie King! How are you?"

"Fine. The question is, how are you?"

"Regarding the Lexapro?"

"Yes."

"Well, I have to admit, despite the dry mouth it gives me, it has lightened my spirits a bit."

"Good."

"But I still want to go through with my plot, as you put it."

"Figures."

"You're not going to help me with this are you?"

"I can't. It would go against all I hold to be sacred as a physician and a friend."

"I still don't know why you can't see this from Peta's perspective."

"Peta wouldn't want you to do this. In fact, I've got half a mind to call her."

"Don't you dare!"

"If that's the only way I can keep you from hatching this cockamamie plan, I just might."

"Richie King! I am old enough to make this decision for myself."

"Age has nothing to do with insanity, Miss Pearly."

He sure hit the nail on the head with that one!

"I'll think about it some more, then," I say, only to put him off. "How about that?"

"Well, it's the only offer on the table, so I guess I'll take it."

"Besides, I have to see Matthew off to college in the

fall. That gives us a couple of months. Also, Peta says she doesn't want us to do anything until the new year anyway. She wants one more Christmas for sure. We had an uncle who died on the operating table during a simple tonsillectomy."

"Oh. Well, I'll be calling you for updates."

"I'm sure you will."

A Psalm of Life, by Henry Wadsworth Longfellow

TELL me not, in mournful numbers,
  Life is but an empty dream!—
For the soul is dead that slumbers,
  And things are not what they seem.

Life is real! Life is earnest!
  And the grave is not its goal;
Dust thou art, to dust returnest,
  Was not spoken of the soul.

Not enjoyment, and not sorrow,
  Is our destined end or way;
But to act, that each to-morrow
  Find us farther than to-day.

Art is long, and Time is fleeting,
  And our hearts, though stout and brave,
Still, like muffled drums, are beating
  Funeral marches to the grave.

In the world's broad field of battle,

In the bivouac of Life,
Be not like dumb, driven cattle!
Be a hero in the strife!

Trust no Future, howe'er pleasant!
Let the dead Past bury its dead!
Act,—act in the living Present!
Heart within, and God o'erhead!

Lives of great men all remind us
We can make our lives sublime,
And, departing, leave behind us
Footprints on the sands of time;

Footprints, that perhaps another,
Sailing o'er life's solemn main,
A forlorn and shipwrecked brother,
Seeing, shall take heart again.

Let us, then, be up and doing,
With a heart for any fate;
Still achieving, still pursuing,
Learn to labor and to wait.

Now why did Joey have to paste that poem into his journal? It leaves me more confused than ever. *Life is real, life is earnest, and the grave is not its goal. Dust thou art, to dust returnest, was not spoken of the soul.*

The Catholics believe that a person who commits suicide goes to hell. I know because Shrubby's Catholic, and he told me that years ago. Does having your only working kidney removed really constitute suicide? My goodness, if I handed my piece of wreckage on the open seas to a fellow survivor of a maritime tragedy, I'd be a hero.

So what's the difference?

Peta throws up in the bathroom. I stand at the doorway.

"Oh, Pearly, this is awful."

"You're underdialyzed."

"Must be."

"Let me get you some Coke to settle your stomach." She shouldn't be drinking Coke, but how much will a little bit hurt?

I hurry into the kitchen and pour a cold glass. Our first setback, but we'll make it through.

"Drink this, and I'll call the nephrologist."

I dial the number.

"Is she retaining fluid?" the dialysis nurse asks.

"Are you retaining fluid?" I yell.

"I think so!" she hollers back from the bathroom.

"She thinks so."

"Okay. Bring her in, and we'll take a look at her." We schedule an appointment for the afternoon.

I tell her as she washes her face and brushes her teeth.

"I guess my kidney function has decreased even more."

"I guess so. Peta, let's do the operation. Please take one of my kidneys."

"I don't think I'm ready for that yet, Pearly."

"Why?!"

"I don't know. I just don't feel right about it. Not yet."

"Have you even thought about it?"

"Not much, I admit. Pearly, I said I didn't want to do this until after the new year."

"Well, start thinking. Promise me you'll at least do that."

She nods. "This nausea is awful."

"There's nothing worse than that feeling."

"I just feel so helpless at times like this."

"I know you do, Cousin. Let me help you."

"Like I said, I'll think about it. And please, whatever you do, Pearly, don't badger me about it, okay?"

I smile. "Okay."

"And don't forget Uncle Stewart."

"You won't die on the table."

"It isn't me I'm worried about."

Oh, great.

Peta is singing in the choir! It's an old tune my grandma used to sing called "Blessed Assurance."

"Blessed assurance, Jesus is mine."

She's an alto. It's her first time singing with the group. They even changed the practice times so she could get home to the dialysis machine. I didn't know church people could be so accommodating.

She sings the song from her heart, believing every word. "Jesus is mine. Oh what a foretaste of glory divine. Heir of salvation, purchase of God."

Yes, that's Peta, an heir of salvation. Purchased of God? I read a passage of Scripture the other day that says Christ was crucified before the foundation of the world. God planned it all even then. Christ bought our souls with His blood before He even spilled it out.

That astounded me for some reason, proving once again that nothing happens by accident.

"Filled with His goodness, lost in His love."

Yes, Peta is lost in His love. Her eyes are closed, and her voice blends with the others, mostly older folk, their voices twittering when alone, but blended together, singing strong, harmonies sure after years of practice.

I wipe away the tears, some string from my mind to my heart tautened, drawn utterly tight.

Oh, Jesus.

Peta throws her purse onto the kitchen counter. "What's for supper, Cousin?"

"Nothing with cheese in it, I can tell you that."

"Oh, what I'd give for even a small chunk of cheddar."

"Well, how about a grilled pork chop and steamed broccoli?"

She makes a face. "If you insist."

"Have a seat at the table, and I'll make you a cup of tea."

"That sounds like just what I need."

I fill the kettle and place it on the stove. "It's a beautiful day."

"Perfect. I've always appreciated the weather, you know that. But the world is different now. Here we are, in the middle of August. There's a breeze, and the sun is shining on the water right outside our door. Can we eat outside?"

"Sure. If the food isn't all that exciting, the least we

can do is make the atmosphere the best we can."

We continue in our comfortable silence. I pour the tea, it steeps, Peta smiles. I like this. I like enjoying small moments. I like assigning more significance to them than ever before.

"How was the choir?" Peta asks as she fixes her tea.

"Wonderful!"

She dunks the tea bag in her cup, up and down. "I still can't believe it. Peta Kaiser singing in the church choir. And it's even more farfetched that you were sitting there in the pew listening."

"You think so?"

"Oh, Pearly. Religion was annoyance to me. To you it was an abhorrence."

"Really? Did I come off like that?"

"Oh yeah. I never heard Joey mention God without seeing you roll your eyes."

What a shame.

"I think your conversion is even more striking than mine," she says.

"Thing is, I don't know whether I'm converted or not."

Her brows rise. "Why is that?"

"I don't know. I haven't experienced a big lightning bolt, or some huge inner relief, you know, like you felt."

"Do you believe?"

"Yes. But the Bible says that even the demons believe."

"Do you love Jesus?"

"I think so. I know He loves me, so that's a step in the right direction."

I sit down across from her.

She says, "Well, I think you're farther along than you think you are."

"Let's hope so."

"Pearly, do you pray?"

I nod. "I know it doesn't sound all that hot to God, though. I don't know the lingo."

She laughs. "That's funny!"

"Why? You should read Joey's journals, his prayers, they're beautiful."

"But that was Joey. I have a theory about prayer. Now it may just be something I've concocted to make myself feel better, but I'll lay it on you." She takes a sip. "I think the most beautiful prayers to God are those when we are so full of pain or joy or wonder that we don't even have words within us. Then we just communicate, heart to heart."

"I've had enough of those."

"That's good. Me too. Especially lately. Sometimes I'm just too tired to even do more than feel."

"Oh, Peta."

"It's true. But I'm actually thankful for this illness. It woke me up."

"I think Joey's death woke me up too."

"It did."

I love the way Peta's so sure about things.

Silence stills the air again. I should put the pork chops on, but I'm enjoying this. I'm thankful, that's it. And it fills me. And it really is a prayer.

"Pearly? I've been thinking about the transplant."

"Really?"

"Yeah. I think I'd like to go through with it."

"I'm glad, but why?"

"You don't deserve this life."

Oh, my gosh. I feel the same way, but to hear someone else say it fills my stomach with lead. What can I say?

"I mean, you don't deserve to be pinned down here with me, making sure all is going fine, handing me towels when I throw up, at the ready to hook me up to the machine if I can't do it myself. You deserve more."

"Oh no, Peta. I enjoy this time together. I don't mind joining you for this ride."

"Be that as it may, Cousin, think of all the fun we could have together if I was healthy too."

But I won't be here. I'll be gone. I mourn quickly. Swallow it down. Peta will do so well, though. "Okay, then. It's settled. I'll work out all the details."

"Good. This is very good. But not until after the new year. I'm still firm on that."

I stand up, lean over, and give her a hug. "You're going to be a great healthy person."

"Yeah," she mumbles into my shirt. "Better than ever before."

Greater love has no man than this. Now I'm the one who feels like throwing up.

I'm done! I'm off the cigarettes. Been down to three or five for over a year, and now it's final. I am a non-smoker.

I hate it. I miss it.

But anyway, I figure I'd better be in good shape for

the surgery so all goes well for Peta. I can't go into cardiac arrest or something before they take the kidney, I have to be able to die on the table after all is finished.

I call Richie to get him off his trail. He's called several times this summer, but I didn't fool him. At least I don't think so.

I wait for at least fifteen minutes on long-distance hold, to the delight of AT&T, or whatever they're called these days. Finally he picks up.

"Richard King," he says, all official.

"Oh, don't be formal with me, Richie."

"Miss Pearly!"

"You haven't checked in for at least four weeks."

"Been busy. Besides, you've been sounding very good. That Lexapro still working?"

"It's great. But I've got some good news. I've quit smoking completely."

"Good! I can't believe it."

"Me either."

"What about the plot?"

"You don't mess around, do you? Well, Peta doesn't want to go through with it, so my hands are tied."

Yes, I lied.

"Good for her. Would you go through with it if you could, though?"

"I don't think so. I've been going to church regularly."

"Hallelujah, you've seen the light."

"Well, yes. I guess maybe you could put it that way."

"As your friend, not your doctor, I'll tell you I've been praying for you."

"You and a million other people."

"Hey, if it works, it works."

We chat about incidentals for a little while and hang up. I feel better for it, although the lies don't sit very well. So I sit and feel for a while, trying to get a heart-to-heart with God going. Finally I just take my coffee out on the deck, sit in my chair, and enjoy the scenery. I need to soak in as much of this as I can now.

"How in the world are you and two other guys going to fit into this apartment, Matthew?"

"It's got to work, Mrs. Laurel. We're all poor, and the rent's cheap."

"There's no bedroom."

"Yeah, but you can only do what you can."

"Let me help with the rent."

"Huh-uh. No way. You've done so much already."

"But I like doing it."

"I've got to make my own way."

"Fine. But at least let me take you over to Kmart to buy some household things. You've got one pot."

He thinks about this. "All right. But nothing expensive, okay?"

"We're talking Kmart here, Matt."

He laughs as he shuts the apartment door and checks to see if it's locked. It's his home, and if I can't see the value of that to him, I'm a boob.

The shopping trip is a hoot. Pots, pans, plates, cutlery. Lots of paper products. What boy is going to wash up tea-towels every week? I even throw in four packs of paper plates to get them started. Laundry detergent, dishwashing liquid, soap, shampoo, razors and shaving cream. Snack foods too.

Back at the apartment, we begin unloading the car, which, naturally, is stuffed, as it's so small. The skies darken, and summer thunder threatens a downpour. At least it smells that way.

"I read somewhere that women can smell a snowfall, but men can't," I say.

"Really? Weird."

"Yeah. Bet you always wanted to know that."

"Hey, that's a great pickup line."

I shut the trunk, our feet surrounded by bags.

Matthew leans down and begins picking them up. "I still feel bad about this, Mrs. Laurel."

"Don't. I never thought I'd get to send a kid off to college. You're doing me a favor."

He closes the trunk, turns to me, and takes me into his arms, stronger now from a summer on the boat. He feels so much trimmer. I breathe him in. "I appreciate everything," he says, his head way above mine. "You can't possibly know how much."

I pull back and look up at his face. "You're a good boy, Matthew."

He laughs. "You'd have been a wonderful mother. I may just adopt you. I mean, a guy can't have too many mothers."

I stand on tiptoe and kiss his cheek. "Now you're embarrassing me. Let's get this stuff inside before it rains. The last thing anybody needs is soggy paper towels."

He releases me. "Sort of defeats the purpose."

"Let's get inside. We still need to make it to the grocery store."

I let myself into the Havre de Grace house. It smells musty. I open all the windows, the storm over and done with. Naturally it poured as I drove up I-95. Thank goodness Matthew put the top up for me before I left. This car is not a rain car. My nerves feel as if they have split ends now, the way those monstrous, annoying tractor-trailers blew by me without a care in the world.

Peta naps upstairs. She drove herself up here, dialysis machine and all. I need to unload her car, but a cup of tea is in order first off. I rummage through the cupboards and find another old box of Joey's tea at the back. Lord only knows how long it's been lurking back there. Still, Joey bought it, and I need the connection. I lose him a little bit more each day. When this house is sold . . . I look around me.

I really have to gather everything together on this trip. I've put it off long enough. I call Maida.

"I saw you pull in," she says. "Glad to have you home."

"I'll be here for several weeks this time. I'm having a big yard sale."

"Why?"

"How much junk does one person need? Want to have one with me? If I know Shrubby, he's already taken over with his stuff."

"That's for sure. Although I doubt I can get him to part with any of it. I've got some things, though."

"I'll put an ad in the paper."

"Good. Hey, how about you and Peta coming over for dinner tonight? It's been way too long."

"We'll be there."

"Six o'clock would be good for us. That good for you?"

"We've got no plans."

No plans. Well, that's hardly the case. We've got big plans, Peta and me. A plot actually. Richie's right about that. Plans are when both people know everything. Plots contain secrets withheld from a lot of people. Yep, it's a plot all right.

The kettle screams. I quickly rinse out a cup, tear open the box of tea, drop in the bag, and pour the water over it. Time to get to work.

"Pearly, you're never going to sell a thing if you don't stop telling stories about everything to every customer," Maida says.

"I can't help it. They need to know."

"Why? They don't care."

"They should."

"No, they shouldn't. It's the way of things. If you died, some junk dealer would just come in and haul this stuff away. They're things, Pearly. That's all these are to people."

She's right. "I don't want to let them go."

"Then why in world are you doing this?"

"Because I have to."

"No you don't."

"I really do. You just don't see it the way I do."

"Look, I'll man the tables. Why don't you take a walk

or something? It'll be easier on you."

I take her up on the offer. Yes, I'll take a walk. I'll walk and I'll walk and I'll walk. And I'll hear Peta talking about what life will be like after the transplant, and I'll mourn because life is so precious now. I love so many people and am loved back, and I'll come to the conclusion once again that I do not want to die.

My mind resumes consciousness. Is that a knock on the door? I scan the bedside clock: 2:00 A.M.

"Pearly!" Peta yells from her room. "I think someone's at the door."

"I'm getting my robe on now."

The doorbell rings as I run down the steps. I peer out the window and quickly yank open the front door.

"Yolanda?"

"Pearly!"

"Come on in."

She rushes inside. "Matthew's mother is dead."

"Good heavens. What happened?"

"The whole house went up in a blaze. She didn't get out."

"Sit down."

"The kids are in the car. Let me bring them in."

As she gathers up her chicks, I hurry back to the kitchen to put the kettle on and a pan of milk to warm for the children.

"What's going on?" Peta yells.

"It's Yolanda."

"And me on this freaky machine!"

"Matthew's mother is dead. Killed in a house fire."

"Good heavens!"

"That's what I said."

I gather linens and towels and begin making up the sofa bed in the living room. Yolanda enters with a sleeping Clay. "I'll just put him down on the lounger for now." She disappears as three sleepy children file into the kitchen.

"I've got some warm milk for you all. Just hang on a second while it heats up. Have a seat at the table."

The girls collapse into the chairs, Katie laying her head down on her arms. I finish readying the bed. This small house! We need more beds. I run up the stairs.

"Peta, would you mind if Yolanda took the other bed in here?"

"Of course not. I'll get it ready."

"Does your line reach to the linen closet?"

"Sure does. Don't worry about a thing up here."

I run outside and pull the cushions from the porch chairs in the shed. Yolanda's already in the living room with two armfuls of sleeping bags. "Oh, good," she says, eyeing the cushions. "With these hardwood floors I was wondering if they'd really sleep or not."

We lay them out.

"Peta's getting the other bed ready in her room for you."

"I'll take it. I am *so* tired."

"Mrs. Laurel, the milk's about to boil over," LeeLee yells.

I run in and slide the pan off the burner. Darn. Now we'll have to wait until it cools. I reach into the freezer for a few ice cubes. That'll work. At least it's whole milk, and Yo's kids aren't picky.

"I'll be right back."

Yolanda unrolls the last sleeping bag. "We'll talk after we get the kids down," she says.

Thirty minutes later, they're tucked in and sleeping. Of course, Yolanda had them in their jammies for the trip.

I make us all a cup of tea, and we settle in Peta's room for the conversation. I ask, "So what happened?"

Yo shakes her head. "They aren't sure how it started. But they know it was her bedroom."

"Probably fell asleep with a lit cigarette," I say.

"Probably."

"Where's Matthew's dad?"

"He was on second shift at the factory, but they got hold of him. I got wind of the fire at the Rib Room and went down right away. Got there just after he did."

"How is he?"

"Like you'd expect. The house burned down to the ground. It was a wingdinger of a fire."

"Not surprising with all those boxes and junk inside there."

"Anyway, I told him I'd come up and tell Matthew face to face. This isn't news a person should get over the phone."

"We'll go down to campus tomorrow. I'll call him early and tell him to stay at the apartment until we get there."

Yolanda nods.

Peta says, "I'll watch the kids."

"It's all set then." I sip my tea, too much too quickly.

It burns my tongue.

"Nobody deserves to burn to death, Mrs. Laurel, no matter what kind of life they lived."

The Rib Room is dim, closed for the night. The scent of the day's cooking lingers, spicy, sweet, and a bit cloying. Matthew sips on a Coke, his pale face igniting the gloom around us.

"I know. It's horrible."

"Do you think she felt anything?"

"She was still in her bed, Matthew. She probably passed out long before the flames got to her."

I hope that's true. It makes sense. What other explanation could there be?

"It was a good funeral, though," he says. "Lots of people there from the factory."

"Yes, that's true." Truthfully, it was the most depressing funeral I'd ever attended. People in jeans and T-shirts standing around the grave smoking while the minister droned out a reading of the Twenty-third Psalm. But Matthew played his guitar, and that redeemed everything.

"She did like to hear me play," he said. "I have to give her that. She wasn't such a bad mom, I guess."

Well, that sure isn't the truth, but I'd be a fool to say it. "She loved you, Matthew. That's all some women can handle. Who knows what demons she was fighting?"

"Yeah." He taps his fingers on the table.

Cars pass down Main Street, their tires creating a soft whine that's almost musical.

"I sure don't know what I'd do without you, Mrs. Laurel."

I only smile softly.

"Do you remember our conversation by your car that day?"

"Yes, of course I do. It meant a lot to me."

"Well, I guess I'm down to one now."

I wish he'd cry.

Oh dear.

Oh, Pearly Everlasting, what in heaven's name have you gotten yourself into?

And Matthew crumbles, finally weeping. I reach out my arms.

I live a most extraordinary life these days. I am a cousin, a caretaker, a faux-mother, although perhaps not so faux if the love I feel for that boy is any indication. I am an adopted aunt to four wonderful children, and the love I feel for Yolanda merits a category all its own.

I am blessed.

It seems I am compelled to give credit where it is due. All these blessings simply arrived through no action of my own. Except for the guitar lessons, and even meeting Matthew could be categorized as happenstance. Has my life always been filled with such wonder and joy, and I failed to recognize it as such?

Therein lies the crux to my newfound faith. I feel like a child again, reborn into something greater, more glorious, and of a deeper significance. I am George Bailey after he realizes he wants to live. I am watching people from all over come into my house, giving of themselves and wishing me a Merry Christmas.

"Joy to the world, the Lord is come."

I sit in The Winters Run Inn. Christmas lights garland the darkened room, three different kinds: colorful miniatures, white icicles, and a string of red, green, and white rope lights chasing each other over the bar area. A red crepe-paper bell, the kind you see at weddings, hangs from the ceiling. Lots of bottoms perch on chrome stools, most of them still sausaged in winter coats. The room, paneled in plywood, bespeaks a bygone era, and I like it. Any kind of beer you'd like advertises itself via neon signs. Keno too. A karaoke machine sits in the corner, reminding me it's the twenty-first century.

I dropped Matthew and his roommate off at Ice World a little while ago so they can go skating, something I've never been able to do.

So here I sit in the corner near one of the few windows, a 3-D Samuel Adams cardboard Christmas tree keeping me company. The waitress delivers a cup of vegetable soup. It's a beautiful sight, people getting together. Chatting. Smiling. Communing. The skies are gray, and a balmy breeze blows outside.

I take pictures in my head. I want to remember this. I want to remember it all. Joey will love to hear about it, even in heaven, I think.

Peta's encamped up at Maida's house, as my little Tudor has passed into more capable hands. A nice couple from Bel Air, owners of a new bagel shop in Havre de Grace, are making it their own. Already the landscaping looks much better, and when I met them, her eyes sparkled as she talked about the place, all the things she loved inside and out, and the things she would do to make it her own.

The house needs to breathe again, become a work-in-progress, waiting expectantly for yet another change within its walls. A nursery is already in the works, and this satisfies me. Who knows the last time that little house felt the *thumps* of tiny feet running on its wooden floors? Yes, it was good to us all those years. It deserves to breathe again.

The last time I sat here in The Winters Run Inn, Joey sat with me. We ordered fried oyster sandwiches and crab soup. We talked about the new medication his doctor had just prescribed an hour before. Joey felt good about finally getting his blood pressure down. I felt hope for many more lovely years ahead. I didn't know I had less than a year left with him, and I'm glad that was hidden from me.

I've decided to give myself a break regarding my life with Joey, particularly how I pushed his faith aside. Peta said I should, and—well, it's hard not to listen to Peta. I cannot say why God chose this path for me, but I do feel my faith journey has been in the making far longer than it seems. Joey lived it for years, quietly and consistently, and that had its effect, collecting steam for the future when his death, like an explosion, released years of buildup.

I console myself that he knows a little of what is happening down here to me. I mean, if God is love, if He is merciful, He'll let Joey know all those years of prayer weren't for nothing.

"It's just country boys and girls getting down on the farm," hollers the jukebox, and I smile. Country music. Oh, dear.

Near the Sam Adams Christmas tree a sign says, DALE EARNHARDT FAN PARKING ONLY. The waitress asks me if I'm okay, and I simply answer, "I am."

Two of the coated behinds, an elderly couple, rise from the bar. The lady points at a younger man seated next to her. "You behave yourself," she says.

"I'll try."

The waitress pipes up, "You're too late, Ruth. You should have said that four months ago!"

They all laugh. I smile. But I think, "Now what could possibly have happened four months ago?"

Another Christmas dawns, the third since Joey's passing. I'm having trouble with the research on this transplant business. The problem is this: I don't know who to ask. I don't know where a person can start cold on a question like this. So I'm bringing myself up to date. My new computer will arrive next week, and by January I'll be up and running. I sure hope I can figure out how to navigate the Internet. It's really my only hope.

The cabin and the farmhouse teem with visitors, except for Maida and Shrubby, who always stay with his brother Marsh. Matthew brought a friend from school who lives in California and can't afford to get home. Harry's home for the holidays too. This year, instead of Mason jars with potpourri and twinkle lights, we settled on ceramic Christmas trees. He paints them, and I install the tiny plastic lights and lamp works. He tells me which colors go where, and when those things light up, they are like nothing I've ever seen. He chooses the most offbeat glazes, and they come out like works of art. Now Peta would berate me for this, but I took them down to Christmas Spirit in Ocean City and showed them to the buyer. She gasped. "How much?"

I shrugged. "Well, they cost us about fifteen dollars to make, and then there's the time to consider."

"I'll give you thirty apiece, advertise them as one-of-a-kind, and I'll make a good profit. Plus, I like getting local stuff in here if I can."

"Thirty-five?"

"Deal."

We shake hands, and I am amazed. "Well, okay then! We have about twenty of them in the car."

"Let me have them."

Harry helps me unload, the lady cuts us a check, and we're off, seven hundred dollars heavier in the pocket-book. Harry wants to go Christmas shopping. So where do we go? To the ceramics store to buy more supplies.

Now, Christmas dinner consumed and no bad oysters along with it, Harry hands a package to each person, including Brett from California. Everybody delights in their Christmas tree, and all the outlets in the down-stairs of the farmhouse are suddenly engaged. We turn off the lights and sing "O Christmas Tree," little Ireland's voice, high and clear, guiding us all.

Yolanda walks over to me and slips her arm around my waist. "To quote Linus, 'This, Charlie Brown, is what Christmas is all about.' "

"I heard that."

She laughs and pulls me tight, her many brass bangles jingling like bells.

I click on the connect button, wincing in advance at the sound to come as the computer connects. Oh, isn't that the most hideous noise? Well, I guess everything comes with a price.

I had the computer installed at the farmhouse so Peta could use it too. She's already become an e-mail junkie three weeks in, communicating with a stay-at-home mom in Kentucky, two other polycystic kidney disease folks, and a computer specialist in Scotland. The way she connects at least five times a day, you think I'd be used to this noise.

But hey! I got on.

I pull up a site called Google because it's one of those search engines and I like the name. I type in the words "assisted suicide, legal, and Europe." It's midnight and it's taken me this long to gather up the courage to get things in motion. Peta's making a list of all the things she'll do in her new life, chattering all the time. She's formed a relationship of her own with Yo, and they're already planning a trip to the beach in the summer. That will be nice for them. I asked her if it's okay if Matthew stays down here and works again this summer, and she said, "Of course, Pearly, whyever not?"

So he's taken care of for a while. I started putting my assets together with his name on them too. Things on this end are almost set to go, if I can just find a surgeon to agree to the rest. The Google search is finished, and I see that I may have more than one country from which to choose.

Mom and Dad are arguing. They don't do it much, and only about Harry.

"When's my turn, Valerie?" he says. "How much longer will I be put in storage for the sake of that idiot?"

"That idiot, as you call him, is your *son,* Carl."

"I wish to God—"

"Don't say that. Don't ever say that to me again!"

The door slams, and the car door opens. I peer out my bedroom window expecting to see my father getting in. But it is Mom. She whirls in the spring breeze, shaking her fists toward the kitchen door. Her heel catches in the turf, and down she goes.

"Go get her, Daddy," I whisper. "Go get her. Please."

But she stays in solitude, sitting up and pounding the ground with her fists. I know she is crying.

I pull back, leave my bedroom and crawl in with Harry. He snuggles against me and smiles in his sleep.

You're so lucky, I think.

Mortis Placidus. That's their name. Peaceful death. An oxymoron, really. We're all afraid to die. At least I am.

So we've gone back and forth in e-mails. This is far more complicated than I realized. I thought I'd just be able to die on the operating table. But from what? Kidney failure takes a long time. I'd have to build up the toxins and await a grueling death. And this isn't an option anyway.

Here's the way it will work, the way it will be if I convince them I'm a worthy candidate: I'll have the operation, get checked out of the hospital, and go back to a Mortis apartment where I'll take an overdose. I have to do it myself. That's the law. And, of course, with the newfound condition of renal failure, I'll be a prime candidate for death with dignity.

Switzerland is quickly becoming the death capital of the world for foreigners, thanks to Mortis. The legislature is concerned, not wanting their country to be known as *the* place to go for assisted suicide. I don't blame them.

Isn't it amazing what you can find out on the Internet?

It's Valentine's Day. I thought I'd be more depressed because Joey always made a huge to-do of Valentine's Day. Flowers, candy, dinner out, and a thoughtful gift I didn't even know I wanted until he gave it to me. But this year I made loads of valentines. Sent a bunch off to Luray with a giant box of candy. Even one to Matthew's father. Sent a box off to Havre de Grace for Maida and Shrubby and the biggest care package you've ever seen for Matthew and his crew. They have a hard time getting dates, being such nice guys, so hopefully brownies, candy, and cards will ease the pain.

We hosted a Valentine's dinner here at the house with Harry and some of the older, single choir members at church. The pianist sat down at the old upright, and we sang until eleven o'clock, a downright ghastly hour for many of these folk.

Yes, love was in the air. It may sound corny, but it's true.

I'd forgotten how much I love the song "Shine On, Harvest Moon."

I sit down to pencil a note to Yolanda's LeeLee. She has a tough time with the girls in school. Well, I know about tough times with schoolmates, so much so that I feel that I am an expert in the subject.

The phone rings.

"Mrs. Laurel?" The accent is foreign, heavy.

"Yes?"

"This is Brigitte Hofmann in Switzerland."

"Oh, my!"

"Sorry to disturb you. Is this a good time?"

"Yes, it's fine. Your English is excellent."

"Thank you. The society tries to make a phone call before we decide on whether or not to help someone. It helps to hear the voice, you see."

"I'm sure it does."

"Now you have quite an interesting request and one which, I might add, will take a lot of planning to execute."

Execute. That's quite a choice of words!

"I see."

"Yes. We have a record of your correspondence so far, but I'd like to hear you tell your story if you don't mind."

"Not at all."

I tell her everything. Joey's death, Peta's illness, and I play up my ingestion of antidepressants.

She listens in silence, and I keep going, trying to fill in the quiet gaps because, well, that's just the way I am.

She tells me they'll get back to me shortly, after a decision is made. "We've never had a case like this before, you see. There are a lot of logistics involved here. But we do have a surgeon in the society who might be open to this. Much of it will hinge on your depression. We do help in cases of mental illness, which is, of course, even more controversial than terminal diseases, you see."

"Yes, I can see that."

After we hang up, I sit still for a while, realizing that my life is in their hands.

I set pen to paper. I'll leave this note for Peta when she returns from Switzerland. Hopefully it will explain a lot. And hopefully it will reassure her that her life is precious and she must resume it with all vigor as planned. I will write a letter to each person I love and hope they understand why I can't go back now, why I have to do this. Dear God, I wish there was another way, but how can I tell Peta the surgery's off? How can I tell her why?

My biggest regret by far is leaving Matthew. He doesn't deserve this. But he's strong, and Peta and Yolanda will step into the gap.

Dear Peta,
By now you'll know that I did not survive the transplant. You do not yet know why because I instructed the doctors to tell you I died of heart

failure, and in the end, I guess we all do. But you deserve to know the truth.

I only had one good kidney. The other one was the size of an infant's and didn't function. At the time I offered the transplant, I truly wanted to die and saw this as a good way to do so, to sacrifice a life not worth living for one that is. So I offered.

And then, life began to open up for me! I found faith, love, and even hope, all those things, and the world became beautiful once again. It's still beautiful, Peta. Use this gift to the fullest. Don't let your anger at me sabotage what you can and should do with your good health. I'm so excited for you.

In any case, I did this because I love you. You have to know that. We've been through a lot together these past couple of years. You've become my best friend and companion. But seeing you struggle has been harder than you can imagine. I yearned to comfort you, to heal you, and now I have.

Just remember, I'm with God now, and Joey, and you know I have much to tell him. We'll be catching up for a good long time, and heaven knows, we'll certainly have a lot of that.

While I'm frightened at what lies ahead, I know there's much to look forward to. Keep singing Cousin, keep praying, keep loving. You have so much to give. Take care of Harry and Matthew, too.

Love, Pearly

A representative meets us at the airport in Zurich and

escorts us to the apartment. It is a secretly located apartment and very nice. Clean and sparsely yet comfortably furnished, as the Web site promised. Two bedrooms, one for the patient and the other for the normally accompanying family member, sprout off the back hallway.

Our escort says little, his eyes crinkling in the rearview mirror every once in a while at Peta's excited chatter. That's also something new about Peta. She chatters happily now. A beautiful sound.

We set her machine up in one of the bedrooms for tonight and open our bags. A box of dialysis solution has already been delivered.

The rooms possess that spare European aura. Clean, flat surfaces like islands in a sea of cream and tan. Peaceful and without fuss or excess.

Peta gazes around her, breathes in deeply, exhales loudly, and shakes her head. "Isn't this the blandest apartment you've ever seen?"

"Well, it *is* owned by the hospital."

Lie. Lie. Lie.

"True. I'll sure be glad to get back home."

"We only left yesterday."

She says nothing in response.

"Ready to go?" I ask a few minutes later after freshening up in the closet-sized bathroom. We need to talk to the doctors today, sign the papers and such, and then we'll be free for dinner out on the town. Brigitte is taking us then, and I want to enjoy my last meal. I'm trying to be matter-of-fact about all this. It's hard, don't get me wrong, but I'm succeeding to some extent, for Peta's sake.

"I can't believe this is my last night on this thing."

"It's wonderful, isn't it?"

She nods. "Thank you, Pearly. Thank you for giving me this chance."

I just sit down next to her and band my arms around her. I wonder what whispers now through her head, but I don't want to ask. This is hard enough. It would be so much fun to experience life with the new Peta Kaiser.

"Let's go," I say. "We don't want to be late for our appointments."

Naturally, we have two different surgeons. Mine belongs to Mortis. Hers? I don't know. Maybe so, maybe not. It doesn't matter.

Dr. Tran Reinhardt shows me into his office. "Mrs. Laurel, we meet face to face!"

"Yes, we do."

"Have a seat. I must tell you that it's a good thing you're doing for your cousin. She seems like a wonderful person."

"Yes, she is."

He folds his hands and lays them on his desk. "Now, I have to ask you one more time, are you certain you wish to go through with this?"

I nod.

"All right then. I have some papers for you to sign, releasing the society from all legal recourse."

"I expected that."

He slides them across the desk and hands me a gold pen.

I stare at the pen. I stare at the form, realizing I'm literally signing my life away. A year ago I would have welcomed this.

"There aren't many people who would go to such lengths," he says.

"Well, with my husband gone . . ."

"Yes, that is a great consideration."

He's all sympathy. Good-looking too, with dark hair cropped closely and stunning hazel eyes.

I sign then, quickly and with a bold hand. Pearly Kaiser Laurel. The living dead.

"Surgery is tomorrow morning at eight. We'll begin preparing you around six. You can change your mind at any time before we begin."

"Thank you, I'll remember that."

He searches in his drawer, pulls out a tin of mints, and offers me one.

Mints. At a time like this. Crazy Europeans.

I shake my head. "And death by the barbiturates is peaceful?"

"Very."

"No pain?"

"No."

"How long does it take to die, Dr. Reinhardt?"

He places a mint on his tongue and returns the tin to the drawer. "Between thirty minutes and two hours. But believe me, Mrs. Laurel, you'll go off into unconsciousness well before two hours. I promise you. It will be easy and relatively quick."

"Yes. Compared to a lifetime lived."

He smiles, and I wonder about his children and his

wife as I look up and notice their smiling faces in a photo on the shelf behind him.

We enter the hospital at 5:45 A.M. It is quiet and cold. All is modern and generic and very smooth. Smooth windows, white walls, smooth shining floors. A place to slide right on into the inevitable. I should have more courage. I should tell the truth.

Peta looks scared. "What if something bad happens?"

"Well, there's always that chance, Cousin. Nothing's guaranteed."

"That's the truth."

What if something bad happens? What if Peta dies on the table like Uncle Stewart? What could be worse? I'd then become a walking, breathing visual aid of guilt, this open target for any meddling mother seeking easy satisfaction.

Tell her right now, Pearly! There is another way!

But what can it be? I would think it would be evident, but so far nothing obvious has surfaced.

"Well"—she stops by a row of cushioned waiting-room chairs in the lobby and turns to me—"thank you. Thank you for doing this."

I pull her into an embrace, trying my best not to heave the massive sob of dread gathered in my throat. I feel so tight, so aware. Her hair, still long, smells clean and feels soft against my cheek. I breathe her in, wondering exactly how many breaths I have left. I tell her I love her. She returns the words.

We continue walking.

"Have you ever counted the moles and liver spots on your hands, Peta?"

"No, why?"

"I was just wondering."

"Have you?"

"Yes."

"How many do you have?"

"Fifty-eight blemishes altogether."

"One for each year!"

"Yes. Exactly."

"You're a piece of work, Pearly."

"More than you know."

For some reason, I never pictured commencing the dying process in a backless hospital gown, naked and skinny underneath, looking more like a plucked chicken than ever. For some reason, I wanted to die with that mirrored shawl around me, my own equivalent of dying with your boots on. I wrote in my letter to Yolanda that I wanted her to have it. She'll wear it too.

But yes, I will wear it when I die. It's folded neatly in my suitcase back at the apartment.

I sit on the gurney, then lie down, the knots in the ties of the gown poking into my skin. Peta's in another room, probably doing the same thing. Oh, I can't wait for her to send that dialysis machine back to Baxter! No more boxes or tubing, and they'll eventually remove that freaky abdominal catheter, too. How she hates that thing, and who can blame her? "I feel gross with this thing coming out of me," she has said many times. All that will be over for her.

Dear God.

I can only pray. Heart to heart.

I hear Yo's voice again. *There is another way.* Heart to heart.

The IV already impales my arm, and they're wheeling me toward the operating theater. I look up. The ceiling lights slide by, and the chin of the orderly gyrates as he chews a piece of gum. It's a perfect, narrow U, his chin, and I focus on it, noticing the stubble underneath and a small nick probably acquired during a quick shave the day before.

They transfer me to the table, and I try to help by digging my heels in and pushing off. Dr. Reinhardt takes my hand as soon as I'm settled. "Ready?"

"Yes."

"Are you certain?"

"Yes."

Lie. Lie. Lie.

"Let's get started then, all right?" He pats my hand. "Let me introduce you to the anesthesiologist, Dr. Wang."

Dr. Wang smiles. "I'll take good care of you, Mrs. Laurel."

He looks just the way his name would suggest. Only he speaks with a German accent. What a juxtaposition.

"Please do."

"You're very brave."

"Thank you."

I cry out again inside, begging wordlessly.

I begin to shake uncontrollably.

"It's just the fluid going in, it's cold," Dr. Wang says.

But I know it's more than that. Oh, God, please help me. Come to me out the back kitchen door and get me here as I lie on the ground.

"Now count backward from ten," he says.

And I do. I mean, time stands still under anesthesia. By the time I get to five, I'll be waking up, ready to lie some more.

I forgot that your hearing is the first sense that returns after general anesthesia.

"Mrs. Laurel?"

I can only groan.

"Blah, blah, blah," in Swiss or something.

I groan again.

Then, "Oh, sorry. You made it through the surgery fine."

I just want to sleep. I have a lot to think about, but all I want to do is sleep.

I manage to mutter, "My cousin?"

But no answer emerges through the mist, and I assume the nurse has walked away.

Nobody will tell me anything about Peta. And why not? Don't they say the surgery is harder on the donor than the donee? Something's wrong. She's dead. Like Uncle Stewart.

I push the nurse's button again. She enters my room five minutes later.

"Yes?"

"I want to see my doctor, and I want to see him right away. Something happened to my cousin, didn't it?

Why won't anybody tell me anything?"

"Yes ma'am." She gives me a brisk nod and hurries out.

Thirty minutes later, Dr. Reinhardt arrives. "How are you feeling, Mrs. Laurel?"

"Fine for a dying person. When will the transport back to the apartment arrive?"

"There's been a change of plans, I'm afraid. Your cousin had a heart attack. There was no transplant."

"A heart attack?"

"She will be fine. We have her under observation."

A heart attack?

"And my kidney?"

"Is still inside you. Word came before we removed it, so we immediately stopped the surgery and stitched you back up."

Oh, my. Oh, my.

I take a few deep breaths.

Oh, my.

"So what will happen?"

"She's in no condition for surgery, I'm afraid. Apparently, she has severe blockage of her arteries and may even need valve replacement. They'll be running tests on her over the next few days. Catheterization, chiefly. We'll know more after that, but don't be surprised if she needs open heart surgery."

"Oh, my. Poor Peta."

"I'm afraid you'll be in Zurich a while, Mrs. Laurel. And most likely they won't want to risk a transplant in the future."

There is another way.

I lay my head back on the pillow. "Thank you, doctor."

Thank you, God.

Poor Peta!

Yes, it's all my fault. But I'll make it up to her. I will. And I'll convince myself that heart attack was meant to be anyway.

Isn't that so?

It's been nonstop for poor Peta, and yet I just sit and sit. She cried when she heard the news. "Why couldn't it have happened after the transplant and not before?"

"I don't know."

Another lie.

"We'll get you through this, Cousin."

"They won't do a transplant now."

"We'll get through that, too. We're in this together."

"Okay."

"How do you feel?"

"How do you think I feel?"

"That's the Peta I know and love! You'll get through that open heart surgery fine."

"They say the recovery won't be easy, not with my decreased kidney function and all the fluid I'll gain."

"You'll get through."

"I have to. Somebody's got to take care of you, Pearly."

"That's right. You remember that."

So here I sit in the waiting room while Peta's chest is spread wide open, obscenely exposed to the wide world.

The society moves our belongings to an apartment provided by the hospital. This one isn't nearly so nice, but I'm finding it's a good place for prayer and contemplation. I plead wordlessly with God tonight, that He'll spare Peta during the surgery, that all will be well. If it doesn't go well, I will never forgive myself. Could I have searched harder for the way out? The answer is yes. I could have just told the truth.

And the truth shall set you free.

I can hear Maida now. "Be thankful that heart attack happened at a hospital."

Yes, I suppose there is that.

And Yolanda? "Pearly Everlasting! Maybe God used your harebrained plot to put Peta in the right place at the right time! Remember '*All* things work together for good!' Saint Paul couldn't have been wrong."

To which I'd answer, "And why not?" Just to get under her skin.

This thought makes me smile as I look out my window over a quiet, midmorning street. Zurich is so lovely.

"I'm sorry, God. I'm so sorry."

I feel a sugar-coated love pull me into its sweetness, not an easy-guiding move, but a quick, jerky pull. And I am warm and filled with hope.

We pull up to the farmhouse. All is quiet and still.

"I never thought I'd be so glad to get home," Peta says, thinner than ever but with good color.

"You said it." It's good to see the place, so familiar

and kind. "Let's get inside and then I'll unload. I want to put the kettle on."

I escort her up the steps. She's so frail, but I'll fatten her up. It's my job. I've got a lot of jobs now.

The afternoon sunshine reflects the sky onto the windowpanes of the kitchen door. "What would you think if I just moved in over here, Peta?"

"Good. We could bring Harry home too."

"You wouldn't mind?"

"Are you nuts? Did you lose your brains over in Zurich?"

I laugh. "Get in there, you old curmudgeon."

I unlock the door and settle her at the kitchen table. What a ritual we've already developed. What a beautiful thing.

I put the kettle on and hear a crash from the living room.

"What was that?" I say.

"I don't know. Do you think an animal got in while we were gone?"

"Let's hope that's all it is."

I'm not all that great at moments like this, moments that can be benign or frightful. "I'll go see what it is."

"I'll go with you, Cousin. You've got that look on your face."

"Oh, Peta."

We tiptoe across the kitchen floor, and I push the swinging door open a crack.

"Surprise!"

Oh, my!

I look at Peta, her eyes shining, and we push the door

open completely. They're all there. All of them. Even Matthew's roommate, Brett, from California.

"Oh, my goodness, you all!" I shout.

"Welcome home!" Yolanda runs forward. "You all are a real sight for sore eyes!"

Hugs all around! Oh, good, squishy warm big hugs with lots of tears in between. A reunion of hearts and souls. A regular mishmash of sentimentality that will be remembered for years by everyone.

"Well, you tried!" Maida says as we all fill our plates with her food and Yolanda's too.

"I guess it's all you can do."

"Yeah. That's right. I thought it was very noble of you, Pearly."

"Thanks, Maida."

"In fact, I don't think many people realize how very noble it actually was."

I look at her sharply. Her eyes narrow, and she pulls a slip of paper from her pocket. "I found this while I was stripping the sheets in Peta's room. Sitting right there on the dresser as pretty as you please."

"And you read it?"

"Of course I did! And all the others you expected Peta to give out. You are a *mess!*"

I say nothing. She's read it all.

I fill my plate with ribs, potato salad, macaroni and cheese, and green beans. Pickled beets too, which I love, and I surely do hope Maida will say nothing else. I don't want her to ruin the relief I feel, the joy, the anticipation of what life will be. I don't want her to be my party pooper.

So I decide to take control. "I'd like to have that back."

"I figured that. But I ran into Salisbury and made a copy just in case."

"Maida!"

"I'm only kidding with you, Pearly. Here. I wouldn't dream of telling Peta or anybody else. Not even Shrubby, who I'm learning just can't keep a secret."

"That's the truth."

We saunter into the kitchen, our plates full. I grab us each a Coke, and we sit down at the table.

"Just tell me one thing," Maida says. "What on earth possessed you to do such a thing?"

I think for a bit. "I think I blamed it on love at first. But when it comes down to it, I was just too scared to go on. This seemed to be a noble way to go."

"Oh." She bites into a rib. "Oh, these are good."

"Uh-huh."

"So then, why are you so happy now? Your plan failed."

"Well, Maida, a funny thing happened along the way. I realized I didn't want to die after all, but I didn't know how to tell Peta it was all off. Thank goodness it worked out like it did. For me anyway. Peta will still suffer, and I wish there was something I could do to ease it. Other than being around."

"Pearly, that's the most any of us can do. My mother always said that half the battle in life is simply showing up."

"That I can do."

Yolanda's voice echoes from the family room.

"Pearly Everlasting!"

"Yeah, Yo?"

"Come take a picture of the cake. We've all decided you need to get going as family chronicler."

I shrug at Maida and arise from the table. "Why not?"

As I enter the room, Yolanda hands me a camera. "What's this?"

"Your new digital camera! Anyone willing to give up a kidney deserves a little present!"

Harry sits and smiles, nodding. Matthew gives me a hug and a peck on the cheek.

"Well then, let me hide in the corner a bit and look at the instructions for a couple of minutes."

Yolanda puts her hands on her hips. "And nobody better even think about touching that cake!"

It doesn't take long. These things practically run themselves. I take a picture of a large sheet cake sporting a hot air balloon and the words, "Up, Up, and Away." And I assemble the whole group around it.

Yes, the family chronicler. And what a crazy family it is. There are twelve of us now, and only three related by blood. But to my way of thinking, that isn't a prerequisite, not anymore. They love me, and I love them, and that's all there is to it.

And Joey would approve. No doubt about it. In fact, I think he'd proclaim the whole thing quite brilliant. I fish in my tote bag for the diamond tie pin, and I attach it to the strap of my new camera. The list lies folded in the corner of the bag, one item left to do. Beside it rests my photo album.

I stand tall in the middle of the living room. "I'd like

to make an announcement concerning this year's Easter dinner."

Peta says, "Listen up, everyone. This is family business."

"We're all going to Haussner's, and we're going to order one of every single thing on that menu, and we'll raise our glasses to Joe Laurel and thank him for changing our lives for the better."

"Hear, hear!" shouts Yolanda.

And three weeks later, we do just that.

I withdraw the list from the tote bag, the only item left inside besides the final picture in the photo album. Joey and me saying our vows, hands clasped together, ready for a lifetime of love. I lay them both on his grave.

"Hi, Joey. I finally came."

I sit down next to the headstone. "I'm done. I finished it all, but you know that already, don't you?"

How can I be sure? Well, I don't know, but I'm positive he sees, because faith is like that. Faith takes what you know in your heart to be true, runs it around inside your brain with the things you know are false, and, without bothering to ask permission, fills your soul with hope and assurance until you know, without a doubt, that what you believe to be true . . . is exactly so.

About the Author

Lisa Samson would like to write here that she is an award-winning author. And indeed she has won many awards, including: first place in the sixth-grade art contest in 1976, as well as "Most Spirited Cheerleader" in 1982. Both the blue ribbon and the trophy are nowhere to be found. Instead, she counts husband Will and their three children, her siblings, family, and friends as her life's greatest rewards. Next in line would be her twice-weekly trip to Starbucks near her home in Maryland.

Center Point Publishing
600 Brooks Road • PO Box 1
Thorndike ME 04986-0001 USA

(207) 568-3717

US & Canada:
1 800 929-9108

CRANSTON PUBLIC LIBRARY